Hate To NEED You

Hate To Need You

This work is a piece of fiction. Names, characters, places, and incidents are the product of the author's imagination or are used fictitiously. Any resemblance to actual events, locales, or persons, living or dead, is entirely coincidental.

Published by Rae Quinn
Cover Illustration by Emma Emerson

ISBN: 979-8-9913334-6-7

Sometimes second chances are worth fighting for.

Chapter 1

ELLIE

The ringing in my ears intensifies as the lights seem to grow brighter by the second. Sweat trickles down my back, provoking a small, involuntary shiver to ripple through me. My breathing is erratic, as if I've just run a marathon, and my heart is racing. My eyes flutter open, but the bright lights make it impossible for me to see anything in front of me. Someone grabs my hand and yanks it into the air before bowing down, causing my body to replicate the action.

Finally, I can see a sea of people sitting in rows, clapping and whistling. The familiar sights of the theatre dance through my vision, and I'm immediately pushed back into the present. Looking to my left, I recognize the person that's holding my hand as he waves out to the crowd. Freddie looks to me with a huge grin, his eyes sparkling with the excitement of a little boy finally receiving the candy he'd been begging his mother for for hours.

Looking back into the crowd, it finally hits me. I've just performed on my first big stage in New York City as a lead character. People are clapping and cheering... for me. For my performance. I'll never get tired of this feeling. The feeling of fulfilment and joy that takes over my body after a great show. It feels impossible that I'm actually here, standing on this stage in front of hundreds of people who came to see me perform. It's surreal.

I wave, mimicking Freddie's movements with a massive smile on my face as a tear falls down my cheek. This is why I do what I do. This feeling is worth all the rejection and heartache. My eyes catch on a few familiar faces in the crowd. My best friends, my mother, and my brother sit in the front row, their smiles as wide as mine as they cheer for me, and I feel so full. I have everything I want, everything I need right here in front of me.

When the curtain closes, Freddie pulls me into a bear hug, lifting me off of the ground and spinning me around. Freddie and I have grown quite close these past few months of rehearsal. We played love interests in the show, but unlike his character, Freddie does not like women. Our friendship has become so important to me, and I appreciate the time we've spent together. He travelled all the way from Wisconsin to be here, despite not having his parents' approval. I admire his ability to go after what he wants, even if others don't approve.

Freddie sets me down but keeps his hands on my arms, holding me in place. A piece of his brown hair falls into his face as his blue eyes lock on mine. I don't think the smile has left his face since the end of the show.

"That was fucking incredible! Holy shit, they loved it! They loved you!" he shouts, and I have to chuckle at his outburst.

"And you! You were amazing. That was the best either of us has ever performed. It was awesome, and the way you executed that quick change? I mean, I've never seen anything like it!" I tell him, and I mean every word. We've rehearsed a thousand times. Late nights, sometimes past midnight, twelve-hour days, seven days a week. It all came together tonight.

"Elenor, darling, absolutely flawless," our director, Mr. Lemaire tells me, throwing a long arm around my shoulders. I involuntarily hold my breath as a whiff of his terrible coffee breath permeates in the air. Mr. Lemaire is nice enough, and he's never done anything sketchy to me personally, but he treats a lot of the male cast members a bit harsher than the women.

"Fredrick, your performance fell flat. I could have used more from you."

Case in point. Freddie rolls his eyes. He performed just fine and we all know it, but no one dares to argue with the great Sacha Lemaire.

"It's just Ellie, and I think his performance was wonderful," I say, standing up for my castmate. Unlike many here, I am not afraid of Mr. Lemaire. He may be a world-famous stage director, but he is not above any laws, nor is he superhuman. He could potentially blacklist me from performing in New York ever again, but I don't think he would. I'm his best performer and he knows it.

I've been performing in small shows here and there ever since I graduated college a few years ago, and it's been amazing to be able to work in the area I received my degree in. However, it doesn't exactly pay the bills. My family may be wealthy, but I do my best not to mooch off of them too much.

"This is why you're the actor and not the director," Lemaire says condescendingly as he bops my nose. "Anywho, I must be going. I have reservations. Ta ta, mes petites marionettes."

Freddie and I watch as Mr. Lemaire exits the stage, and once he's gone, the air in the room seems to grow a bit lighter.

"Incoming," Freddie says under his breath, his eyes looking over my shoulder in the direction Mr. Lemaire exited. Before I can ask what he means, I'm being lifted into the air, flailing like an idiot.

"Put me down, you sasquatch! You're crushing my ribs!"

"Who you calling sasquatch, pipsqueak?" my brothers familiar voice asks. Once I'm safely on the ground, I turn to face my group of supporters.

"You did great out up there, Ellie Belly," Holland teases. Having a twin is some people's dream, and it's pretty cool sometimes. Having someone who shares a lot of the same feelings, emotions, and thoughts as you can be fun, except when you have to share a birthday, a cake, a gift. That's when having a twin sucks ass. I got lucky I guess, since Holland is a guy, we didn't have to share many toys, so that's pretty nice.

"Thanks, and don't call me that," I demand. He's had that stupid nickname for me since we were like three. I have no idea why, but I think it's because it rhymes.

"Seriously, my bestie is practically famous! Look at you, performing in New York and shit. This is awesome, El!" Lainey squeals while giving me the biggest hug, as if we didn't see each other last night.

"Can I get your autograph?" Gwen chimes in, fanning herself with her playbill.

Gwen and Lainey are two of my very best friends. I've known Lainey since we were like, eight. Gwen came into the picture our freshman year of college at Ellington University, and the three of us have been inseparable ever since. We're even more inseparable now that Lainey decided to date my brother, which would be weird if we hadn't all seen it coming. They've bickered and fought since they were kids, and I always knew there would be something between them. I'm honestly surprised it took them this long to finally do something about it.

"Ellie, honey. You did an amazing job. I always love seeing you perform, baby. You're incredibly talented," my mother says with a smile, bringing me in for a tight hug. I squeeze her back, loving the way she feels in my arms. I love my mother. She's always been there for me, and she's always been one of my biggest supporters. She wasn't exactly thrilled when I told her I wanted to go to college for theatre, but she still supported my decision. She's been to every performance I've ever had, including the dumb musicals I was in between the ages of five and seventeen.

"Thanks, Mom. I'm glad you could make it."

Mom smiles, running her hand over my hair and down my cheek with a small smile.

"I wouldn't have missed your New York debut."

It would seem to some on the outside looking in that my life is pretty perfect. I have a good job that I actually enjoy, I have friends and a mother who love and support me. I would agree with them, however, there's some things about my life that aren't so peachy. My family wasn't always supportive of my theatre endeavors. Mom was worried I would never be able to find work, not that I really needed to work because Mom and Dad have old money. Mother never worked a day in her life; she didn't have to, and my father made sure of that.

Dad owned a multi-conglomerate of several different types of businesses, most of which were not exactly legal. I'm pretty positive he was part of the mafia. I'm not happy he's in prison for life, of course. He is my father, however that doesn't excuse what he's done. Especially since my mom had absolutely no idea that he was dealing with so many illegal activities. So, when we found out, thanks to Holland, it came as a shock.

"Who's ready for some drinks?" Holland asks with a grin, throwing his arm around Lainey's shoulders.

"Oh, I'm so ready. Sitting in those seats for two and a half hours made me thirsty," Lainey winks at me dramatically. "Maybe we can find you a man."

"She doesn't need a man, she's a strong, independent woman," Gwen chimes in. She's not exactly wrong. I don't want a man; I don't need one.

"You have to get back on the horse sometime, El," Lainey tells me, tossing her brown hair behind her shoulders.

"No, she doesn't. El's better without a guy dragging her down," Holland says.

Rolling my eyes, I begin to gather my things from the row of cubbies all of the cast members keep their belongings in backstage. Slinging my bag over my shoulder, I start to walk out of the theatre.

"Screw a man. Let's go get drunk," I declare.

Holland's right. I don't need a guy dragging me down or distracting me from doing what I love. My rehearsal schedules are crazy. My voice lessons, dance lessons, and acting lessons keep me more than busy when I'm not actively in a show. I have no time to entertain a man, and why would I want to?

Chapter 2

ELLIE

My head throbs and the room spins as my eyes flutter open. That fifth lemon drop shot was definitely a bad idea, but Lainey can be persistent. Honestly, she really didn't have to try that hard. The combination of the post-show high, being with my friends, and thinking of he who shall not be named really set me up for failure. I try not to get blackout drunk when I go out because I like to be aware of my surroundings, but last night was an exception, I guess.

The buzzing of my phone on the nightstand adds to the pain in my head. Grabbing it, I blink a few times as I wait for my eyes to adjust to the brightness of the screen. I first check the time and see that it's only eight in the morning. Who would be calling me this early?

Once the number comes into focus, I realize I don't recognize it and send it straight to voicemail. I don't have time for that right now. I just woke up, and I feel like I was hit by a bus. The last thing I need right now is to talk to a stranger on the phone. It's probably just a scammer trying to tell me that I owe them thirty thousand dollars or something. If it's that important, they'll leave a voicemail.

Groaning, I toss my phone on the pillow next to me and stare up at the ceiling. Sunlight peaks through the blinds, but not enough to make me wish I were dead. What does make me wish I were dead is the loud knocking on my bedroom door.

"Go away," I say, my voice sounding groggy. Instead of going away, they do the complete opposite and enter the room without invitation. Lainey prances over to the bed and plops down at my side with a grin.

"Good morning, sleepy head. You look like shit," she giggles. Narrowing my eyes, I glare at her.

"I hate you."

"You love me," she states with certainty.

"No, I don't. I hate you and your husband."

Lainey laughs. "You mean your brother?"

"Yes."

She jumps off the bed, pulling my arm in a poor attempt to get me to move. I'm dead weight right now, and there is absolutely nothing that could get me to move out of this bed.

"Why is Dean Ashby calling you?" Lainey asks, her face pulling into a concerned expression.

Shooting upright and completely regretting it a second later as the pain seeps into my brain, I grab my phone and watch as the unknown number leaves a voicemail.

"I have no idea," I tell Lainey honestly. We graduated years ago. I have no clue why our old dean would be calling me personally. Did I not actually graduate? Was I missing credits and they just caught it?

The thoughts swirl around in my head, progressively getting worse by the second before Lainey grabs my phone and begins to listen to the voicemail aloud.

"Hello, Miss Monroe. This is Dean Ashby calling. I was hoping we could discuss an opportunity I might have for you. Please call me back at your earliest convenience. I look forward to speaking with you." The voicemail ends and my head reels. What the hell kind of opportunity is he talking about? Lainey and I share a questioning glance before I snatch my phone from her and re-read the voicemail translation.

"Should I call him back?" I wonder out loud.

"Well yeah, I want to know what this opportunity is," she says with excitement. Staring at the phone for a few more seconds, I finally decide to hit the call button. I have no idea what he's going to say, or why I'm the one he's calling, but I'm about to find out. Setting the phone on speaker, it rings a few times before a masculine voice answers on the other end.

"This is Martin Ashby speaking."

My heart stutters and I suddenly forget how to speak. Come on, Ellie. Use your words. Lainey stares at me, giving me a 'what the hell are you doing' kind of look.

"Um, hi Dean Ashby. It's uh, it's Ellie Monroe. I was just calling you back. I apologize for missing your call. I didn't recognize the number," I stutter out. Shaking my head in shame, I wait for Dean Ashby's reply.

"That's quite alright, Miss Monroe. I'm glad you called back. I wanted to discuss something with you. Is now a good time?" I nod, forgetting that he can't see me.

"Yes, now works." When did I become so awkward? I'm not usually so awkward, and Lainey knows it too by the way she's looking at me.

"Great. I was wondering if you'd be interested in taking on the role of the director for our theatre program here at Ellington University?"

I'm sorry, what? Did he just ask me to be the *director?* As in, I'd actually be in charge, *and* I'd be getting paid? Lainey's eyes widen and a grin grows on her face.

"Director? What happened to Professor Littman?"

"Professor Littman had her baby this past weekend. She specifically requested that I call you to be her replacement," Dean Ashby explains. Professor Littman was my favorite professor out of my four years at Ellington. She gave me the confidence to continue my passion for theatre. I knew she liked me, but I never thought she'd ask for me personally to take over for her. Is this really happening?

Lainey makes a 'come on, give the man an answer' gesture, urging me to continue the conversation.

"Oh, wow. Dean Ashby, that would be an amazing opportunity. But I don't think I have the qualifications to lead a class," I cringe at my stupid response. Why am I trying to talk him out of hiring me?

"Oh, don't worry about that. I know you'll be the perfect person for the job. Honestly, I'm in a bit of a bind, Miss Monroe. You'd really be helping me out," he tells me.

Gritting my teeth, I mull over my options in my head. I could stay here and continue auditioning for musicals and plays in the area and have no steady income, or I can work as a director and have a guaranteed paycheck. I'd be crazy not to take it, right?

Lainey nods silently. She's been grinning so long I'll be surprised if her face isn't stuck that way.

"We can provide you with housing as well, so you don't have to worry about that," Dean Ashby adds.

"Could I think about it?" I ask, hoping that he'll say yes so I can have a moment to take it all in and actually weigh the pros and cons.

Dean Ashby clears his throat before saying, "I will need to know by end of day today, or I'll have to look elsewhere, Miss Monroe."

Nodding, I reply. "Yes, sir. I understand."

When we've hung up, I look up to see Lainey staring at me, her eyes wide in shock. She looks as if I just told her I was miraculously pregnant after not having sex for a year.

"Why are you looking at me like that?"

"Are you crazy? Take the damn job!" she shouts, standing from the bed. I'm honestly surprised by her response. I thought for sure she'd be against it since I'd be leaving her here.

"You think I should?" I ask.

"Hell yes! You'd be a director! An actual director of a play at Ellington. You've always wanted to direct. I don't see why you wouldn't go for it," she shrugs, her eyes seemingly searching my face for the reasons of my uncertainty.

She makes a good point. I have always wanted to direct. I've always wanted to prove to everyone, to prove to myself, that I could do it. I have the opportunity right at my fingertips, so why am I hesitating?

Lainey sits back on the bed right in front of me, grabbing my hands in hers. She looks sincere, her dark curls framing her model-like face. I've always been jealous of that face. Somehow, Lainey never had an awkward phase, and I don't understand how that's possible.

"You've always been weird with change, and this is a big step. You need to do this, okay? It could end up being the best decision of your life," she urges.

"Or the worst," I reply under my breath.

"Hey, I'm the pessimist in this friendship, not you. Look, I believe in you, El. You can do this."

With a deep breath, I look down at my phone, picking it up and making a life changing decision.

When the other line picks up, I immediately say, "I'll take it."

ELLIE

"I hope you find these accommodations to your liking, Miss Monroe. This was the closest house we had to campus," Dean Ashby explains, walking me through my new home for the next semester. I was able to convince him to let me try it out for one semester before agreeing to anything more than that.

Apparently, Professor Littman has decided that she's not coming back to Ellington University after her maternity leave, so the position is fully open now. I plan on using this semester as a trial to see if this is something I can actually do, and if it is, maybe I'll consider doing it full time.

When I told my mom that I was going back to Ellington, she was ecstatic for me. I knew she would be. It's an actual job with an actual paycheck. Gwen was sad I was leaving the city, but she was also really happy for me, and my brother was thrilled.

My twin has always been my biggest supporter, and I have always thought how lucky I am to have a brother who cares about me. Of course we fight and bicker as all siblings do, but as we've grown up and have had to deal with our family drama, we've learned to stick together.

Dean Ashby brings me into a grand dining room that is attached to the large kitchen. This place is almost as nice as my mom's house, which is crazy since this is a college campus. I guess that's what you get when you go to a school that charges an arm and a leg for tuition. You can't get into Ellington University unless you have money, you know someone, or you get a scholarship. Fortunately for Holland and me, our father attended Ellington and was an Elite. Being an Elite meant wealth, power, and brotherhood. Once you're inducted into said brotherhood, you're in it for life, and so are your children. Specifically, the sons.

Holland is what they call a Legacy. Since our father was an Elite, Holland is too. We were given no other choice but to attend Ellington. Lainey got in because her parents are richer than God, and Gwen was there on a scholarship.

I take in the space around me, noticing the intricate details in the old wood. The atmosphere is inviting and full of charm, with a sense of history that feels comforting rather than intimidating.

The grand entryway opens into a bright, airy foyer where natural light streams in through tall windows, warming the polished wood floors and highlighting the elegant staircase that curves gently upward.

To the right, a sunny sitting room is equipped with a beautiful area rug and cheerful patterned wallpaper. The fireplace is old and looks like it hasn't been used in years, but it still serves as a decorative focal point. The framed artwork on the walls looks as if it's from the late eighteen hundreds era, which gives the room a sort of spooky feel.

The dining room is spacious but comfortable, with a long wooden table that gleams under a simple chandelier. The China cabinets display neatly arranged dishes and glassware. As we make our way upstairs, I notice that each of the four bedrooms are spacious and thoughtfully decorated. I thought there would be more bedrooms, considering how large the house is.

"Yes, this is amazing. I wasn't expecting something so..."

"Spacious? Yes, well, you're an alum, and you're helping me out a great deal. You deserve a decent living space. Of course, you'll be sharing said space with a roommate, so you'll be grateful for the extra space," he explains. My heart freezes in my chest at the mention of a roommate. I couldn't have heard him right. There's no way he forgot to mention that I'd be living with someone, right?

"I'm sorry, roommate? You didn't mention anything about a roommate when we spoke about me taking the position."

Dean Ashby has the decency to look sheepish, knowing he conveniently left that part out. Running a hand through his grey, thin hair, he looks at me with guilt in his eyes.

"Unfortunately, we hired someone around the same time as you and promised you both housing. An oversight on our part, as we found that there was only one house available. Since the space is so big, I figured you would both have your own space. Your schedules are drastically different, so you probably won't even know he's here most days."

Blood rushes in my ears as I take in everything he's just said.

"Did you say he? As in a him? As in a guy? As in, the roommate I didn't even know I was going to have is a male?" Is this even legal? Can he even do this? Dean Ashby cringes at my sharp tone.

"I know this isn't ideal, but please understand that the intentions on my part were good; we just did not realize the lack of housing until it was too late."

My blood boils, and everything in me wants to say screw this and walk out, but I need this gig. This could be really good for me, and it could open up a lot of doors.

"Dean Ashby, I'm really not comfortable with this. Isn't there literally anything else we can do? I'll live on campus, I don't care," I plead desperately.

"Unfortunately, all of our dorms are occupied, Miss Monroe." His bushy brows furrow, and his cheeks pinken.

"Please, just give this a chance. I've met him, of course, and he is quite the gentleman. He's very professional. He's here to work and that is all. If you ever have any issues with him, notify me immediately and I will have him removed from our faculty."

Sighing, I nod. I don't think I'm going to win this. Maybe there really is nothing he can do. If I want to keep this job, this is something I need to endure. Who knows, maybe the guy will be really nice, and he won't end up killing me in my sleep.

"Is he aware of this arrangement?" I ask, crossing my arms over my chest. Dean Ashby looks at the ground nervously, his weight shifting from one side to the other.

"Not exactly."

"Oh my god, you can't be serious." My jaw drops at the audacity of this man to assume two strangers would be perfectly okay living together for an entire semester against their will.

As I mull over all the ways I could probably sue for this, I hear the sound of the front door opening and closing in the distance. Dean Ashby smiles as if this is completely normal and he didn't just throw a huge wrench into my life.

"Speak of the devil. We're in the kitchen!" he shouts in the direction of the front hall.

A tall, muscular man appears in the kitchen where Dean Ashby and I stand, watching in strained silence. The man's brown hair falls in his face, his muscles contracting as he reaches up and pushes it back.

His eyes look from Dean Ashby over to me, taking me in from head to toe.

My heart beats wildly in my chest. It can't be. This is not happening.

"You didn't tell me there would be a maid here. My bags are at the front door," he tells me with a smirk. He either thinks he's being funny, or he's being completely serious, which makes this situation ten times worse. Dean Ashby clears his throat before stepping forward to confront the guy.

"Oh, she's not a maid," he gestures to me. "This is Ellie Monroe. Ellie, this is Jamie Patterson. You two will be sharing the space for the time being until we can set up other accommodations."

Jamie nods slowly, looking from Ashby then back to me. He assesses me once more, and I can feel my face burning. The way he looks at me is so intense, and it's kind of making me uncomfortable. I just hope he argues this arrangement. Maybe Dean Ashby will reason with him more than he did me.

Finally, Jamie shrugs. "Fine by me."

My eyes widen in shock and horror. 'Fine by me'? Did he really just agree to this?

"I call top bunk," he says with a wink. The smug smirk on his pretty face makes me grind my teeth to keep from saying anything.

Jamie freaking Patterson. Out of all the men in this world, how did I end up having to room with Jamie Patterson? This must be some sort of cruel joke, right? There's no way I can share a house with this man. Not him. Not the guy that broke my heart all those years ago.

Chapter 4

JAMIE

Her face twists in disgust, causing a smirk to grow on my face. She's clearly pissed off, and my nonchalant attitude is making her blood boil even more. A strand of her blonde hair falls into her face as she looks between the Dean and me, looking completely appalled.

Dean Ashby must realize Ellie's about to blow because he begins to reassure her.

"There are plenty of rooms in the house. No need to share one," he says, his tone soft and careful, as if he's trying not to set her off.

I know there's a shit ton of rooms in this place, but I honestly wouldn't mind sharing a bed with little Miss Priss.

I can't tell if she even recognizes me. It's been years.

I mean, she looks incredibly angry, but that could be because she also wasn't aware that she'd have a housemate. What are the fucking chances that I take a job at the one place my ex-girlfriend is working at? I knew she went to school here, but I had no idea she was also an employee. It's like the universe said, 'screw you, man", and threw me to the wolves. And by wolves, I mean Ellie Monroe. The one that got away.

More like the one I dumped because I thought my career was more important than my relationship with her. To be fair, it was senior year of high school, and I was going into the NHL. She couldn't honestly expect that we'd go off to school together and live happily ever after at eighteen, right? But the way she's glaring at me says that might be exactly what she thought.

Her complexion pales when I make eye contact with her, her weight shifting from one leg to the other uncomfortably. I can tell she has no idea how to proceed, and yet she has so much to say. This is going to be fun.

Am I pissed that I wasn't aware of a roommate? Hell yeah, I am. That wasn't part of the deal. I never agreed to a fucking roommate. In fact, it took a lot of begging on Mr. Ashby's part to even get me here in the first place.

Being a coach for a college hockey team was not on my bucket list.

I'm Jamie fucking Patterson, a right winger for the Rhode Island Storm, one of the greatest teams in the NHL. There's no reason I should be teaching ungrateful douchebags how to play hockey.

Ellie's eyes roam my body until they stop right at my knee where a black brace wraps around it, making it possible for me to stand upright. Right, that's why I'm here. Her eyes shoot back up to my face, her cheeks reddening at being caught.

"I'm going to settle in. I have a lot to prepare for my first class on Monday. Thank you, Dean Ashby, for showing me around." She picks up her bags and begins to head for the stairs. Before heading up, she turns around and looks at the Dean. "I expect this issue to be resolved as soon as possible."

With that, she disappears up the stairs, leaving me and the Dean standing in the kitchen. He clears his throat and fixes his tie before turning to me. I've never met Martin Ashby, but something tells me he's not usually this unsure of himself. He strikes me as the type of asshole who grew up wealthy and never struggled a day in his life. Someone who expects people to fear him. Well, I don't fear anybody, so if he expects to be able to run over me, he's dead wrong.

Ellie didn't seem to be afraid of him, and I wonder if that's because he was her dean for four years or he's in her father's pocket. I'm not an idiot, I know what her family does. Or did, I'm not sure if that's still going on or not.

In high school, though, I pretended I didn't know there was something off about her father and the wealth he had. I pretended that Ellie's family was perfectly normal.

But I knew there was something off with them the minute I stepped foot into her world.

"I'm truly sorry about this misunderstanding, Mr. Patterson. This is not how I wanted your first impression of our wonderful school to be. I am working on getting this remedied immediately," Dean Ashby tells me.

I believe he'll do what he can, but I don't know if I'm in a rush for him to figure it out. This might not be ideal, and I may have been a bit aggravated at first, but it's Ellie. Having her as a housemate could either be insanely distracting or incredibly entertaining.

"Don't worry about it, Martin. It is what it is," I assure him. He nods graciously.

"Are you ready to start this weekend? The boys are excited to have you," he smiles. I'm sure they are. A famous hockey player coming in to take over as coach? What guy wouldn't be excited about that? These little pricks have no idea what's coming.

I've never coached a team before, but I've been playing hockey since I learned how to walk. I know everything there is to know about the damn sport, and I know what it takes to make it to the big leagues.

If they think daddy's money and a pretty face is going to get them to the NHL, they have another thing coming.

"Yep, I'm looking forward to getting up and running. Are they good?" Ashby grimaces before regaining his composure.

"They're okay. But they need to be great. Our lacrosse and rugby teams have been performing exceedingly well, and our hockey team needs to meet that same standard of excellence. Other schools are laughing at us, and I won't let that stand. Those boys need to be whipped into shape, and fast. I know you're going to help get us there, Mr. Patterson."

With that, he pats my shoulder before turning and heading out of the kitchen. When I hear the door click shut behind him, I exhale a deep breath. I remove my jacket, setting it on the back of a chair at the outrageously large island. Pulling a water bottle from the fully stocked fridge, I rest against the counter as I take a sip.

When Martin Ashby called me and offered me this position, I laughed. I couldn't believe he thought I'd want to coach. I've never taught anything. I've never been good enough at anything to be able to teach it. Hockey though? I can play some damn hockey.

A few hours later, I'm lying in bed watching a rerun of some shitty sitcom when I hear a floorboard creak from outside my door. Ellie's been so quiet, I'd almost forgotten she was even here.

Deciding to check it out, I climb out of bed, careful not to put too much weight on my bad knee and open my door a crack. Ellie walks down the hall to what I assume is her chosen room, wearing a fucking robe. Her hair is wrapped in a white towel on top of her head. All I can see are her legs. Her long, tan, freshly shaved legs. Legs that were once wrapped around my...

Jesus, Jamie. Get your head out of your ass. This is the first time I've seen her since we were eighteen. I didn't think it was possible for her to get any hotter, but here we are. When I saw her standing in the kitchen, I'll admit I didn't recognize her right away.

Her blonde hair passes her shoulders now; she always kept it at her shoulders. Her eyes somehow look even greener, and her body has filled out in all the right places. My god, she looks like a dream. So different yet exactly the same. Although the attitude is new.

I take a small step closer, and my damn knee betrays me, giving out under my weight and causing me to tip forward. I grab onto the door frame trying to steady myself, but the noise must have attracted Ellie because she stops in front of her door to face me. She holds a mug in her hands, the robe is tied tightly around her waist, and her expression is both curious and pissed off. Shit.

"What the hell are you doing?" she asks accusingly. "Were you watching me?"

Straightening, I lean against the door frame and try to act as if my heart isn't pounding out of my chest. I didn't mean for her to see me, but now my cover is blown. I shrug, crossing my arms over my chest.

"No," I say simply. Obviously, we both know it's a lie. Ellie rolls her eyes, and I feel my dick swell a bit at the action. Who knew I liked a woman with attitude? I mean, don't get me wrong, I haven't been celibate all these years. I was in the NHL for Christ's sake.

I slept with my fair share of beautiful women, but none of them stuck out to me. I didn't have time for a girlfriend, and I never let myself get distracted. Hockey came first, and it still does. Women are a distraction, and any distraction could take me away from my goal, which is to heal my knee and get back to my team.

When the injury happened, the doctors told me I'd probably never play again. With a Medial Collateral Ligament tear, it was already risky. It wouldn't have been so bad if I hadn't ignored it for weeks and kept playing through the pain. The team doctor told me it was stupid and reckless to continue playing with this sort of injury, and our coach was absolutely furious.

When they told me I would have to have surgery and I'd be out for months, if I can even return, I threw a chair at the wall of coach's office. I'll admit, it wasn't my finest moment. However, being told you can't play the sport you've lived for your whole life can be jarring.

Ellie uses her free hand to tighten her robe. "Then why are you standing in the doorway like a creeper?"

"I heard something, wanted to check it out," I say, which isn't completely a lie. I did hear something, but I knew it had to be her. What else would it be?

She takes a few steps closer until I can smell her floral shampoo and fruity body wash. My mouth waters at the thought of running my tongue up her thighs and tasting her... God, I haven't gotten laid in a while.

"You need to leave," she demands, stone-faced.

I'm taken aback by her bluntness. I wasn't expecting her to say that, and I honestly don't know how to reply. I don't want to leave, not now. Now that I know she wants me gone.

"Can't do that, sweetheart."

Her eyes never leave mine. She's staring me down so intensely, I'm not sure what she's thinking. It honestly looks like she's ready to murder me, but that can't be. Sweet little innocent Ellie, she couldn't hurt a fly. She's always been quiet and reserved, except when she's on stage. That's where she thrives, or at least, she used to. I haven't kept up with what she's done since high school. Okay, that's a lie. I thought about her more than I should have after the breakup. I'm the one that broke it off, but I still loved her. I just knew I couldn't be what she wanted me to be at that time.

"And why not?" she asks, her brows furrowing together, making her look more cute than intimidating, which is what she's trying to be.

"I have a job to do. Gotta whip this hockey team into shape, according to Ashby."

"Why are you here, Jamie?"

"I just told you. I'm coaching the—" she cuts me off.

"I don't mean here. I mean, why are you at Ellington? Why aren't you with your fancy hockey team and your fancy friends, with your fancy new cars and girls?"

Is that a hint of jealousy I hear in her tone? It can't be, right? It's been years, and she told me she hated me.

"Injury. Can't play. Ashby called a few weeks ago after word spread that I was on medical leave. Said he needed a new hockey coach and knew I was local. I told him no at first, but my mom convinced me it'll give me something to keep my mind off things."

Ellie rolls her eyes. "You knew I went here for college."

"It's been years since you graduated, Ellie. How could I have known you'd be here now?"

"I don't know. Maybe you've been stalking me or something," she shrugs. I laugh at the thought. I may have kept tabs on her, but I wouldn't say I was stalking. At first, I didn't think about her or us at all. I left, signed to the Storm, fucked my way through puck bunnies, and had a blast. I took it all in, the fame, the money, the girls. Ellie was my first love. Hockey was my life. It is my life, and that took precedence over everything else.

"I was too busy to stalk you, sweetheart."

"Was it worth it?" she asks, her tone as sharp as a knife.

My brows furrow. "Was what worth it?"

"Leaving me behind. Was it worth it?"

Is she seriously asking me if going to the fucking NHL was worth it? Hell, yes it was worth it. I put everything I had into this god damn sport. I spent my whole life dreaming about getting to where I'm at now. Well, maybe not where I am at this very second because the way Ellie's looking at me is actually kind of scary.

"Ellie, you can't be serious." Her expression turns to one of regret, as if she's realizing that she's not being logical.

"I'm sorry. I know the NHL was your dream. I'm glad you got there. You worked incredibly hard. I just... I wish I could have been there."

A sharp pain makes its way through my chest as guilt settles in my stomach like a weight. I really did love her, but we were kids. I would have never made it if she were with me. She wanted a family, kids and a dog, and white picket fence. I would have given everything up for her and I knew I couldn't do that. Not after all the work I'd put in. My dad would have killed me if he were alive.

I never thought I'd see her again, let alone be living with her. This was not something either of us could have seen coming. I never thought I'd have to face what I did again. The way I left things was shitty, even I know that. I was a complete asshole, and I could've gone about it completely differently. Yet, I didn't, and I broke her heart.

She looks down at her feet, and when she looks back up, I can see the tears forming in her eyes. Fuck, I didn't want her to cry.

"You just left. You left without a word. I woke up and you were gone. We had dinner, fell asleep under the stars, and then poof. Four years gone, without an explanation. What was I supposed to think?" Fuckkk. I really am a piece of shit.

"I was immature. I should have talked to you. I should have, I know. But it was easier to just disappear..."

Tears stream down her cheeks freely now, and I can tell she's pissed at herself for crying. She's always been a 'cry when she's angry' kind of girl.

"Easier for you..." she mumbles lowly while looking me in the eyes. Shaking her head softly, she turns around and begins to walk away. Part of me wants to beg her to stay. I feel like there's so much more I need to say, but I know nothing's changed. I still can't be with her, and she's better off without me.

"Ellie," I call after her before I can stop myself. She freezes but doesn't turn around. "I'm sorry."

Without a word, she walks to her room, opens the door and slams it shut.

Well, fuck.

Chapter 5

ELLIE

At eighteen, if anyone would have told me that I'd see Jamie Patterson again, I would have told them they had no idea what they were talking about. Seeing Jamie again was like seeing a unicorn. It would have been a one-in-a-million chance. I had no idea where he went or what he was doing. One minute we were in love, the next he was gone as if he never existed.

I'm not stupid, I knew he wanted to go to the NHL. It had been his dream for as long as I can remember. Him and his dad would watch games together on the couch, and they never missed a Storm home game.

Jamie would drag me along with them and I'd watch his face light up every time the team made a goal.

When his dad died, his drive to play grew. He'd practice day and night. I saw less and less of him, until eventually, I stopped seeing him at all. He wasn't the Jamie I knew anymore. He was someone I didn't recognize, but I loved him. I thought I was going to marry him. Imagine my shock when he fell off the face of the earth. He could have at least had the decency to break up with me to my face. Lainey threatened to hunt him down and chop off his dick on numerous occasions. She couldn't stand seeing me so depressed. It took months for me to finally feel like myself again.

I vowed to never watch hockey again in fear that I'd one day see Jamie on TV and completely lose it again. I had no idea if he went off to college or if he ended up in the NHL like he'd always dreamt of. I told Lainey and Holland to keep their mouths shut if they ever found out anything about Jamie and what he was doing. Of course, my idiot brother can't keep a secret and let it slip that Jamie was drafted to the Storm. That was the last time I thought about Jamie Patterson.

When I got to college, I focused on my classes and my friends, living my life and having fun like a college girl is supposed to. Yet, every time a guy would flirt with me or try to get intimate, I'd freeze up. I'd think about Jamie and how much I loved him. How badly he hurt me. I did end up dating a guy for a while though.

Ty was an asshole, but he was attractive, and it pissed Holland off that I was with him. We only dated for a few months before he cheated on me with the next best thing. I honestly think he was only with me because he wanted to piss off my brother, so it worked for both of us. I wasn't heartbroken over the loss of Ty Manning. Not like I was over Jamie.

Running my hands through my hair, I take a deep, shaking breath and press the Facetime button on my phone. It rings twice before Lainey's face lights up my screen.

"Bitch, you never called me last night. I thought you died," she squeals.

Rolling my eyes, I say, "You're so dramatic. I'm alive, I just... got distracted."

Lainey's eyes narrow, and her expression turns suspicious.

"What's wrong? Why do you look like that?" she demands.

"What do you mean? Like what?" I ask, feigning innocence.

"Like you've seen the ghost of Christmas past. What happened?" How does she know everything? I seriously don't get how she can tell that by just looking at me. I mean, we have known each other since we were kids, but still. She can read people better than anyone I've ever met.

"Nothing happened," I lie.

"Ellie Morgan Monroe. Tell me what's going on."

I deflate, lying back on my pillow and deciding it's better to tell her now than her showing up and finding out that way.

"He's here," I say ominously, not wanting to say his name out loud, as if it'll change the fact that he's here. Lainey moves closer to the phone, looking intrigued.

"Who's there?" I cringe inwardly, knowing what her reaction is going to be.

"Jamie..."

Her eyes practically bug out of her head in shock. I'm betting that's the last name she thought I'd say.

"Jamie Patterson? Like, from high school?" she asks, and I nod.

"That would be the one."

"What the fuck is he doing there?" Shrugging, I play with the ends of my hair, a nervous habit I've had for years. That's one of the reasons I kept it so short most of my life. I've let it grow out recently, not only because I actually like the way it looks, but because I haven't had the time to go to the salon.

"He's the new hockey coach. But that's not all," I pause, taking in a breath before continuing. "We're housemates."

"You're WHAT?" she yells into the camera. Yep, there's the reaction I was expecting.

"Shhh!" I shush her, looking around my room as if Jamie's going to pop in any second. "He could hear you!"

"What happened?" I hear a male voice ask before my brothers face pops into view next to Lainey's.

"Jamie's there. They're living together," she explains.

I watch as Holland's face turns red and turn the volume down on my phone, hoping it's low enough so Jamie can't hear what he's about to say.

"Jamie fucking Patterson?! What the hell do you mean you're living together?!" Holland seethes. He's hated him ever since we broke up, naturally.

"It's not like that!" I defend quickly. "You know how Dean Ashby promised housing if I took the job? Well, apparently there was a mix up and there was only one available. Apparently, Ashby hired Jamie around the same time, and he obviously offered him a place to stay too."

Lainey and Holland share a disgusted glance before looking back at the screen.

"Tell Ashby that he needs to figure something out ASAP, or he'll be hearing from me," Holland threatens. Holland's always been protective, and he's literally always had my back. He'd take the fall for things I did when we were kids just so our dad would yell at him more than me. He's warded off stupid boys since we were teens, and when I started dating Jamie, he threatened to kill him if he hurt me. Obviously, Jamie is still alive so that was an idle threat, but he meant well by it.

My father never conducted his business dealings around my mother and I, but he brought Holland in at a young age. I knew whatever was going on was shady, but I learned never to ask questions. Holland learned how to defend himself real quick, and he grew up unafraid of the world and what it could do to him.

Granted, my father never exactly told Holland that what he was doing was illegal, so Holland only thought he was following in dad's footsteps. He was devastated when he found out dad had been lying to him about everything since the beginning.

I know for a fact Holland would show up here and threaten everyone involved in this misunderstanding, but it's not necessary.

"I did. He is. He assured me he'd keep an eye out for a new location, and he'd let me know as soon as one becomes available. In the meantime, I'm stuck with—"

"A lying, conniving pussy who left you without a fucking word and broke your heart," Holland spits, his tone hot like fire. He's pissed, and rightfully so. So am I.

"Yeah..." is all I can say. This whole situation sucks, but at this point it's out of my hands. I can't do anything about it, other than leave. That's not happening though. I'm not letting Jamie take this away from me. I'm just going to ignore him and pretend like he's not even here. It shouldn't be hard, right? Our schedules are probably so different, and this house is so big we'll most likely never see each other. I just need to figure out his routine and avoid being in the same vicinity as him.

The next morning, I make my coffee and sit at the massive island in the middle of the kitchen while scrolling through videos of my friends from my theatre company back in the city. I've been keeping Freddie posted on what's been happening here, and he's told me several times how much of a 'lucky bitch' I am for being roommates with a hot hockey player.

He's not quite understanding the fact that this particular hockey player broke my heart.

My first class is today, and I'm starting to feel really nervous. I'm not sure if it's imposter syndrome or what, but I'm feeling highly underqualified to even be here right now. I mean, I know what I'm talking about, and I have the experience. What I don't have is teaching experience or director experience. However, they say the best way to learn is to do, so here I am. Taking a deep breath in, I take the last sip of my coffee and watch one more video before stuffing my things in my bag and hopping off the chair.

The alarm I set on my phone to remind me to grab food goes off and as I attempt to turn the damn thing off, I run into a hard body, causing me to stumble back. When I regain my composure, Jamie is staring at me like I'm some new species of animal he's never seen before. My heart begins to race, and I have to mentally remind myself to breathe because I think I've forgotten how. His brown hair curls under the hat he's put on, backwards might I add. His sweats and black t-shirt make his muscles pop, and my eyes land on the one spot they shouldn't. I look away quickly, hoping he didn't catch me staring at his dick.

"Watch where you're going," I say, knowing full well that I ran into him because I was trying to turn off my stupid alarm. He knows it too because a smirk grows on his face.

"You ran into me, Sweetheart." My heart stutters at the pet name. He doesn't get to do that. He doesn't get to try to flirt and call me cute names and act as if everything is fine.

It's not fine, and I won't pretend it is. I know that might be petty, but I don't care. What he did was way worse.

"Why are you even here?" I ask accusingly.

"Gotta get to work," he shrugs, walking past me and into the kitchen, heading directly to the fridge. Opening it, he pulls out a protein shake, and I watch as his bicep flexes as he shakes it. God, when did he get so buff? All that time in the gym really paid off, I guess.

"Work? You have practice now? It's nine in the morning."

He nods, grabbing a gym bag from off the floor. "Yup. Early morning practices are the best. Gotta get the blood pumping and shit," he explains, his velvety smooth voice like a drug. He always had a deep voice, and now it's more manly. It's really annoying.

"Is this going to be like, a normal thing?" I query. His brows furrow as he takes a sip of his shake, never breaking eye contact.

"Why? You wanna keep tabs on me?"

"No, I want to avoid having to see you as much as possible," I reply, but I don't think I even believe that.

He chuckles, the sound bringing me back to when we were sixteen and laughing together about some video we'd just watched. My heart aches at the thought.

"Whatever you say, sweetheart." He makes his way to the front door, grabbing a hockey stick that had been leaning against the wall.

"Don't call me that," I call after him. He turns around with a teasing smile.

"What should I call you then?"

"Nothing."

Chapter 6

ELLIE

I step outside right as Jamie shuts the door behind him, immediately regretting not checking the weather before I left. A gust of cold wind slaps me in the face and sends my hair flying in every direction. Great. Perfect. Exactly what I needed on my first day trying to prove I'm not some imposter pretending to be a professor.

The campus is still quiet this early, only a few students walking toward the arts building, backpacks slung over one shoulder, earbuds in, half-asleep. My stomach twists. I used to be one of them and now I'm supposed to lead them?

My shoes crunch against the gravel as I cut across the quad, the smell of damp leaves and cold air filling my lungs. Ellington has always been beautiful this time of year. Fall in Connecticut is one of my favorite things. It may be chilly, but the vibrant colors and falling leaves make up for it. The town of Seabrooke is small. There're two gas stations, a liquor store, a small grocery store, and the college. Ellington is known for its beauty and old architecture. It feels different now, walking through it as a faculty member. Everything feels...bigger.

I'm halfway to the theatre building when my phone vibrates in my hand. Lainey's contact name pops up on the screen.

Main Bitch

Main Bitch: *Have you killed him yet?*
Me: *No, but I came close.*
Main Bitch: *Well, if you do, don't get caught.*

Rolling my eyes, I shove the phone into my coat pocket and hurry down the steps toward the side door reserved for faculty.

My chest tightens as I swipe myself inside. The familiar scent of sawdust and paint hits me immediately, but that calming feeling it usually brings me is lost. The hallways feel narrower. The bulletin boards on the walls seem more cluttered, and every footstep echoes as if announcing, 'You don't belong here.' I swallow hard.

Walking into the rehearsal studio, I watch as students take their seats, and I'm hit with a wave of nostalgia so strong I nearly choke. I don't know how I got here, but if I stand here any longer, these people are going to think I'm mute.

Stepping up onto the stage, I clear my throat and wait for their attention. When they all turn and stare, heat rushes to my cheeks.

Pushing through the panic that has taken over my body, I say, "Good morning," but it comes out so quiet I can barely hear myself.

I try again, clearing my throat once more.

"I'm Ellie Monroe. I'll be taking over for Professor Littman this semester." A ripple of whispers takes over the room. I see some nods, and a few confused faces. They're probably freshmen wondering if I'm a senior covering a student-led meeting.

"I... I know this might be a surprise to some of you," I continue, "but this is going to be a great semester. I'm excited to get started."

A girl with purple hair and glasses raises her hand.

"Yes?"

"Are you even old enough to be teaching a college class?" she asks, her nose scrunching in disgust. Seriously? That's how we're going to start off? My stomach lurches as I try to think of how to respond.

"Um, yes. I am."

Another student in the back of the room, a guy with a beanie and long hair raises his hand before asking, "Are you like, famous?"

I chuckle. At least his question wasn't so rude.

"No, I'm not. But I do perform in New York City."

A few students exchange impressed looks. Purple Hair sits up straighter. Maybe she'll accept me now. Something in my chest loosens, just slightly.

Before I can continue, the door opens from behind me. I turn, expecting a late student or something, but what I see instead is Jamie striding into the room like he owns it. Why does he have to be so... him?

He's sweaty from practice. He pushes his hair out of his eyes, his sweatpants hanging dangerously low on his hips as a handful of hockey players trail behind him like puppies, laughing too loudly, joking, bumping shoulders. Why the hell is he here? In my space? Why does the universe hate me?

Jamie stops when he sees me, smirk already forming. "Hi, Sweetheart."

Twenty heads swivel toward me.

"I told you not to call me that," I grit through my teeth. I step toward him, whispering sharply.

"Get out."

"Just saying hi. Didn't know we'd be office neighbors too," he winks before turning to his players. "Let's go."

They all follow, throwing glances over their shoulders like they've just witnessed an episode of some drama show.

The second the door closes, the room erupts with whispers and soft gasps, eyes darting between me and the exit.

Purple Hair raises her eyebrows. "Sooo...who's that?"

"The hockey coach," I answer stiffly.

"And you're together?"

"No," I say immediately. Too immediately.

She grins like she definitely does not believe me. The others settle in more eagerly now, watching me like I'm suddenly a walking plot twist. Wonderful. Exactly what I wanted on my first day. Speculations of me dating another faculty member, one that I can't stand to be in the same room as.

I inhale deeply and clap my hands once, shaking any thoughts of Jamie out of my body.

"Let's get started."

The class begins and my heart eventually slows. I dive into warm-ups, scripts, vocal exercises. For the first time all morning, I feel like myself again. By the time class ends, several students are lingering to ask questions. My chest aches in a good way and I finally feel like maybe I can do this.

After saying goodbye to my students, I gather my things, still smiling as I step into the hallway. I immediately slam into a very solid, very familiar wall of muscle.

Jamie grips my elbows, steadying me. "Really? Twice in one day?" You've got to be kidding me! So much for barely ever seeing each other.

I shove his hands away.

"You need to stop being everywhere."

"It's a hallway, Ellie."

"Then pick another one."

He laughs soft and low, the kind of laugh I used to fall asleep listening to, and the ache returns.

"I heard your class," he says. "Sounded good."

I blink. "You were listening?"

He shrugs, jaw tightening. "Walls are thin."

"Well, I don't need your approval," I snap.

"Didn't say you did," he pauses, eyes flicking over my face. "You crushed it, though."

The compliment hits harder than it should, and I hate that it does. Before I can respond, he steps back, hooking his gym bag over his shoulder.

"See you at home," he says simply.

And then he's gone, leaving me alone in the hallway with my heart hammering against my ribs.

Chapter 7

JAMIE

I don't know what possessed me to stay and listen to her class. I don't know why I talked to her about it afterward. I don't know why I feel like I have to be close to her. I saw her in that kitchen, in the hallway in that robe, and it was like a wave came crashing down on me, pulling me under with the tide. I don't even know who she is anymore, yet I feel like I need to. That pisses me off more than anything, because I know I need to focus all of my energy on healing and getting the hell out of here.

If I'm being honest with myself though, I think a big part of me knows that I'm never going to play professional hockey again. At least, my knee injury is most likely never going to heal enough for me to play like I used to. I'm probably better off here coaching than straining my knee by playing back-to-back games and practicing twenty-four seven.

I'm still doing physical therapy three times a week and having it checked weekly to make sure its healing properly. However, even with all that, I just have this aching feeling that my Storm days are over.

Practice is brutal.

These kids have talent, they're just lazy and spoiled. They coast through drills like mommy and daddy are waiting on the sidelines with juice boxes and participation trophies.

"Hey, Coach?" one of the defensemen pipes up. "Are we gonna stay on conditioning all practice?"

"Yup," I say curtly.

"That's like... all we've done for an hour," the guy that I now know as Jacob Rostolvic says as he comes to a stop in front of me, sweat pouring down his face.

"Good. Maybe you'll finally grow some lungs."

A groan ripples through the team.

"You think you'll make it to the NHL whining like little babies? You want to compete? Earn it."

They groan again, but they skate harder.

Eventually I grow tired of watching them skate back and forth and decide to end practice for the day.

When they finally file out of the locker room their legs are Jello and their egos are bruised. Good. They need it.

I drop into the chair behind my desk and roll up my compression pants to check my knee. Even under the brace, it's swollen. It'll be worse tomorrow.

I breathe through it, waiting for the pain to dull, but it never does.

By the time I make it back to the house, the sun's dipping low and I'm starving. I don't expect Ellie to be in the kitchen, sitting at the island with her nose in paperwork. She looks so focused, and when a piece of her blonde hair falls into her face, she quickly tucks it behind her ear.

She looks up the second she senses me, eyes narrowing like I'm a problem she doesn't have the energy for.

"What?" she snaps, not even attempting politeness.

I grab a water from the fridge. "Nothing. You look busy."

"Good observation."

I bite the inside of my cheek. Alright. She's pissed. That's fair.

I lean my hip against the counter. "You know, the attitude's new."

"No," she bites, her head snapping in my direction. "What's new is you being here."

Her voice cracks a little, and it guts me. I know she must hate me, I know I didn't think things through when I left. I don't blame her for not wanting anything to do with me.

I step forward before I can think better of it. "Look, Ellie—"

"No." She raises a hand, palm out. "You don't get to stroll back into my life and pretend this is normal. We are not normal. This situation isn't normal."

A beat passes before I can get myself to reply, and when I finally do, all I can say is, "Okay."

That seems to surprise her. Her eyes flick to mine, guarded but curious.

"Ellie, I'm not trying to pretend nothing happened," I say quietly. "I know what I did. I know how I left. And I'm not asking you to be okay with it."

She looks down at her papers, blinking rapidly like she's refusing to let emotion win.

"Then what *do* you want?" she practically whispers.

The truth sits heavy on my tongue. Something I haven't let myself think about in years, something I didn't even know I wanted until I saw her standing there in the kitchen.

"Nothing," I say instead. "We're coworkers. Housemates. I won't bother you."

It feels like a punch straight to the gut saying it out loud. But maybe it's what she needs. Maybe it's what *I* need.

She swallows once, then nods tightly. It seems like there's so much she wants to say, but she's fighting with something inside herself.

"Good." With that, she gathers her things and heads toward the stairs.

"Ellie?" I call after her before I can stop myself.

She pauses, just barely. I know everything in her is telling her to keep moving, but I also know she needs to hear what I'm about to say.

"I'm not trying to make your life harder."

She doesn't turn around. "You don't have to try."

Then she's gone, leaving me in the kitchen with nothing but my throbbing knee and a growing ache in my chest that I don't have a name for. I rub my brace like it'll somehow fix the past too. No such luck.

Well, that could have gone better.

My phone buzzes in my pocket, distracting me from the self-deprecating thoughts swimming around in my head. Pulling it out, I see it's my mom.

"Hi, Mom," I say, trying to sound more upbeat than I feel.

"Hi, honey. I just wanted to check in to see how your first day as a coach went. You didn't push the kids too hard, did you?"

I chuckle as I think back to the guys dripping in sweat, walking out of practice like they had sticks up their asses.

"It went well, mom."

"How's the knee? Are you settling in? Did you eat today? Remember what Dr. Larson said. Don't push it," she says hurriedly. Mom always worries. She's been like that since I was a kid. I think it has to do with the fact that I'm an only child, so she feels extremely protective over me. It got worse after dad died. I know she's lonely.

"The knee is the same, and I'm settling in fine."

I hear her sigh of relief on the other end. "You know I worry about you, honey."

"I know, mom. I'm okay, really. But I gotta go. I need to shower and stuff," I say, hoping she'll accept that, and she does.

An hour later, I'm showered and lying in bed answering a slew of text messages in the team group chat.

Rhode Island Stormies

Connor Grieves: *That call was seriously fucked. The ref had it out for you, Calli.*
Billy Callahan: *I'm telling you, I've never been so personally victimized in my life. Felt intimate. Didn't consent.*
Theo Cramer: *Maybe he was into you. You do have that "problematic but charming" energy.*
Billy Callahan: *Please. If he wanted me, he could've just bought me a drink instead of a penalty.*
Connor Grieves: *Honestly, the way he blew that whistle? Aggressive.*
Wilder Ranslavic: *A little too aggressive. Man really said 'watch this'.*
Billy Callahan: *Meanwhile I get slammed into the boards and he just... looks away. Classic.*
Connor Grieves: *You were asking for it wearing those tight-ass pants.*
Billy Callahan: *These thighs are a public service.*
Theo Cramer: *I hate this team.*
Connor Grieves: *You love us. Especially when we're sweaty and angry.*
Theo Cramer: *Don't flatter yourselves. I'm only here for the adrenaline and unresolved tension.*
Wilder Ranslavic: *Same. And the post-game showers.*
Connor Grieves: *Wow. Straight to jail.*
Theo Cramer: *Says the guy who stripped his jersey off the second the buzzer hit.*
Connor Grieves: *It was hot. Physically. And emotionally.*
Billy Calhahan: *Refs screwed us, but at least we looked good losing.*
Wilder Ranslavic: *That's the real win.*
Connor Grieves: *Hey Patty, you alive?*

Billy Callahan: *Yo, Patty. You would have shit yourself if you were there tonight.*
Theo Cramer: *I miss Patterson. He kept you idiots in check.*
Wilder Ranslavic: *Same.*
Jamie Patterson: *I leave for ten minutes and the team goes to shit.*
Billy Callahan: *We need you, daddy.*
Jamie Patterson: *You are seriously mentally ill.*

God, I miss those guys. When I joined the team six years ago, I never thought I'd be this close to my teammates, but we really are like brothers. Callahan and I were drafted together, Theo and Wilder were on the team before I got there, and Connor is the rookie. We get along great on and off the ice. It's better that way when you're constantly travelling together.

The guys don't know about Ellie or the life I had before coming to the Storm. It was never really a topic of conversation. All they know is that I never wanted to be tied down. Theo and Callahan are married men, and Wilder has a long-term girlfriend that he's been with since high school. It's only Connor and I that are the single ones, and Connor is probably going to fuck his way through his rookie year anyway.

When I went out on LTIR, I thought I'd be sitting at home alone wallowing in self-pity. I never expected to end up coaching.

The last thing I expected was Ellie. No, correction. The last thing I expected was *living* with Ellie.

How is it possible that I haven't seen her in years, and the minute she's in front of me again, I feel like I need her?

There's gotta be some psychological word for that right? I mean, yeah. She looked like a goddess, and seeing the way she's turned into this... this woman. This accomplished, beautiful woman. I'm actually proud of her.

She's doing what she always wanted to do, and I know she worked her ass off to get here. Her perseverance always impressed me. It inspired me.

She never knew that, and she probably never will. But Ellie Monroe, she helped me keep going even when I wanted to quit. She thought I was training so hard to keep my mind off my dad, but I was only trying to be more like her.

And then I left her.

What a fucking idiot.

Chapter 8

ELLIE

My first week as a director went better than I expected. I half expected myself to fail and run away screaming, never to return again. I thought for sure the students would laugh at me, call me an imposter and revolt.

But that didn't happen. In fact, they've been great. They seem really excited to start the auditioning process, and I'm excited to watch them give it their all. I know what it feels like to stand in front of a director and have to place everything else aside to focus on becoming someone else for a few moments.

Acting is one of the most vulnerable things you can do. Not only are you trying to portray someone else, but you also have to make people believe what you're saying and doing.

You have to put yourself out there and be prepared to get rejected hundreds of times. Your entire life is on display, and you're doing it all in front of thousands of people.

People who judge you for every move you make; what you wear, what you eat, how much you weigh, how you spend your money. I'm not a famous actress, I'm not on TV or in the movies, and stage acting is much different from film acting. I have seen both sides of things, and my stance has never changed. Being an actor is not for the weak.

It's long, gruelling rehearsals, late nights studying lines and blocking, getting to know the character you're playing. I wouldn't trade it for the world, though. I love that I get to do this every day. I love that I chose this path for myself, and I love that I never gave up. I didn't exactly expect that it would bring me back to Ellington to direct, but here I am. I am proud to be where I am.

I'm at the coffee shop on campus when I get a text from Lainey, once again asking if I've murdered my new roommate yet. I swear she just loves the drama of it all. If she were here, she'd be having a field day. I reply with a quick 'nope' and shove my phone in my bag. I'm trying to study this cast list and get an idea of what each character is like so I can mentally cast some of my students. They haven't auditioned yet, but I like to have an idea of who would be good playing who.

The café is quiet today, with only a few students scattered at the small tables in the dining space. One works on their laptop while another eats a scone, seemingly watching something on their phone. The space smells like freshly brewed coffee, one of my favorite smells in the entire world, and the lights are dim. I absolutely love spending time at a café. Whenever I go to a new city, I have to try out their local cafés to see who has the best coffee. I would say I'm kind of like a coffee connoisseur.

I've been avoiding the house since my conversation with Jamie the other day. He knows what he did. He knows how he left me without a word. He'd said he's not asking me to be okay with it, but if he's not asking for forgiveness, what does he want? Obviously, the rational part of me knows that he's not here for me.

There's a huge possibility that he wants absolutely nothing from me and he's just here to do his job. He had no way of knowing that I'd be here, nor would he have cared. He's not here for me. I know that. I don't want him to be... at least, I think I don't want him to be.

God, why did he have to show up here? Why him? Why *me*? I spent so long trying to leave him in the past, and now he's here? Out of absolutely freaking nowhere, might I add.

Have I done something awful and this is how God is punishing me? Forcing me to share a house with the man that obliterated my heart?

A part of me still hates him for what he did to me, what he put me through. He doesn't even know that half of it.

The sleepless nights spent curled up in a ball crying. The memories I had to erase from my mind. The time I had to spend telling myself that it wasn't me, it was him.

At eighteen, he was my world. I saw my future, and he was in it. To have that ripped away so suddenly without a reason, that was the cruelest thing he could have done to me. To someone he claimed to love. Because it was easier for him to just leave without a trace? What about me?

Jamie was selfish and cruel. What he did was so completely out of character for him and I think that's what shocked me the most. Looking at him now though, who knows who he is. I'd heard things throughout the years of how well he was doing in the NHL.

He was apparently a big star, which is no surprise. I always knew he would be. I never wished for him to fail, that's just not who I am. But I hated him, and nothing could have changed that. Not him coming back, not him apologizing.

Taking a deep breath, I try to push thoughts of Jamie out of my mind. I will never let him consume my thoughts again. Although, when I saw him walk into my classroom the other day, all sweaty and dressed in sweats and his Rhode Island Storm shirt, I almost fainted.

I actually had to hold my breath, because how the hell can someone look that good while simultaneously looking like a wet dog? That should be impossible.

Yet there he was, looking all God-like and masculine. I'm sure he's had women fawning over him for years since becoming a big hockey star. Not that I care, of course. It's just an educated guess.

There's no way he doesn't have a whole line up of women waiting for him to come back to the team and give them what they desperately want from him. I bet he can't wait to get back to them, too.

Jeez, I sound like a jealous girlfriend. Jamie can do whatever the hell he wants with whoever he wants. I don't give a shit. He's nothing to me but an annoying thorn in my side that I have to deal with while I'm here. Once the semester is over, I'll be gone, and Jamie will no longer be an issue.

I'm halfway through my latte when the bell above the café door rings again. I don't look up right away. I don't need to. Something in my chest tightens instinctively, like my body has learned his presence before my brain can catch up.

"Ellie."

Goddammit.

I close my eyes for a brief, traitorous second before lifting my gaze. Jamie stands a few feet away from my table, hands shoved into the pockets of his jacket. He looks... mischievous. Almost as if he's playing a game and he's the only one that knows the rules.

"I'm busy," I say, gesturing pointedly to the stack of papers in front of me.

"Yeah. I can see that," he says, shifting his weight and glancing around the café like he's suddenly aware we're in public. "I won't take long."

I sigh, irritation flaring hot and fast. "What do you want, Jamie?"

He pauses, his jaw tightening.

"Dean Ashby called," he says. "About the housing."

My stomach flips. Against my will, hope sparks.

"And?" I ask carefully.

"And there's nothing available. Yet," he grimaces like he knows exactly how that'll land. "He said maybe mid-semester."

The hope fizzles out, leaving behind something bitter and sharp.

"So, we're stuck," I say flatly. Jamie winces a bit, like my reaction was expected but disappointing.

"For now." He nods once. "Yeah."

I stare at him for a long moment, then look back down at my notes. "Okay."

"That's it?" he asks, clearly thrown.

"That's it," I repeat. "Now, if you'll excuse me. I have to get back to work."

He huffs out a quiet laugh. "You always do that."

I look up sharply. "Do what?"

"Avoid having a conversation," he shrugs and my blood boils.

"What is that supposed to mean?"

"It means that even back then you avoided talking to me whenever we had to talk about something serious. Like when I told you I wasn't going to Ellington because I wanted to focus on hockey. You completely skirted around that entire conversation for weeks."

My eyes water, and I hate myself for being so emotional. He's right. I did avoid that conversation for as long as I could because I knew it was only going to end one way. And it did.

"I don't know what you're talking about," I lie, packing up my papers in hurry. I want to get the hell out of here before I start crying. He doesn't get to see me cry.

Something flashes across his face. Regret, maybe. Or guilt. Or both. He pulls out the chair across from me and sits before I can stop him.

"I'm not here to fight," he says. "Or... whatever this is."

"Then why are you here?" I demand, keeping my voice low.

"I just... I wanted to let you know that Ashby called. We're living together, Ellie. Pretending the other doesn't exist isn't exactly working."

"It works great for me."

"Bull," he quips.

My grip tightens around my coffee cup. "You don't get to tell me how I feel."

"I know," he says. "I'm sorry."

The word hangs between us, fragile and thin. I don't know if I even believe him.

I scoff. "You already said that."

"I know," he says quietly, leaning forward slightly. "I just... I meant it. Then and now."

I study his face, searching for the boy I loved, the man I lost, seeing a stranger in front of me. He looks tired. Older. The cocky edge is still there, but dulled, like it's been worn down by pain and disappointment and a knee that quit on him.

"You disappeared," I say quietly. "Do you know what that does to someone?"

His throat bobs. "Yeah. I do."

"Then why?" my voice cracks despite my best efforts to keep my freaking emotions under control.

He looks down at the table, fingers curling into fists. He looks like he's at war with himself, and damn me, I feel bad for him.

"Because I was scared," he admits. "Because if I stayed, I would've chosen you. And I didn't trust myself not to."

The unexpected confession hits me square in the chest. The thought of him choosing me over something he'd worked for his entire life makes me both happy and devastated.

"That doesn't make it better," I whisper.

"I know," he looks up again, eyes steady. "But it's the truth."

Silence settles between us, heavy with emotion. Like neither of us knows what to do or how to feel, and we're just... lost.

I shake my head, pushing my chair back. "I can't do this. Not right now."

"Ellie, come on."

I stand, slinging my bag over my shoulder. "Just leave me alone, okay?"

"Ellie," he says as I turn away.

I hesitate, just for a moment.

"When are you going to admit to yourself that you're kind of glad I'm here?"

Is he for real? Did he actually just ask me that? Right when I was starting to feel like he was human again?

"Never."

With that, I walk out of the café before he can say anything else.

That night, the house is quiet in a way that feels intentional. I cook pasta for one and eat it standing at the counter, scrolling mindlessly through my phone. Jamie doesn't come into the kitchen. I would think I was home alone if it weren't for his car in the driveway. When I finally head upstairs, his door is closed.

Good.

I shower, change into pajamas, and crawl into bed, staring at the ceiling as the events of the day replay in my mind.

'If I stayed, I would've chosen you.'

The words refuse to leave me alone. I squeeze my eyes shut. It doesn't matter. It doesn't change what happened. Love doesn't excuse abandonment, and apologies don't erase years of healing I had to do on my own. Still... my chest aches. Why am I like this? Why can't I be more like Lainey? Or Gwen even. They would tell him to fuck right off, I know they would. Why is that so hard for me to do?

As I'm finally drifting toward sleep, a soft knock sounds at my door. My heart jumps straight into my throat.

I sit up quickly, every muscle tense. "What?"

"It's me," Jamie says quietly through the door. "I uh... I just wanted to let you know that I'm heading out early tomorrow. Away game. I won't be back until late."

Relief washes over me, swift and undeniable.

"Okay," I say.

There's a pause and I think he's gone, but a moment later he says, "goodnight, Ellie."

I don't reply, I just wait until I hear his footsteps retreat down the hall and listen as his door latches shut.

I lie back down, staring into the darkness, trying to convince myself that the quiet doesn't feel lonely.

Trying, and failing to ignore the truth settling deep in my chest. Jamie isn't going anywhere. We're stuck together and I'm going to need to get used to it or this is going to be a miserable fifteen weeks.

Chapter 9

JAMIE

The locker room smells like sweat, disinfectant, and testosterone which is both familiar and grounding. It's easier here. Simple. Skate, shout, sweat, repeat. No complicated emotions. No history lurking around every corner.

And yet, Ellie's still in my head. Her voice. The way she looked at me in the café, like she was bracing for impact even while standing still. Like I was something dangerous she hadn't learned how to disarm yet.

I shouldn't have gone to see her. I especially shouldn't have told her the truth. 'If I stayed, I would've chosen you.' What the fuck was I thinking telling her that? I knew it wasn't going to change anything. She wasn't going to automatically forgive me with that one confession. It wasn't going to go back to the way things used to be before I fucked it all up. Do I want it to?

I think on that for a moment. Do I want things between us to go back to how we were before I left? Did I ever really stop loving her? Was this all a part of the universes plans to get us back together? Was it fate? I mean, Jesus, I don't know. I sound ridiculous. Ellie's just a girl. She's a distraction from the goal. But even I know I'm lying to myself. She's not just some girl. She's Ellie Monroe. She's my first love. She's my first... everything.

I remember our first time together. How scared she was. She'd asked me if it would hurt, and I didn't know what to tell her. I'd heard that it could pinch the girl a bit, but it wouldn't last. I wanted to make it special for her. Of course, it was as special as it could be for a quickie in her bedroom before her parents came home. We had to stay quiet since her brother was in the next room.

"We're going to get caught," I told her.

"We'll be quiet," she'd argued.

"I don't want to hurt you, El."

"You'd never hurt me."

God damnit, did I fuck that part up. I did hurt her, and she'd never trust me again. I don't even know why I'm so caught up on this. Ellie wants nothing to do with me, and I have a career to focus on. She is the last thing I should be thinking about right now.

"Coach."

I glance up to see Jacob Rostolvic hovering near the bench, helmet dangling from his fingers.

"What?" I say roughly.

He winces. "You're scaring the freshmen."

Good.

"Lace up," I tell him. "We're running drills."

Groans echo through the locker room, but no one argues. They learned fast that I don't bluff. On the ice, everything quiets in my head. The scrape of blades, the rhythm of passes, the sharp crack of puck against stick. It's the only place my thoughts don't spiral. My knee burns, but I welcome the pain. It reminds me I'm still here. Still useful.

For a moment, I can almost pretend this is enough.

The bus ride to the away game is loud and chaotic. Music blares from someone's speaker, and the guys chirp back and forth, shoving each other like overgrown children. I sit near the front, scrolling through my phone without really seeing anything.

My mom's name pops up in my notifications.

Mom

Mom: *Did you eat today?*

I smirk faintly.

Me: *Working on it.*

Mom: *That's not an answer.*

Me: *Yes, Mom.*

Three dots appear, disappear.

Mom: *I'm proud of you.*

I lock my phone and lean my head back against the seat, staring at the ceiling. I wish my dad were here. He'd tell me to stop feeling sorry for myself. He'd say pain is temporary and legacies last forever. He'd always pushed me to be the best, to get up even when things got tough. My dad was my biggest fan, and the truth is... without him, I would've never made it to the NHL. I would have never gotten to be the Storm's number one right winger. My life would be drastically different if my dad hadn't been there to shove me in the right direction. I miss him every god damn day.

The game was rough. Kind of like how I'm feeling right now honestly. I want to say I'm shocked, but I'm not. These boys don't have enough drive, not yet.

We lost by one point, and the boys are pissed. They should be, that was God awful. They played like absolute dog piss.

"You had them," I tell them in the locker room after. "You let off the gas. That's on you."

They nod, breathing heavy, sweat dripping. They know I'm right.

When the bus finally pulls back onto campus late that night, exhaustion weighs down my bones. I'm ready for a long shower and my bed. Game days are always a lot, but when you're the coach, it feels different. Like everyone is counting on you to make sure the team wins.

The house is dark when I unlock the door, making sure I stay quiet in case Ellie's sleeping. I don't want to wake her. It'll probably just piss her off more.

I toe off my shoes and head to the kitchen for water. As I twist the cap open, I notice something on the counter.

A plate, covered with foil.

I stare at it like it might disappear, blinking a few times.

Underneath the foil is pasta. Still warm enough to steam faintly. No note. No explanation.

Just food.

My chest tightens.

I lean against the counter, staring at the plate longer than is reasonable, something dangerously close to gratitude swelling in my throat. Ellie has always taken care of people without asking for anything in return. I think acts of kindness might be her love language.

I eat slowly, like if I rush it, the moment will break. When I'm done, I wash the plate, dry it, and set it carefully back where I found it.

Hesitantly, I grab a pen and a scrap of paper.

'Thanks. J'

I leave it beside the sink, hoping it doesn't feel like too much.

Later, lying in bed, knee throbbing, ceiling staring back at me, I let myself think about her. About the way she stood in front of her class, commanding the room. About the way she looked at me like I was both familiar and foreign. About how she didn't soften when I apologized, but she didn't shut the door completely either. That scares me more than her anger ever did.

Because if there's still space between us, even a small one, I don't trust myself not to step into it.

I turn onto my side, jaw tight. I came here to heal. To wait out the injury. To figure out what comes next if hockey is no longer my life. I did not come here to fall back in love with the girl I broke.

As sleep finally drags me under, one thought repeats louder than the rest.

I don't think I'll have a choice.

Chapter 10

ELLIE

My stomach is in knots, and I feel slightly nervous as I set my things on the table that sits directly in front of the stage. It's audition day, and even though I'm not the one auditioning, I still feel like I could throw up.

I can literally feel the nerves radiating off of my students. Auditioning is kind of like standing on the edge of a cliff with your eyes closed and waiting to either fall to your death or fly.

Okay, maybe that's a bit dramatic, but where better to be overly dramatic than the theatre? Speaking of dramatics, I stupidly left out a plate of pasta for Jamie last night.

Why the hell did I do that? I don't care if he eats or not. But something in me was telling me that he'd probably be hungry after the long bus ride home. Curse me being an empath.

What I wasn't expecting was the note he left me.

'Thanks. J.'

I mean, what is that? He didn't need to say anything. He could have just eaten the freaking food and left it alone. But he left a note. I don't know why that feels so... significant, but it does. It feels like an olive branch. A creaky, old, chipped, weak branch, but a branch, nonetheless. Lainey is going to lose it when I tell her what I did. One thing about my best friend is she's unforgiving. She holds grudges, for a long time.

Once when we were kids, she'd let me borrow her scooter. Well, I was riding said scooter and hit a rock. I'd fallen off, but not before bringing that damn scooter with me. It got all scuffed up, and she was pissed. She didn't talk to me for three whole weeks. She still brings it up to this day.

Okay, I really need to focus today. No more thoughts about Jamie and his stupid note. This is my first real task as a director, and I do not want to fuck it up.

The stage is a blank canvas. No sets or costumes, just a plain old stage with long red curtains and a lot of potential. The sounds of students practicing lines, pacing the room, and doing vocal warmups fills the large space.

What people don't realize is how gruelling the audition process can be. When you buy tickets to a show, you don't think of how the actors got their parts or the work that needed to be put into it.

You see this perfectly polished, rehearsed show in front of you, and you have no idea the hard work, blood, sweat and tears that were put into getting it that way. That's the point. That would take your audience right out of that fantasy world that you're trying to portray.

Once I'm all set up and ready go, I begin to call students up one at a time. The first audition is rough. The second is worse. The third surprises me in a good way. I jot notes quickly, my mind already reshuffling possibilities. It's exhilarating and exhausting all at once, watching these students bare themselves for three minutes at a time. For a fleeting moment, I wish I were them. Auditioning for a new show and feeling the hope and drive they're feeling right now. Although, I'm kind of enjoying being on this side of things.

The morning flies by in a blur of monologues and half-sung songs, and only a few mental breakdowns. I would say this went really well for my first time holding auditions. These kids really have the heart for this, and I absolutely love that. I offered notes, encouragement, and smiles when I could tell someone was nervous.

By noon, my coffee is cold and my voice is hoarse. During my lunch break, I sit alone on the edge of the stage, flipping through my notebook. Names circle my brain, refusing to stay neatly assigned.

Casting is like a puzzle. One wrong piece and the whole picture feels off.

My phone buzzes on the stage next to me.

Main Bitch

Main Bitch: *How's auditions?*

Me: *I'm still alive. Barely. Send more caffeine...*

Main Bitch: *I'm sending my good vibes. Haven't gotten an update on he who shall not be named. You haven't fallen back into his lap, have you?*

That makes my smile falter, because the truth is that I don't hate him as fiercely today.

Me: *I left him a plate of food last night.*

Main Bitch: *You did what now?*

Me: *He had an away game. He got home late, so I just left him some left over pasta. I was gonna throw it out anyway...*

Main Bitch: *Oh, Jesus El. You don't need to feed him!*

Me: *He left a note...*

Three little dots appear as Lainey types back her reply. I knew she'd freak about the food. It's like me saying 'hey, I forgive you. You can fuck me now.'

Main Bitch: *A note?! What the hell did it say?*

Me: *"Thanks. J."*

Main Bitch: *That's it?*

Me: *Yes...*

Main Bitch: *What the hell?*

Me: *I know.*

Students begin to filter back into the auditorium, and I quickly tuck my phone away before I can spiral and stand, rolling my shoulders. Work first. Always.

Auditions finish just before dusk. I thank the last student and close the door, the sudden silence ringing in my ears. My body feels heavy, but it's the good kind of tired, the kind where you feel like you've worked the hardest you possibly could.

My walk home is quiet. The light breeze is cold and unforgiving, but the fresh air feels nice on my skin. When I arrive back at the house, I pause before unlocking the door. What if he's right there? What will I say to him? Do I want to see him?

Slowly, I unlock the door and push it open. Light from the foyer envelops me as I step inside the warm home. I set my bag down on the floor before removing my coat and shoes. As I make my way into the kitchen to begin dinner, I hear laughter. Jamie's laughter.

I pause.

It's different from how I remember it. Deeper, more masculine. It catches me off guard.

Jamie's sprawled on the couch, his bad leg stretched out carefully, watching something on TV. He looks so relaxed. My chest warms. He's looked like he's had this huge weight on his shoulders since he got here. This is the first time I've seen him not so stressed. I can understand why he'd feel so burdened. Being stripped of the thing you love can do that to a person.

He looks up suddenly, obviously hearing me walk into the room. Sitting up slowly, a toothy smile appears on his face. I recognize that smile, and my heart skips.

"There she is," he says, a teasing lilt to his voice. "You survived?"

"I did," I reply, releasing a long sigh.

"That bad, huh?"

"That good," I correct. "Which is somehow worse."

I head into the kitchen, instinct pulling me there. He follows, hovering in the doorway like he's not sure he's invited. He wasn't, but for some reason, I don't tell him not to.

I pull out a water from the fridge, popping the cap off and taking a small sip. Jamie leans against the counter, watching me carefully as if any move he makes could spook me and I'll run. To be fair, I don't know if he'd be wrong in thinking that.

"I'm sure you did great," Jamie says simply, as if it's not possible that I could fail at anything. My cheeks heat and I just know they're red which makes me blush more with embarrassment.

"Thanks..." I tell him, looking down at the counter. I fidget with a crumb as we stand there in an awkward silence.

"Ellie," he begins, slowly taking a step toward me. I back away, a little too quickly, and begin pulling ingredients from the fridge.

"How was practice?" I ask, trying to change the path of conversation. I could tell whatever he was about to say would have brought my mood down, and I do not want to feel sad right now. I had a good day, and I will not let him ruin it. He stops in his tracks.

"Great," he shrugs. "They're terrible."

I snort. "Promising start."

"I told them if they keep skating like that, I'm switching them to ballet."

I pause mid-reach. "You did not."

"I totally did."

We both chuckle before our eyes meet and my heart stops. The way he looks at me is so intense. I hate it. I don't like the way it makes me feel. Like I'm willing to forgive him and let him ravage me. I think he can tell that my resolve is wavering because he looks like he wants to do exactly that.

He stands straight and grabs his jacket off the back of one of the chairs at the island. "I'm heading out. Team thing."

It's so sudden, I don't know how to react. It's like he feels like he has to remove himself from this situation before he does something he'll regret. Something we might both regret.

"Okay..." I say timidly.

He hesitates by the door, then turns. "Hey, Ellie?"

"Yes?"

"You don't look like someone who almost ran away screaming after week one."

I blink. "Yeah?"

"Yeah," he says. "You look... solid. Like you landed where you're supposed to."

The compliment causes butterflies to erupt in my gut, and I feel like I lose all train of thought.

"Thanks," I reply.

He nods, satisfied, and heads out. Once he's gone, the house feels... emptier. I can't explain it, but I almost wish he didn't have to go.

Leaning against the counter, I stare at nothing, my heart doing that annoying, traitorous flutter again.

This version of Jamie, this playful, confident, version that's not asking for forgiveness is far more dangerous than the broken one. This version makes me forget why I built walls in the first place.

Chapter 11

JAMIE

Fuck.

I groan loudly as Jared bends my knee in a way it shouldn't be bent. I don't care how many degrees someone has on their wall or how many times they say it's 'part of the process.'

If I wanted to be slowly tortured by elastic bands and someone leaning over me, counting reps with a smile, I would've signed up for it willingly. Instead, I'm here lying on my back, knee exposed, my pride in pieces.

Physical therapy should really come with a waiver that says, 'may cause rage, existential dread, and the sudden urge to throw things.'

I knew this wasn't going to be a pleasant process, but the pain is unimaginable. I have a pretty big pain tolerance, and this is whooping my fucking ass.

This is supposed to help you, Jamie. Keep going.

Jared hands me a foam roller the size of a small missile.

"Quads today," he says cheerfully. "You're tight."

"No shit," I mutter.

"We're going to mobilize the joint a bit, then work on strength."

He presses his thumbs into the muscle above my kneecap, and I swear I see white.

"Jesus fuck," I gasp, hands gripping the edges of the table. "You trying to kill me?"

"That's scar tissue," he says calmly, like he's talking about a mildly inconvenient coffee stain. "Breathe."

"I *am* breathing."

"No, you're talking."

I clamp my mouth shut and stare at the ceiling, counting tiles to keep my mind on something other than the searing pain. There's a crack shaped like Florida. I've memorized it. That's how often I'm here. Jared works methodically, unapologetic. Every press sends heat shooting through my leg, sharp and deep and personal.

"This wouldn't be necessary," I grit out, "if my knee wasn't a piece of shit."

"It's not a piece of shit," he replies. "It's traumatized. And this wouldn't be as bad if you'd come in sooner."

I bark out a humorless laugh. "Join the club."

He pauses, glancing up at me. "You doing okay mentally?"

I scoff. "Fine."

He doesn't push. That's one thing I'll give him. He knows when to back off. The truth is that my thoughts have been all over the place lately. Not being able to play, being away from my team, seeing Ellie again. It's all taking a toll on me. It's hard not to be negative when a shit ton of negative things are happening to you.

We move to the bars next. Assisted squats. My least favorite.

"Slow on the way down," he instructs.

"I'm going slow."

"You're cheating," he accuses.

"I am *not* cheating."

"You're shifting your weight."

"Because it hurts."

"That's the point."

I lower myself another inch and my knee screams as I feel a deep grinding sensation that makes my stomach flip. My hands shake as I grip the bars, sweat rolling down my spine.

"Fuck this," I snap, standing up so fast it makes my head spin.

"Jamie," Jared warns. "Sit back down."

"No. I'm not doing this today."

He steps in front of me, voice steady. "You don't get to quit when it gets hard."

Something in me snaps.

"My entire fucking career is over because of this knee," I bark, jabbing a finger downward. "I think I'm allowed to tap out of a goddamn squat."

The room goes quiet. Jared doesn't flinch. He doesn't argue. He just nods slowly. I'm sure he's used to people freaking out on him. I know I lost my cool for a second, but I fucking hate this shit. I'm twenty-seven years old. I have a whole life to live, and one stupid accident is going to ruin it for me.

"Sit," he says. "We'll reset."

I do, my chest heaving, jaw tight, shame creeping in behind the anger. I stare at the floor, blinking hard. After a minute, he speaks again.

"You know why this feels worse than games or injuries, right?"

I don't answer.

"Because you can't brute-force it," he continues. "You can't push through and win. You have to slow down. Let your body lead."

I laugh bitterly. "That's not how I'm wired."

"I know." He meets my eyes. "But it might be how you survive this."

That sits heavy in my chest.

We finish the session quieter after that. My leg throbs, but the anger dulls into something heavier. Something like grief.

As I'm pulling my brace back on, Jared says, "You're not failing."

Feels like I am.

"You're adjusting," he adds.

Doesn't feel like that either.

Later, in my car, I sit with the engine off, my forehead resting against the steering wheel. I used to measure my days in goals, assists, wins. Now it's reps completed, degrees of motion gained, and pain tolerated.

I fucking hate it.

But worse than that, I'm terrified that this is it. That one day soon, someone's going to tell me that my knee did everything it could. That hockey did everything it was going to do for me. And then what?

I start the car, my jaw clenching as I think of everything I've lost.

I'll be back here in two days. I'll do the squats. I'll grit my teeth and count the tiles and let Jared dig his thumbs into my scars because if I stop showing up then it's really over. And I'm not ready for that yet.

The drive home is quiet. I don't blast music like I usually do. I just listen to the sound of the turn signal clicking and my thoughts doing laps I can't keep up with.

When I get home, Ellie's car is already in the driveway.

My chest tightens. I knew she'd be here, but for some reason it still shocks me that it's her.

Inside, the house smells like her vanilla perfume. She's had the same scent since high school, and I love it. It's familiar and sweet and... it's Ellie. I shut the front door a little harder than necessary, toeing off my shoes and leaning against the wall for a second while my knee throbs in protest.

"Jamie?" she calls from the direction of the kitchen.

"It's me," I call back.

"You okay?" she asks tentatively, as if she's mad at herself for wondering about my well-being.

"Fine," I call back automatically.

I'm a damn liar, but she doesn't need to know that. I round the corner and find her standing at the counter in one of those oversized sweaters that swallow her whole. Her hair is up in a messy bun. She's wearing no makeup. She's beautiful. She's always been beautiful.

That realization hits harder than it should.

Ellie studies my face, her eyes narrowing slightly.

"You don't look fine."

"Physical therapy was shit."

She gives me a pensive look. "That bad?"

I shrug, heading for the fridge. "Depends how much you enjoy being humbled by rubber bands."

I grab a water, twisting the cap off with more force than necessary. Ellie leans back against the counter, arms crossing loosely.

"Is it helping?" she asks.

"Feels like it's making it worse, but Jared says it's helping."

"Is that your therapist?"

"Yup. He's an asshole, but he knows what he's doing."

There's a beat of silence that feels awkward.

I don't know how to act around her. It's like I want to be close to her, but I don't know how to be. It seems like she might understand where I'm at too. I think she wants to be near me too, she's just too proud to show it. She would be smart to ignore me and run away. I broke her heart; I don't deserve anything from her. But I don't know if I can go back to pretending she never existed.

"Ellie. I'm sorry if it feels like I'm hovering," I admit. "Or saying the wrong thing."

She considers me for a moment, then sighs. "I know this isn't easy for you."

I swallow. "It's not exactly a dream scenario."

"No," she agrees. "It's not."

She turns back to what she's doing, clearly done with our conversation. I should leave it there. I know I should, but me being me, I don't.

"Hey Ellie?" I ask timidly, feeling like an ass for even asking what I'm about to ask. If my teammates could see me now, they'd call me a pussy.

She turns back at me, her eyes glistening. "Yes?"

"Will you ever forgive me?"

I see the sharp intake of breath as she mulls over how to answer my shit question.

"I don't know," she replies softly, turning around and organizing silverware in a drawer. That's it. That's all I'm going to get from her. That's all I deserve. I nod even though she's no longer looking at me.

I head upstairs, my knee aching, and my heart doing something stupid in my chest. Physical therapy might be tearing me apart piece by piece, but Ellie... Ellie is doing something worse.

She's reminding me of who I was before everything broke.

And I'm not sure I can afford to remember that guy.

Chapter 12

ELLIE

Rehearsals have officially started, and I have officially begun to regret all of my life decisions. Trying to direct twenty eighteen- and nineteen-year-olds to act out exactly what you've pictured in your head is not easy. They either don't want to listen, or they want to do their own thing. I appreciate the art of acting and putting your twist on characters, but as the director, they need to take into account my directions.

The lead female character, Sherri Martin is a go getter. She's sweet but she's ambitious. She gets what she wants, and she never has to ask twice.

After an amazing audition, I cast April Lewis, a beautiful, brown-haired girl with big blue eyes and an ambition that reminds me so much of Sherri.

However, since rehearsals started, she's been lacking. I'm not sure if it's nerves or what, but this is not what I thought I'd be getting from her.

After rehearsals end, I ask April to stay back. She slings her bag over her shoulder and meets me at my desk in the corner of the auditorium. She looks weary, like she anticipating bad news.

"Hey. What's going on up there?" I ask, a hint of worry in my tone. "Sherri is supposed to be this strong-willed woman who never takes no for an answer. You've been acting—"

"Like I have no idea what the hell I'm doing? Yeah, well... I don't," April interrupts, crossing her small arms over her chest in defeat. Something tugs in my chest at her forlorn expression. Damnit, Ellie. Why did I have to say anything?

"No, it's not that. It's just... is everything okay? You did so well with your audition. That's why I gave you the part. You don't seem like yourself."

She nods slowly. "Yeah, I just... I get so nervous when I'm up there. Auditions are a breeze for me, but once I actually get the part I... I don't know."

"You feel like you have something to prove?" I ask, knowing exactly how she feels. April nods and looks up at me through hooded lids. She looks like she's about to cry, and that's the last thing I want.

"I get that. I get the same way. I do great during auditions, but once I'm officially given the part, I feel like I have to prove to everyone that I deserved it."

Kind of like how I feel like I need to prove to everyone that I deserve to be here as director.

"Yeah, and sometimes I just feel like maybe someone else would have been a better choice for the good of the show," she sniffles. I know how she's feeling. The self-doubt, the feeling of never being good enough, that worry that everyone is thinking you don't belong. It's terrible, and it's something every actor goes through. Hell, it's something every person goes through.

"Listen," I begin, placing a soothing hand on her shoulder. "You deserve this part; do you hear me? You are perfect for this role, and I don't want you to ever doubt that again. I gave you this part because you earned it. You are incredibly talented, and you were meant for this. Don't ever make yourself feel small to allow others to shine. You deserve to shine as well."

A small smile tugs at the corners of her lips as she wipes a tear away. I feel a huge sense of relief when she nods.

"Okay. Thank you, Professor Monroe. You're really good at this directing thing," she tells me, and my heart swells at the reassuring compliment. She has no idea what that means to me.

I smile brightly. "Thank you, April. I'll see you tomorrow. We'll start fresh, okay?"

April nods with a grin before walking out of the auditorium and leaving me alone with my thoughts. A sense of pride washes over me and I feel like less of a fraud than when I first got here.

The hair on the back of my neck stands as I feel the overwhelming feeling of being watched. I scan the auditorium, looking for any remaining students or lurkers. I don't see anyone, so I go back to writing notes for tomorrow's rehearsals.

"That was really great advice," a familiar male voice says, scaring the living shit out of me. A yelp of surprise leaves my lips as I erupt from my chair, and a chuckle comes from Jamie who is now standing in front of me. His crystal blue eyes rake over me before landing on my face. I feel my entire body heat at his assessing gaze. How long has he been here? Why is he even here?

Jamie shoves his hands into his pockets and takes a step closer effectively crowding my personal bubble. God, he smells good. Like cologne and shampoo. I notice his wet hair and clean outfit. He must have been at practice.

"What are you doing here?" I ask accusingly. For someone who swore he'd keep his distance and leave me alone, he's doing a shit job at it. Sometimes, I think he only told me that to get me to calm down. His eyes sparkle with mischief. It's like he knows his presence puts me on edge and he enjoys making me uncomfortable. Asshole.

"Practice ended. I was walking by and heard your little pep talk with the cheerleader. It was good advice, sweetheart. You should take it," he shrugs.

"Don't call me that. And she's not a cheerleader."

He takes a step closer, and when I take a step back, I run into my desk. He has me trapped, and suddenly I feel claustrophobic.

"Whatever you say, sweetheart," he winks.

"Seriously, you should really take your own advice. 'Don't ever make yourself feel small to allow others to shine.' It's... poetic," he repeats my own words back to me. The grin on his face makes me irrationally annoyed.

"Are you making fun of me?" I ask, offended.

"No, I'm being serious. I think I need to remember that myself."

A laugh bubbles out of me before I can stop it, and now Jamie looks like I've offended him.

"What?"

"You feeling small? You've been cocky since the day I met you. Especially when it comes to playing hockey. You've always been so sure of yourself and your talent," I tell him, and immediately regret it as I watch his expression change from playful to disheartened.

"Yeah, well. Not so much anymore."

"You'll play again," I try to reassure him, but I have no idea if that's even true. From what I've heard, his injury is pretty severe and there's a good chance it won't heal right, and he'll never play hockey again. At least, not the way he used to. I can't imagine how he feels.

Jamie snorts. "My knee is fucked. The chances of me getting back on the ice are slim, and everyone knows it. My coach, my teammates, the fans. They all know it, and no one wants to say it out loud. My career is over, Ellie. So no, I'm not so sure of myself anymore. In fact, I've never felt as unsure of myself as I do right now."

He lets out a defeated breath as I stand and stare at him in awe. Who would have ever thought I'd be standing in front of Jamie Patterson again?

Who would have thought he would be admitting to being imperfect? My heart aches for him and the level of uncertainty he's facing.

"Jamie..." I begin but trail off as he takes another step closer to me. I realize I have nowhere to go as my butt lands on my desk. He stands so close I can smell the mint on his breath from the gum he's been chewing.

"You want to know one thing I am sure about?" he whispers. My heart pounds in my chest and my breath hitches at his closeness. I can feel his body heat radiating off of him and it feels warm and inviting.

Stop it, Ellie. Jamie is not warm *or* inviting. He is heartless. Although now I'm not so sure about that. I haven't seen him this down since his father died. I'm pretty sure that's the last time he ever gave a shit about anyone but himself.

"What?" I ask, curious of what he'll say next.

"I'm sure you'll forgive me," he says, all confidence and nerve. And there he is, the arrogant son of a bitch.

"And what makes you so sure of that?" I ask, my voice unsteady, because apparently, I've forgotten how to breathe with him standing this close.

"Because I'm going to do everything in my power to make it impossible for you not to."

My heart does a summersault, and butterflies erupt in my stomach. He seems so confident, like it's not even in the realm of possibility for me to stay mad at him forever.

As much as I want to prove him wrong, I fear that he may actually be right.

I may not be strong enough to stay pissed at him forever. I don't know if I even want to.

ELLIE

The hot water cascades over my skin while the scent of my shampoo and body wash wraps around me. It was a long day, and I'm ready to lay down and go to bed. After Jamie left me in the auditorium reeling from our conversation, I sat alone in the quiet, dark room for an hour before finally heading home.

"Because I'm going to do everything in my power to make it impossible for you not to."

What the hell does he mean by that? Why does he want me to forgive him so badly? He didn't care how I felt back then, why would he care how I feel now?

The questions swirl around in my head like a tornado. Could I even forgive him? I mean, I can already feel my resolve cracking just from being around him. What does that say about me?

I'm weak. I'm weak and stupid and I know if he continues being in my orbit, I'm going to fold and I will forgive him.

Even if I do forgive him, I won't let him in again. I need to get through this semester without any hiccups. He is an unexpected hurdle that I need to face. Maybe if I do forgive him, he'll leave me the hell alone and the weight that feels like a constant reminder of him will be gone. I can move on and focus solely on what I came here to do which is direct this show and prove to myself that I can do this.

Jamie Patterson is not going to get in the way of my dreams. I will not let him dictate my thoughts. Even though that's exactly what he's doing right now. He's gotten into my head and he knows it.

He was so close. So damn close to me today, and I could feel every fiber of my being clawing at me to reach out and touch him. Feel him. Every part of me wants to say fuck it and forget about our past.

I haven't been that close with a man in forever, and I'd forgotten how good it feels to have someone so close to you. We never touched. His hands were gripping the desk on either side of me, his face was inches from mine, but we never touched. I could feel the tension between us, which means he felt it too.

I don't know what had gotten into him. This whole time he's been keeping his distance, yet he came to see me after practice to what? To tell me that he knows I'll forgive him? He really is a cocky asshole, isn't he.

Frustrated with myself for the thoughts and feelings overtaking my body, I scrub my skin a bit too hard in hopes that the feeling will take away the dull ache between my legs as I think of Jamie.

I lay wrapped in my towel on my bed as a scroll through my phone, stopping to watch a few silly videos here and there. The screen lights up with Lainey's picture as my phone vibrates in my hand.

"How goes it, Professor Monroe?" Lainey asks with a teasing lilt to her voice. I chuckle before rolling my eyes.

"Just peachy," I say sarcastically.

Her face twists in question. "Did that asshole Patterson do something? Are you okay?"

"He didn't do anything. Not yet at least. He's just..." I trail off, trying to think of the right words.

"Don't let him get into your head, Ellie." Too late.

"I know, I'm not. He's just everywhere and it's getting difficult to avoid him," I explain. "He showed up at my rehearsal today."

Lainey's eyes widen. "For what reason?"

"He said he was passing by," I shrug, twirling a piece of wet hair around my finger nervously. "He told me he knows I'll forgive him."

She scoffs. "He what? Why would he say that? There's no way in hell you're going to forgive his stupid ass."

My eyes dart away from the screen and I feel my cheeks heat as Lainey glares at me through the screen. I can't lie to her, and I don't know if what she says is true.

"Ellie Monroe. You are not going to forgive that man, right? He may be a hot hockey player, but he hurt you. He does not deserve your forgiveness. You're too good for him," she declares. I know she's right. I know what he did, and I know the pain he caused. I just... he seems so different from the boy I knew. Sure, he's still cocky and a bit arrogant. He knows how to push my buttons and what to say to get me riled up. Jesus, I don't even know why I'm entertaining this.

"I know, Lane. I know. He's just... I don't know."

"If you say different, I'm going to slap you," she warns. "He is no different than when he left you without a word. You may not have kept up with his hockey career, but I did. He's an asshole on and off the ice. He is an arrogant jerk, and you are better than that."

She's obviously right. I'm not stupid, I know it would be idiotic of me to think that Jamie is a 'changed man' but honestly, people *can* change. Hell, I know I've changed since I was eighteen. I'm not that quiet, naïve little girl anymore. I know what I want, and I go after it. I don't let anyone walk all over me, even if I am a bit of people pleaser.

Despite what my brother may think, I am capable of standing up for myself. I am perfectly okay with telling someone to back the hell off if I don't enjoy their presence.

However, even when I'm telling Jamie to leave me alone, deep down, I don't think I mean it.

"I know," I agree with her, knowing this conversation isn't going anywhere. I love my best friend, but sometimes I feel like her strong opinions make it hard for me to talk to her.

She wouldn't understand the conflict I'm having because she's the type of person to cut you off if you cross her. She's not weak. Not like I am. "I'm gonna get to bed, Lane." '

Lainey nods. "Okay, Ellie Bear. Remember you're a boss ass bitch and you are better than him. Love you," she says before hanging up and leaving me in the quiet of my bedroom.

Groaning, I flip onto my side and shove my face into my pillow before letting out a small, muffled scream.

I'm frustrated with myself and with Jamie and with this whole situation that could have been avoided if I had just told Dean Ashby I couldn't do this. But where would that have gotten me? I'd be back in New York trying to make it as an actress without a steady income. At least I'm doing something here. I feel important, and these kids seem to enjoy having me around.

A soft knock on my door has me jumping up so fast I swear I gave myself whiplash. I check the time on my alarm clock on the nightstand. It's 10:30pm. Shit, did Jamie hear me scream? I thought I'd masked it pretty well with the pillow. I didn't even know he was home. Damnit. Do I answer or should I just pretend I'm asleep?

Pretend you're asleep, Ellie. Do not open the door. Do not open the...

Before I can stop myself, I'm up out of bed and heading for the door. I hesitate for a split second, taking a deep breath and trying my best to make it look like I've been sleeping. I grip the handle and pull the door open slightly, revealing a wet haired Jamie. His eyes roam up and down my body as if he's assessing me to make sure I'm unharmed.

"I, uh... I thought I heard a scream. Are... are you okay?" he stutters, his gaze locking onto my face. He looks worried, but uncertain too—like he's not even sure he has the right to ask.

"A scream? No, I didn't hear a scream," I lie, leaning against the doorframe with what I hope looks like nonchalance. God, I'm an idiot.

His eyes shift, dropping briefly to my chest before slowly drifting back up to my face. "I was asleep."

His head tilts, brows knitting together as a smirk tugs at his lips.

"You were asleep," he repeats. I nod.

"I was."

He crosses his arms, his veiny, muscular arms, and my attention snags on them far longer than it should.

"In a towel?" he asks. Heat floods my face.

I glance down, suddenly aware of my bare legs and the white towel wrapped around me—one I'm only now realizing I've been clutching tightly shut.

"It's a new sleep trend," I mutter. "Very breathable." God, Ellie. Stop talking.

His lips twitch, like he's fighting a smile. "Very breathable," he repeats. "I'll have to try it sometime."

"You should," I say quickly.

He laughs under his breath, shaking his head. "So let me get this straight. You were asleep, not screaming, and just happened to wake up... like this." He gestures up and down my body.

"Correct," I nod, knowing I'm full of shit and he knows it. His eyes flick to the towel again, then back to my face.

"You know, most people put on clothes when they answer the door."

"Most people don't expect surprise wellness checks in the middle of the night."

He hums, clearly enjoying my embarrassment far too much. "Right..." he says skeptically.

"Yep."

He grins. "Alright," he says, lifting his hands in surrender. "No scream, no emergency. Good to know."

He turns to leave, then pauses, glancing back over his shoulder.

"But if you *do* scream," he adds, smirk firmly back in place, "I'll come running."

"Please don't," I shoot back.

His grin widens. "No promises."

When he's finally down the hall and tucked away in his room, I shut my door behind me and slowly fall to the floor. What the actual hell just happened? Was he being flirty? Of course he was, Ellie. You were in a towel in front of him.

How did I not realize I was still in a freaking towel? I'm never going to live that down. He is never going to let me forget this.

After quickly getting dressed and ready for bed, I lie down and wait for sleep to overtake me.

I'm half asleep when I hear another soft knock on my door. What the hell is it now? Before I can get up, my door slowly creaks open and Jamie slips in. The room is so dark, I can barely make him out, but I can feel the mattress sink as he sits next to me.

"What are you doing? Get out of here!" I tell him, but he doesn't move. He just sits there; his gaze locked on mine.

"Ellie..." he rasps, almost like he's in pain. Like he can't control himself. My heart hammers in my chest and the room spins as his body heat radiates into me. The smell of his soap and shampoo overtake my senses as he leans down, his face coming into focus.

"Jamie... what are you—" he stops my question, smashing his lips against mine and my body feels like it's on fire. All of my nerve endings are firing, and it feels like an electric current is surging through me. Holy hell. Jamie Patterson is kissing me.

Why is Jamie Patterson kissing me? And why the hell do I not want him to stop?

Chapter 14

ELLIE

The kiss is a total shock to my system, a jolt of electricity that melts my annoyance into something hotter, something needier. I'm kissing him back. I don't even try to push him away. I let him melt into me, and I don't know why. Probably because I haven't felt something this good in years.

Jamie's hands grip my waist, pulling me closer, and I can feel the hard line of his body against mine. His chest is warm, and his muscles taut beneath my fingertips. He deepens the kiss, his tongue demanding entry, his breath hot against my mouth.

A moan escapes me, my hands tangling in his brown hair in an attempt to pull him closer. It's been so long, yet it feels like no time has passed at all. His kiss is familiar, yet different. It's hungrier, more grown up. Like he's confident in himself and what he's doing. He breaks the kiss, trailing kisses down my neck, his teeth grazing my skin, sending shivers down my spine. I arch into him subconsciously, my breasts pressing against his chest, my nipples hardening at the mere brush of his lips.

Jamie reaches under my shirt and cups my breast, his thumb flicking my nipple. I inhale sharply, my head falling back.

"Jamie," I whisper, my voice thick with need. God, what has gotten into me? Why am I allowing this?

His smirk is visible even in the dim light, his blue eyes dark with desire. He pushes me back onto the bed, his hands moving lower, slipping into my sleep shorts. His fingers lightly brush the edge of my panties, and I shiver, my body already responding to his touch. Tell him to leave, Ellie. Tell him to get the hell out of your room and never speak of this again.

Except, I don't do that. Instead, I let him move his hand further down until he's cupping me. I'm so wet, and my pussy is throbbing for him like the desperate whore she is. Bad, bad idea Ellie.

He hooks his fingers into the lace, pulling my panties down my legs, his eyes never leaving mine.

"I've missed this," he growls, his voice rough and raw with longing. He presses a kiss to my inner thigh, his lips warm against my skin. I squirm, but my legs fall open as he teases me with his lips, his breath ghosting over my clit.

"Jamie, please," I practically beg, my hands gripping the sheets. Jamie chuckles, a dark, dirty sound, before his mouth closes over my clit, his tongue flicking, sucking, and driving me wild.

I can't help the cry that leaves my lips as my hips buck against his face shamelessly. He eats me out, his fingers digging into my thighs. His tongue is relentless, his mouth devours me, and I can feel my orgasm building, coiling tight in my core. I'm so close, I can feel the heat in my cheeks burn. But instead of bringing me there, Jamie pulls away, his throbbing cock pressing against my thigh.

"Not yet," he murmurs, his lips brushing my ear. His voice sends a shiver down my spine as a mix of frustration and anticipation begin to make their way through me. Why on earth would he stop?

He positions himself at my entrance, his tip teasing my wetness. Peering up at me, he waits until I nod before sliding inside me in one slow, deliberate thrust. I moan so loudly, I'm glad no one else lives here because they definitely would have heard me. My nails dig into his back as he fills me. His cock stretches me, fitting perfectly after all these years. He begins to move, his hips snapping, his dick pounding into me, relentless and primal and I meet him thrust for thrust, my walls clenching around him. My breath comes in ragged gasps.

"Harder," I demand, my voice sounding far too desperate, and he obliges, slamming into me, the bed creaking under our weight. The room fills with the sounds of sex and once again, I'm close. So fucking close. To my surprise, Jamies reaches between my legs, his fingers finding my clit and rubbing circles.

"Cum for me, Ellie," he growls, his voice a command. His words pushed me over the edge. I shatter, my body convulsing and my pussy clenching around his cock as I scream his name. Jamie follows, his thrusts stuttering before he pulls out and cums on my stomach. His groan vibrates against my neck before he kisses me lightly.

I jolt awake, my body aching and my pussy throbbing. Sitting up too quickly, I scan my room that is now basked in morning sunlight. It's empty. There's no sign of Jamie or any nefarious activities. It was a *dream.* A freaking dream!

Relief floods me, along with a bit of disappointment at the fact that none of it happened. I shouldn't feel any disappointment. This is good. I didn't sleep with Jamie Patterson. Why am I dreaming about it though? Do I want to sleep with him? I mean, who wouldn't? The guy is seriously hot *and* he's a hockey player. But I can't. I won't.

Taking a deep, calming breath, I fall back onto my pillow and stare up at the ceiling. The dream felt so real, so vivid. I don't know how I'm going to be able to look him in the face and pretend that I wasn't dreaming about his dick ramming into me just hours ago. Of course, he can't know about this. His ego can't handle growing any larger, and my pride can't take that kind of hit.

After my cold shower, I throw my hair up into a ponytail and put on my outfit to go to rehearsal. I always try to dress in comfortable clothes so I can easily move around and show the kids the correct blocking. We do have a choreographer that goes over the dances with them, but I'll occasionally get up there and show them some moves.

Slinging my bag over my shoulder, I make my way downstairs. Clashing around in the kitchen catches my attention. A glass smashes on the ground, and when I turn the corner, I see Jamie leaning over the counter, breathing hard.

"Jamie?" I say, taking a cautious step toward him. He doesn't look up; he doesn't even move. I set my bag down on the floor and take a step closer until I can see his face. His eyes are closed, and his jaw is tight. He looks like he's trying to keep himself from breaking down, and my heart squeezes. I don't know what's wrong, but I don't like seeing him so worked up.

"Jamie, what happened? What's wrong?" I ask with a bit of hesitation. His eyes stay shut, his chest rising and falling with each breath.

"Go away," he mumbles under his breath.

"Jamie, I—"

"I said go away, Ellie."

I take a step back at his dark tone. There's clearly something wrong, and he's not exactly ready to talk about it.

"I'm sorry, I just..."

"Jesus, Ellie!" he shouts, finally looking up at me, his eyes are full of rage and hurt. "Just get out of here!"

I jump, taking another step back, and stepping on something sharp. I hiss, and Jamie's attention goes down to my foot. My bleeding foot. Shit, I stepped on a shard of glass.

"Damnit," I say through gritted teeth. Pain radiates through my foot as I hobble my way over to one of the stools at the island, careful not to step on anymore glass.

"Shit, Ellie. Fuck, I'm sorry," Jamie rushes out, moving to the counter and wetting a paper towel under the sink. He sinks down to his knees, careful to not put too much pressure on his injury, and slowly blots the bottom of my foot with the towel. I try to keep a brave face, but God, this hurts like hell. I watch as Jamie delicately wraps my foot in the paper towel.

"There's no glass in there, so that's good."

"Yeah, that's good," I agree, eyeing him carefully. His anger from before has vanished, and it's replaced with... concern? His face twists as he looks at the blood seeping through the towel.

"I'm sorry. I shouldn't have snapped at you," he apologizes. I nod. I don't know what made him snap, but it can't be good. The Jamie I knew was never a hot head. He didn't yell or fight. Then again, I don't know this version of him. Maybe this Jamie does.

"It's fine," I reply.

Jamie shakes his head. "No, it's not. I shouldn't have yelled at you like that. I just... I got some bad news and I'm clearly not handling it very well. But you didn't deserve that. So, I apologize."

At the risk of pissing him off again, I ask, "what was the news?"

He sighs, and I watch his huge shoulders bob up and down.

"One of my teammates texted. Said coach is talking about replacing me as team captain. Can't be captain if you're not there, I guess." He shrugs.

"Oh, Jamie. I'm sorry," I practically whisper. He's losing everything he's worked for, and even though I should hate him, I can't help but feel awful about the situation he's in.

"It's fine. I knew it would probably happen sooner rather than later. They had Theo Cramer stepping up as alternative captain. He's a great player, and he deserves it," he admits, seeming completely defeated. I can tell he means what he says, but it's obvious that it hurts him to say out loud.

I place a hand on his shoulder, and he tenses. He looks up at me through hooded eyes, still kneeling at my feet. My heart skips a beat, and goosebumps rise on my skin when his hand brushes my calf. Seeing him this vulnerable, it makes me so sad for him. I know I shouldn't, but I want to hold him. I want to tell him that everything's alright and that he'll be back to himself soon. But I can't tell him that, because I don't know if it's true. So instead, we just sit here in silence with my hand on his shoulder and his finger tracing patterns on my leg.

It feels oddly intimate, and with the way he's looking up at me, it sends a shiver straight down my spine. His thumb traces a slow, absent pattern against my calf, and it's such a small thing, barely anything at all, but my body reacts anyway, heat pooling low in my stomach.

I pull my hand back, breaking the moment like snapping a thread.

Jamie freezes.

His eyes lift to mine, something unreadable flickering across his face before he straightens and rises to his feet. He takes a step back immediately, distance returning like it was summoned on instinct.

"Sorry," he says, too quickly. "I didn't—"

"It's fine," I interrupt, even though my pulse is racing and my chest feels tight. "Really."

We stand there for a beat, the kitchen suddenly too quiet, the broken glass still scattered on the floor.

"I should go," I add. "Rehearsal."

"Yeah," he nods, running a hand through his hair. "Of course."

I grab my bag, careful with my foot, and head for the door. My hand pauses on the knob. I don't turn around, but I feel him behind me.

"For what it's worth," he says quietly, "I didn't mean what I said earlier. Telling you to leave."

My throat tightens.

"I know," I say.

I leave before either of us can say anything more.

Rehearsal is a blur. I go through the motions. Notes, blocking, counts, but my mind keeps drifting back to the kitchen. To the way Jamie looked kneeling in front of me. I know he's going through so much right now, and as much as I want to say he deserves it, I'm not that kind of person. I never wished him harm; I never even talked badly about him. It just... was what it was.

By the time I get home that evening, the house is quiet again and Jamie's car is gone. He's most likely at practice.

I shower, change, and crawl into bed, but sleep doesn't come easily. When I close my eyes, I don't see the dream anymore. I see him exactly as he was this morning. Raw, exhausted, and trying to hold himself together while everything he loves slips through his fingers.

And that's somehow worse, because dreams are easy to dismiss.

Reality isn't.

Chapter 15

JAMIE

I almost fucked up this morning. I was so frustrated with the text I got from Callahan that I didn't think. I yelled at her. I told her to go away, when we all know that's the last thing I want. I just... I didn't want her to see me that way. So vulnerable and fucked up. I've only ever been strong, even when dad died. I kept a brave face for my mom and pretended I was okay, even though deep down, I was dying inside. Bottling up my emotions is pretty typical for me. That's why I enjoy the game so much. It gives me an outlet for all the pent-up rage and aggression.

The rink is loud this morning. Sounds of skates carving into ice and pucks slapping boards fills my ears, and I feel the most at home I've felt in weeks. I may not be able to actually play, but just being here gives me a high. This is where I'm meant to be. Even if these guys are pissing me the hell off. They don't know how to play as a team.

They're sloppy, uncoordinated, and honestly, a bit pathetic. They don't want it bad enough.

I grip the whistle so hard my knuckles ache.

"Line up," I bark.

The sound cuts clean through the noise. Heads snap up and conversations die mid-sentence. Good.

They scramble into place, sticks tapping nervously as they fall into line. I pace in front of them, jaw tight, knee stiff. The ache is there, it's always there, but it's background noise compared to the fire in my chest.

"You look comfortable," I say. "Anyone want to tell me why?"

You can hear a pin drop in the absolute silence. No one wants to answer me, or rather, no one's brave enough.

I stop in front of one of the defensemen, David Andersson. The kid's talented, but like many of the boys, he lazy. He's the kind of guy who expects everything to be handed to him because his dad has money.

"You," I say. "What was your effort last shift?"

He blinks. "Uh—" I don't let him finish. My mood is shit and unfortunately for these guys, they're the only ones I can take my frustrations out on.

"Wrong answer," I snap. "Skate."

He hesitates for a fraction of a second. The other guys watch as if this is a TV drama.

When Andersson doesn't move, I say, "Now."

He takes off, face flushed.

"Everyone else," I add, turning back to the line. "You run until he's done."

Groans ripple through the arena. I hear someone mutter under their breath, but I can't quite make out what they say.

I spin. "You got something to share?"

Their heads go down, and some of them shift uncomfortably. Then, they push off.

I try to focus on the guys skating back and forth, but I can't shut it off. The image of Ellie pulling her hand away. The sound of glass shattering. The word captain echoing in my head like a taunt.

"Again," I shout when the first guy finishes. "That was pathetic." Jesus, I'm a dick.

I blow the whistle and throw pucks onto the ice. They're not done yet. The only way to get them into shape is to play against one another. To put their all into every practice, no matter how they're feeling. They may hate me now, but they'll thank me later.

"Scrimmage. No breaks. If you fall behind, you stay behind."

They play hard as their frustration bleeds into their movements. I know what I'm doing. I know I'm pushing them past the edge. But I also know they can take it, because I had to.

My knee flares as I make my way slowly across the ice, shouting plays and directions at the team. One of the assistant coaches catches my eye, concern flickering. It's obvious that I'm limping, but I push through the pain. I will not show weakness. I refuse.

Blowing the whistle one more time, I say, "Last drill," I say. I watch their sighs of relief as they begin to slow down. They're exhausted now, relying on instinct and muscle memory.

After practice, the locker room is quiet. There's none of the usual back and forth, no laughing and joking, just the sound of the showers and lockers slamming shut.

"Good practice," I tell them. "See you tomorrow."

A few groans fill my ears before I head to my office. Maybe tomorrow will be better. Maybe I can control my emotions, and maybe they'll play like they mean it.

Once the locker room is clear, I walk in and take a seat on one of the benches, remembering what it felt like to sit and get myself psyched up for a game. A helmet sits beside me, and I stare at it as if it's going to blow any second. My heart races and I feel like I can't catch my breath. My hands grip the bench tightly before grabbing the helmet and chucking it at the wall. It smashes, the plastic falling to the ground. My knee flashes with pain, my chest constricts, my ears ring, and the room around me spins as I fall to a pile on the floor.

I flinch when two hands grip my face, forcing me to look into two gorgeous, emerald, green eyes. I didn't even hear her come in, but Ellie kneels in front of me, her face full of concern. I'm sure I look pathetic, but I can't bring myself to care at this moment. The warmth from her palms sends a shiver down my spine as she moves from my face, down my arms, landing on my hands. She squeezes tightly, bringing me into the present.

"Breath, Jamie. It's okay, just take a deep breath," she coaxes. "You're alright."

Her sweet voice breaks through the ringing in my ears. I take a breath, just like she instructed me to do. She nods slowly, a small, worried smile on her lips.

"What happened?" she asks. I don't know how she can be so nice to me after what happened this morning. I don't deserve her kindness. I was a dick, and she should run the other direction.

Instead of answering her question, I ask, "why are you in the men's locker room?"

"I heard a crash, so I came to check it out. Then I saw you." I nod, my breathing beginning to steady and my heart slowing down. Somehow, just her presence has helped the anxiety die down.

Her eyes shift from my face, down my body, probably checking for any injuries. When she finds nothing, she lands back on my face.

"Are you okay?" she asks, worry lacing her voice. I clear my throat, trying to gain some of my dignity back. "Are you still thinking about this morning?"

Pictures of the shattered glass and Ellie's bloody foot flash in my head, my stomach feeling queasy. My eyes dart to the broken helmet on the floor. Fuck, I need to learn to get my anger under control. Two broken things in one day? Ellie must think I'm a neanderthal. I never lash out. I'm calm and collected, I always have been. Until recently. Ellie's never seen this side of me, this side that's filled with rage and devastation. I wonder if she remembers the way I used to be.

There's no point in lying to her. She'll see right through me. I nod. Ellie frowns.

"Jamie, it's going to work itself out. You're going to play again. You just need to keep up with your physical therapy sessions and practice. It'll take some time, but I know you can do it. You're resilient, and I know you're not going to give up now. You've come too far."

My racing heart swells at the pride in her voice, like she's proud of me. I don't understand how she can be so optimistic all the time. Even when she struggles to believe in herself, she believes in me. Why does that make me happy?

Ellie's eyes search mine, waiting for me to respond, but I don't know what to say. I don't have the same faith in myself as she seems to have in me. With the way my knee throbs, constantly reminding me of everything I've already lost and will probably continue to lose, it's hard to believe it will get better.

Her small hands squeeze my forearm, and the longer she looks at me with those big green eyes looking so innocent and beautiful, the more I want to grab her face and kiss her. I shouldn't want to, I know she wants nothing to do with me. Well, I know she didn't, but now I'm not so sure. Things have shifted between us within the few weeks we've been cooped up together. We've talked more, she doesn't run away when I walk into the same room as her, and she actually has full conversations with me.

I know that sounds like the bare minimum, but it's a step in the right direction for us. *Us.* There is no us. It's Ellie and it's me. There hasn't been an 'us' in a long time, and I know that's my fault.

So why is the air between us so thick? Why does this moment feel like it's pressing in on my lungs instead of easing them. I wish I could read her mind, because her face is saying absolutely nothing right now. She's just looking at me like I'm about to explode and she's waiting for the destruction.

Yet, her hand is still on my arm. I can feel every inch of it. It's warm and grounding. The exact same way it used to feel, and that's the problem because my body doesn't know the fucking difference between now and all those years ago.

I don't move, because if I do, I'm not sure she'll stay put. She's like a scared animal. One wrong move, and she'll sprint in the other direction. I'm not ready for her to leave yet. My body is enjoying her closeness, her touch. She's so close I can see the tiny freckle under her left eye, the one she used to hate but I always loved.

Is she thinking the same thing I am? That if we lean forward just a fraction, our mouths will meet. That it would feel so good to be entwined with one another, consequences be damned. Or is she not thinking of that at all? Her eyes are sorrowful, and that worried expression is still etched into her perfect features.

Get it together, Patterson. You fucked it up. You lost your shot. This isn't some clean slate moment. This is a minefield. We're not two strangers circling each other. We're history. We're broken. Because of me.

My chest burns with the urge to close the distance and the knowledge that if I did, she might not reciprocate. Yet, all I want to do is grab her face and remind her that this, whatever this is, has always been ours. That it never really went away, not for me. I may have made the wrong choices back then, and maybe if I'd have made different ones, we'd still be together today. Even though I wasn't thinking of her every single moment of every day, I did think of her. I thought of every moment we'd spent together. I thought of how we'd be if we'd stayed together. If I didn't decide hockey was more important than her. But thinking about what I'd lost didn't change anything.

I'm not the guy she knew anymore, and she's not the girl who once loved me without hesitation. Our lives are so different now. I'm sure this isn't exactly where she'd pictured herself to be, and I know for a fact that this isn't where I thought I'd be. Things are different now, but maybe that's a good thing.

I force myself to lean back, breaking the invisible thread snapping tight between us. The movement feels violent, like it tears something out of my chest. My fingers curl into my palms until my nails bite the skin.

Her hand drops and I feel the loss immediately.

I know kissing Ellie would ruin everything. It would blur lines that are already thin. She lives with me. She works with me. There's no way this would work. I need to keep my head on straight, focus on getting back to the Storm and back to my life. The last thing I need is to start something that I can't finish...again.

I know what I am right now. A mess. A guy spiraling because his body betrayed him and the one thing that ever made sense has been ripped away. I don't get to drag her into that. I don't get to be selfish this time, no matter how much my chest aches when she looks at me with that soft, worried expression, like I still matter to her.

She exhales slowly and stands, putting even more space between us. I want to tell her to come back, to stay with me. But I know I can't.

"Jamie..." she says quietly, and hearing my name like that nearly undoes me. Clearing my throat, I stand, towering over her. She looks up at me, all innocence and determination.

"I'm fine," I say, even though my heart is still racing like I just took a hit I didn't see coming. "Don't worry about me, sweetheart."

She frowns, but I'm already shutting the door, piece by piece. That's what I do. That's what I've always done.

Her jaw tightens. I know she doesn't believe me. She's not stupid. Obviously, I have some issues I'm working through, but I won't put them on her. She doesn't deserve that.

"Okay," she says finally, though it's clear she doesn't mean it. She hesitates for a moment at the door, hand hovering on the handle like she's considering whether to leave or not, and for one terrifying second, I think she might come back.

I don't know what I'd do if she did. But then she leaves. The door shuts, and the silence crashes down hard enough to ring in my ears. I press my hands into my eyes, dragging in a shaky breath.

Fuck, I wanted to kiss her. Not a gentle kiss. Not a maybe. I wanted to devour her. To taste every fucking inch of her. To make her forget why she hates me. I wanted to be inside her. I wanted to feel her body against mine; I wanted to hear her moans as I teased and played with her. I wanted her so badly, it was almost a need. Like I need her to breathe. I've been breathing on my own for years now, and I never realized how much better it is to breathe the same air as Ellie.

But kissing Ellie wouldn't be harmless. It wouldn't be this moment where we both realize what we've been missing.

It would be the beginning of something I'm not sure either of us would survive.

ELLIE

Today has been exhausting. Not only that, but it's been a whirlwind of emotions. I woke up from a sex dream with Jamie, then I ran into him in the kitchen where he freaked out on me, then I find Jamie sitting on the locker room floor having what appeared to be a panic attack. The worst part of all that is the fact that being so close to him made me think of the dream. It made me want it to come true. It made me want him.

I was trying to bring him back to earth from his panic, but all I could think about was his lips on mine and if it would feel as good as it did back then.

Would I like it? Would it make me feel something I haven't felt in a long time?

Those kinds of thoughts are dangerous, though. I shouldn't want him. I shouldn't be feeling any connection to him. But seeing him like that, all vulnerable and broken, it made me want to help him. Curse being a good person.

I don't realize how hard I'm breathing until I fall into my chair at my desk in quiet auditorium.

Idiot. That's what I am. Stupid.

It's been nine years. Nine years of distance, growth, and rebuilding myself into someone who doesn't fall apart over one man. All of that, and I nearly undo all of it on a locker room floor because Jamie Patterson looked at me like I was still his. Like I was the thing anchoring him to the ground. My hands are shaking, and I feel as if I've just run a marathon. I press them flat against the cool surface of my desk and count to five, then ten. It doesn't help. My heart is still racing, my skin still remembers his warmth, the weight of his gaze, the way his breath hitched when I looked at him.

He wanted to kiss me. I know he did; I could tell by the way he was watching me. I could see it in his eyes. That realization lands with a dangerous mix of satisfaction and fear. Knowing that he was having a hard time controlling himself sends a shiver down my spine. Maybe I'm not alone in feeling this connection, this pull to him.

God, Lainey and Gwen would go crazy if they heard my thoughts right now. I know they'll support me in whatever I choose to do, but they'll definitely try to warn me away first.

As I sit in silence, I try to calm myself, but my body won't settle. Every nerve feels awake, buzzing, like it's waiting for something. Or someone. I haven't felt this kind of awareness in years. Not since before everything fell apart between us.

God, Ellie. It was nothing. You were helping a friend. Not even a friend, an acquaintance. Except that feels like a lie. So much for trying to keep my distance. Clearly that hasn't been working out too well for me.

Jamie's face flashes in my mind again, and for a second, I forget about our past. I forget that he was the boy who broke my heart. I forget that he's a famous hockey star. All I can think about is what would have happened if I'd let him kiss me.

Forget it, Ellie. Not happening. He's too busy with work and PT and getting back to his team. He doesn't have time for you. He didn't back then, and he doesn't now. Especially now. He has other things going on that have nothing to do with me. Plus, I have enough to focus on. I need to make sure this show goes perfectly. I said no distractions, and here I am. Letting a boy distract me.

Well, no more of that.

I open up my laptop and look through our upcoming rehearsal schedules, our budget, what we still need for the set. If I'm going to prove to myself that I can do this, I need to be completely focused on the task.

My phone buzzes on the desk and I throw my head back and groan. What now?

Lainey's name flashes on the screen and I swipe to answer it.

“Well, if it isn’t Professor Monroe,” she greets in a teasing tone. I roll my eyes, a smirk forming on my lips.

“If it isn’t the bride to be,” I say, knowing talking about the wedding freaks her out. She is so not the girly girl that’s obsessed with getting married. She’s rather have a shotgun wedding and get the whole thing over with, but my brother is not going to let that happen.

“Why are you still at work? It’s like 6:00. Shouldn’t you be home by now?” she asks, throwing her hair into a curly bun on top of her head.

“I still have work to do,” I tell her, but I’m leaving out the part where I’m afraid to go home because I don’t want to run into Jamie again tonight. Her eyes narrow in suspicion.

“Why do you look like you almost made a terrible life choice?” Lainey says, her eyes narrowing further. “Or a really good one. It’s hard to tell.”

I give her own narrowed gaze. “I hate you.”

Lainey grins. “That’s not a denial.”

I hate how hard it is to lie to her. Scrubbing my hands over my face, I huff out an exasperated breath. The image of Jamie kneeling, breathing hard, eyes staring into my soul, flares behind her eyelids.

“Are you alone?” I ask, hoping my brother isn’t there with her.

She nods. “Yeah, Holland’s at the gym. Why?”

I take a deep breath. Here goes nothing.

“We almost kissed.”

Lainey’s smile vanishes instantly. “Oh.”

“Yeah,” I mutter.

"How almost are we talking?" Lainey asks carefully. I cringe.

"Like, I could feel his breath on my face."

Lainey gives me a look of disapproval which I knew was coming.

"Ellie."

"I know, I know. Don't say it."

"El, you know how I feel about him," Lainey replies. "But that doesn't matter. How do you feel?"

I laugh, sharp and humorless. "That's the problem. I don't know what I feel."

Lainey studies her. "That bad, huh?"

I nod. "It's like my body didn't get the memo that we shouldn't want him."

"Well... do you?" Lainey presses.

"Do I what?"

"Do you want him?"

"Lainey..." I start. She holds her hands up in surrender.

"Hey, I'm not judging. That man is seriously sexy. He's got that whole hot hockey player, bad boy, persona."

I chuckle. "I thought you hated him?"

"I hate what he did to you. But I can't deny he's good looking," she shrugs.

Yeah, she's not wrong. He is undeniably attractive, but he's still so focused on hockey. It's his entire life. How would I possibly fit in?

"By the way, how's he doing? His injury is the talk of the NHL right now."

My throat tightens. "He's...broken."

Lainey winces. "Shit."

"Honestly, I barely recognize him. He's barely holding it together, Laine," I tell her without divulging too much into his private life. "The injury, the coaching. He keeps pretending he's fine, and then he just kind of... explodes."

"I know Holland would be devastated if he couldn't play rugby anymore. Not that he would ever want to play professionally or anything, but he's been playing for so long that it would probably break him to never be able to play again," Lainey says quietly.

I nod. "Yeah, except, Jamie might be able to play again. He just doesn't seem to have the confidence. He's so focused on the fact that his injury might never heal."

Lainey takes a deep breath before exhaling. She looks directly into the camera.

"Look, El. All I'll say is he is dealing with a lot right now. He's on the verge of losing everything he's worked for his entire life. It still seems like his world might be centered around getting back to the NHL. I don't want you to get too attached just for it to—"

"End the same way it did before? I know. That's why I'm not doing anything about anything. We are colleagues and housemates. Nothing more. That's all we can be," I say with as much confidence as I can muster. That's how it has to be.

Lainey gives me a look that tells me she doesn't believe me at all. I don't even know if I believe myself. All I know is that I'm beginning not to trust myself around him, and that's not good because we literally share a space of living.

A door shuts in the background and Lainey looks over her shoulder, then back to me.

"Holland's home. Gotta go, babe. Don't do anything I wouldn't do!" she winks and gives me a knowing smile.

I roll my eyes. "And what exactly wouldn't you do?" I tease.

"Oh, whatever. Bye, bitch," she says before hanging up and leaving me to think about the mental battle currently playing out in my head.

Damnit, Ellie. What did you get yourself into?

Chapter 17

ELLIE

The next morning, I'm sitting at my desk attempting to focus on my rehearsal schedule for the day. There's still so much to do and we're running low on time. This show needs to be ready by the end of the semester, and we're already seven weeks in. We have about six weeks left to nail this thing so we can move into dress rehearsals. To say I'm stressed is an understatement.

Add in the Jamie factor, and I'm screwed. I do not have the head space to deal with both things at once.

To top it all off, I have a meeting with Dean Ashby this afternoon after rehearsal. Something about needing to discuss the 'next steps' for the arts department. Whatever that means.

Finally peaking up from the pile of papers scattered across my desk, I watch the two students on stage finish up their scene.

"From the top!" I call out, my voice echoing through the empty rows of seats. "And please, for the love of God, try to look like you're actually in love, not like you're waiting for a dental appointment."

April and a junior named Leo, reset their positions. They're talented, but I'm almost positive Leo is gay and it's making it hard for them to have a connection. Of course, one could argue that a professional wouldn't let their real-life preferences bleed into their work. But these aren't professionals, they're college students.

They lack the raw intensity their characters require. I know first-hand what that intensity feels like. I felt it in the locker room while staring into the eyes of a man who ruined me.

I haven't seen Jamie since he almost kissed me. Since I almost let him. I've spent the last twelve hours convincing myself it was just the lighting; the close proximity or the fact that he looked so broken, and I've always been a sucker for a project.

My constant need to fix things has always been a problem. Seeing Jamie so destroyed has only made me want to try to fix him. But he's not a puzzle that needs to be put together.

He's not a torn piece of paper I need to tape together. He's not mine, and I'm not in charge of fixing him. That's something only he can do.

"Stop," I call over April and Leo as I approach the stage. They break away from each other like one of them was on fire.

"This isn't working," I gesture between them. They look to each other, confused. "You're supposed to be in love with each other. Where is the passion? The emotion? The tension? I'm getting nothing."

"Well, Professor Monroe, I do prefer sausage," Leo winks and chuckles. April gives him a disgusted look, and I roll my eyes.

"Then act like April has a penis. I don't care. Just give me something. And April, this is the love of your life. He's pushing you away because he doesn't see how anyone could possibly love him. You need to show him he's worth loving. Understood?" I ask, directing my question to both of them. They nod, and I begin to walk away.

"We'll pick this up tomorrow. We have six weeks to get this right. I want you two rehearsing together as much as you can, even outside regular rehearsals. That's your homework, okay?"

"Yes, professor," they answer in unison before exiting the stage.

I know how badly April wants this. How badly she wants to prove herself. I can see she's working hard, but Leo isn't giving her anything to work with. He's not taking it as seriously as she is.

I don't think this class was something he truly wanted to do, more of a filler class than anything. Which sucks for April, because she's really giving it her all. Especially in scenes where she's solo.

Unfortunately, this is a love story, and it's going to need both of them to work at it for it to be believable.

I don't want to push them too hard, because I want to it to be enjoyable for them, but I have a lot riding on this play. Like April, I'm also trying to prove myself, and I need them to cooperate to do that.

My chest tightens just thinking about it. Everything's in someone else's hands, and I can feel my control slipping through my fingers. I'm not used to this, not being the one controlling the outcome, and it's giving me anxiety. I'm not usually an anxious person, but I need this to be perfect.

Hours later, I'm sitting in Dean Ashby's office, my leg bouncing with anticipation as I wait for him to enter the room. When the door opens, I expect Ashby to walk through, but to my surprise, Jamie walks in and takes the seat beside me. What the hell is he doing here? Ashby didn't tell me Jamie would be joining us.

Jamie gives me a cocky smile, and the shift from seeing him falling apart in front of me to the confident man sitting next to me is giving me whiplash.

"Why are you here?" I ask, my tone a little rougher than I intended.

"Ashby told me to be," he shrugs, the smile never leaving his lips. The lips I haven't been able to stop thinking about since yesterday. God, Ellie. Focus.

"Well, great. He must have seen us together in the locker room. He's going to fire us," I begin to panic. Oh god, if he fires me, I'll never be able to show my face again. I'll be too embarrassed. I'd have to tell my friends and family that I was fired for fraternization with a coworker. Shit. I'm so screwed.

Jamie's large hand lands on my thigh, causing it to stop bouncing. It's supposed to be comforting, but it's sending adrenaline straight to my heart. I can't focus when he's this close, especially when he's touching me.

"Hey, he didn't see anything. He's not going to fire us, just calm down," Jamie says, trying, and failing, to get my nerves in check.

Looking down at his hand, I swat it away. "Why else would he call us both in here then?"

"Maybe he wants to give us a raise," he suggests. I glare at him. We both know Ashby didn't call us here to give us a raise.

The door opens once again, and this time, the Dean walks in with a smile on his face. He takes a seat in his big, desk chair and folds his hands together in front of him like he's about to discuss how both of us have broken some sort of rules and we're both being terminated.

"Miss Monroe," he nods towards me, his smile genuine. "Mr. Patterson. Thank you for joining me."

We both nod, and I do my best to smile, even though I feel like my heart is about to pound out of my chest.

"I called you both here because there's something important we need to discuss."

Oh god, oh god, oh god. I brace myself for the bad news.

"Let's get right to it then. This won't take long," he continues. "As you both know, we're piloting a cross-departmental initiative to boost student engagement and donor visibility. Athletics and Arts. Funds have been kind of low since Mr. Steele went to... well, since he went away."

No, no I did not know this. My stomach sinks. I have no idea where this is heading, but I know I'm not going to like it by the way Ashby is smiling.

Jamie shifts beside me. I don't look at him. I don't need to.

"We'll be hosting a campus showcase," Ashby says. "Performances, exhibitions, demonstrations. The hockey program will be featured prominently. Coach Patterson."

Jamie's jaw tightens.

"And Director Monroe," Ashby continues, "you'll be co-leading the coordination."

He isn't serious. This can't be real. He's already trapped us in the same house together, now he wants us to work together?

Jamie stares straight ahead, his expression carved from stone.

Co-leading. With Jamie.

"With respect," Jamie says, his voice level but edged, "we weren't made aware of this *initiative* at all."

Dean Ashby's face flushes. I would definitely remember if he mentioned something about joining the arts and athletics departments. He never once mentioned that when he hired me.

"Did I forget to mention that?" he asks, awkwardly chuckling. I can't tell if he really forgot that he didn't tell us, or if this was his plan all along. He doesn't know our history, so there's no reason he's do any of this maliciously. I'm just not sure how he forgot to tell the two heads of each department that they'd be working together for an event.

Jamie nods. "Yeah, you did."

Dean Ashby clears his throat nervously. "The expectation is that you'll present a unified front. The arts and the athletes working together."

He looks between Jamie and me with a stern expression. Can he see the tension between us? Can he tell there's some sort of animosity there?

Jamie's mouth turns into a slight smirk. Is he enjoying this? I thought he would be pissed. I am.

I'm supposed to be focusing on the play. I'm supposed to be keeping my distance. How is it going to be possible for me to keep my distance from the man if I have to work with him?

"Dean Ashby, I have so much to do for the play and—"

"I trust you'll be able to do both, Miss Monroe. I know you can. Now, let's discuss details."

The meeting continues, the details blurring together. Dates, budgets, talking points, but I'm barely hearing them. I'm too aware of Jamie beside me. Too aware of how much effort it's taking not to react to every shift of his body. To confused as to why he didn't fight back more.

He told me he'd give me space. He told me he wouldn't get in my way. And that's all he's done.

The most frustrating part is, I don't even know if I want him to give me space anymore.

When the Dean finishes his spiel, Jamie stands and shakes his hand. I stay seated for a moment, collecting my thoughts. Then, I stand quietly and walk out the door without another word.

I feel Jamie's presence behind me as I enter the empty hallway. Stopping abruptly, I turn around to face him, ready to set my terms for this damn arrangement I'm being forced into.

Before I can get a word out though, he says, "So," he says in a low tone that sends a shiver down my spine. "Guess we're a team again."

The way he says again makes my heart stutter.

"This is professional," I say sternly.

His mouth curves into a sly smile. He's enjoying this way too much. Holding his hands up in mock surrender, he chuckles.

"Sure, yeah. Professional."

I roll my eyes. "We can coordinate via email. I'll send over the outline." That way, I don't have to spend more time with him in person and risk anything happening between us that I'll later regret.

Jamie leans back against the wall, arms crossed.

"No. We won't."

My pulse jumps. "Excuse me?"

"You want this to work?" he asks. "We meet. In person. No miscommunication."

I bristle. "I'm perfectly capable of—"

"This is my program," he cuts in. "My players. If your department's name is attached, I need to know exactly what you're expecting from us."

I search his face for sarcasm, for provocation but find neither. He's taking this seriously.

"Fine. Tomorrow," I tell him. "Auditorium. Ten a.m. But no funny business."

Jamie's eyes flick to my mouth, then back up to my eyes. My stomach flips.

"I'll be there."

The butterflies in my stomach let loose as I watch the smirk on his face turn into a grin. All of this would be so much better if I actually hated the man. I wouldn't have to worry about feelings or attraction.

Unfortunately for me, I don't hate him. I don't know if I ever really did.

Chapter 18

JAMIE

I watch her hips sway as she walks down the hallway to the auditorium. She's not happy with this little arrangement, and honestly, I don't know how I feel about it. I'm pissed that Ashby didn't let us know about this whole thing earlier. On the other hand, this will force Ellie and I to work together, spend more time together, learn more about the people we are now.

That could either be a good thing or a really, really bad thing. I don't know what to think. I'm not good for her, I know that. She deserves someone who isn't such a fucking mess. Someone who has their shit together. Someone who hasn't already broken her heart once.

But fuck, do I want her.

It's selfish as hell, and I don't care. I can't stop it. Every time I look at her, my body remembers what she tasted like, the way she smelled when she was warm and undone, the sounds she made when she stopped holding herself back. My mouth remembers what it felt like to kiss her. My dick remembers what it felt like to be buried inside her.

She's slowly overtaking all of my thoughts and my focus, and working together so closely isn't going to help matters. But it's not like I can tell Ashby to go fuck himself. I do enjoy the coaching gig, and I'd rather not get canned. So I have to do this. We have to work together, and I have to rein in my thoughts and feelings towards her and stay professional.

Against my better judgement, I pull my phone out of my pocket and pull up her contact.

Ellie Monroe

Me: *We should loop in Facilities. The rink setup will matter.*

Ellie Monroe: *I'll handle it. Focus on your team.*

Me: *You're bossy.*

Ellie Monroe: *I am not.*

I can't help myself. I wish I could take it back as soon as I press send, but it's too late.

Me: *I like it.*

What the fuck is wrong with me?

Three little dots appear and then disappear about four times before disappearing all together. I'm a fucking idiot. She already doesn't want to do this, and I go ahead and say something like that?

I try to imagine her face when she got the message. Was she pissed or was she flustered? Did she smile or grimace? Honestly, she probably rolled her eyes and tossed her phone to the side, not thinking anything of it.

I really don't want to make her life complicated, but for some reason, I need her to know that I'm not that guy anymore. I'm not the guy that up and left her without a word. I'm not the guy that can't balance life and hockey. I've grown, and as much as I want to get back to my team, I also want to prove to Ellie that I'm not the guy she thinks I am. She needs to understand that if she gave me another chance, even though I don't deserve it, that it would be different this time. I wouldn't hurt her.

Later that night, I'm washing my dishes from dinner when Ellie walks into the kitchen. She's wearing tiny shorts and a t-shirt that's so big it almost covers them. My eyes wander down her legs, landing on her pink toenails before making their way back up to her blushing face. She knows I was checking her out, and I don't even care. She can't come down here looking that good and expect me not to look. I'm only human. I mentally tell my dick to calm down before he causes a scene.

Ellie makes her way toward me, leaning over the counter to reach for a plate in the cupboard overhead. She stands on her toes and reaches, but the plate is too far back. I watch her struggle for a moment, her shirt riding up a bit, revealing her ass to me. Goddamn, why'd I look?

She falls back on her heels and huffs in defeat. I smirk, looking down at her and trying not to laugh at the adorable pout on her face.

"Do you need help?" I ask calmly. Her eyes narrow as she glares at me like the answer to that question is obvious. It is, I just want her to ask for it.

"Use your words, Ellie. Do you need me to help you?" She visibly shrinks at the use of her name. She hates asking for help. We have that in common.

She nods, and I shake my head and tsk.

"Tell me," I demand, turning the sink off and wiping my hands on a towel before crossing my arms over my chest and leaning back on the counter.

I watch as the internal struggle she's having fades into resolve.

"Can you grab me a plate?" she asks, and I shake my head.

"Can I grab you a plate..." I wait for her to finish the sentence. She rolls her eyes, and I chuckle. She's annoyed, and I'm finding this kind of amusing.

"Can you grab me a plate, *please*," she asks again, this time emphasizing the please at the end.

I turn around and easily grab a plate from the cupboard, handing it to her with a smile.

"Was that so hard?" I ask her. She snatches the plate from me before walking away and placing it on the counter.

"I want you to bring some ideas to our meeting tomorrow. If this event is going to happen any time soon, we need to come up with a plan," she states, all business.

She places a piece of chicken onto her plate, along with some rice and puts it in the microwave. I lean over the island, watching her as she stares at the microwave and avoids looking at me. When it beeps, she removes the plate and places it back on the counter, all without looking up.

"Why are you watching me?" she asks, cutting her chicken into pieces. She stabs a piece, and I watch as she pulls the empty fork out of her mouth and chews. Why am I hard right now? I should not be hard just watching her eat. There is something seriously wrong with me.

"I'm not," I lie, because it's clear that I am.

"I can see you," she replies, her eyes narrowed.

"I don't know what you're talking about," I shrug, feigning innocence. The truth is, I don't know why I'm watching her, but I can't stop.

"Did you hear me?"

Fuck, what did she say?

I nod. "Yeah."

Ellie glares at me because she knows I'm full of shit.

"So you'll do it then?"

"Yeah, of course."

"Great, I'll let them know you're up for it," she smiles, taking another bite of her chicken.

Wait what?

"Up for what?" I inquire, afraid of what I'd just agreed to. I should have been paying attention to her, but I'm too distracted by the way her mouth moves as she chews her food. I know it can do a lot more than that from firsthand experience, and fuck. Now I'm thinking about blowjobs. Jesus, Jamie.

"The naked photoshoot for the hockey players. I think it'll raise a lot of money," she shrugs and gives me an innocent smile. It takes a moment for my brain to understand what she just said. Did she just say, 'naked photoshoot'?

Standing up straight, I rub the back of my neck nervously.

"Wait, no. No naked hockey players. We can't—"

Ellie cackles. Like throws her head back, slaps her knee, and laughs hysterically. Did she just wipe a fucking tear away?

"You should have seen your face! That's what you get for not listening to me," she wipes at her eyes again before finally settling down. What the hell just happened?

"I told you to bring some ideas to the meeting tomorrow. For the event."

I nod, taken aback by her playful attitude. She hasn't let herself go like this in front of me in forever. I can't remember the last time I've seen her laugh like that. So carefree and real. The sight sends a tingle down my spine. She's beautiful when she laughs. I could listen to that laugh for hours. I want to make her laugh more.

"Right," I say. "Yeah, I'll think of some stuff."

"Good."

She finished her food, cleans off her plate, and places it in the dishwasher before turning back to me.

"I'll see you at ten," she tells me before walking out of the kitchen, leaving me to figuratively bang my head against a wall for not being able to control my thoughts.

I've never been one to lose my mind over a woman. Plenty have thrown themselves at me over the years, but I never felt like I needed them. Not how I feel like I need Ellie. Like if I don't have her, I'll combust.

I feel like a teenager that can't control their hormones. I'm a grown ass man. I shouldn't be struggling to keep it together when she's around. Yet here I am. Trying not to cum in my pants at the image of her lips wrapped around that fork and imagining it was my dick instead.

Lucky goddamn utensil.

Chapter 19

JAMIE

Rhode Island Stormies

Billy Callahan: *Patty, when are you coming back? The new captain is an ass.*
Wilder Ranslavic: *Agreed. He's the worst.*
Connor Grieves: *He tried to touch me inappropriately.*
Theo Cramer: *First off, you're a fucking idiot. Second, I'm right here.*
Billy Callahan: *Oh shit. Here's gramps himself.*
Theo Cramer: *I'm only two years older than you, dumbass.*
Wilder Ranslavic: *And not much wiser.*
Connor Grieves: *Oh shit. Burn.*
Billy Callahan: *Patty's living it up at that fancy university. Too busy to answer his besties.*

Jamie Patterson: *Don't say besties.*

Connor Grieves: *He lives!*

Wilder Ranslavic: *It's a Christmas miracle.*

Connor Grieves: *It's October.*

Theo Cramer: *Patterson, please come get your kids. They're driving me fucking crazy.*

Shaking my head at the stupidity that is my teammates, I toss my phone onto my bed and dry my hair with a towel. Even a cold shower couldn't get rid of the thoughts of Ellie.

I lay in bed, trying to think of anything else. My team, my knee, ideas for the event. But everything keeps coming back to Ellie. How did I go years without thinking about her, to not being able to stop? I mean, that's crazy, right? I want to blame it on the fact that I see her almost every day now, so it's hard not to think about her. But it's not just that. It's like my body is begging me to remind it of what she feels like. There's no way she'd let that happen though. Not now. Not with us having to work together and be professional.

That might be an issue, if I can't seem to be able to keep my dick down. Speaking of my dick, he's hard yet again. Would it be wrong to masturbate to visions of Ellie? I mean, it's not like she'd know. Fuck.

My hand drifts down, brushing against the bulge in my briefs. I hesitate for a moment, but then give in, pulling them down my legs and tossing them aside.

I never said I was a good guy. In fact, I wouldn't say I am. I'm decent, but I did leave the girl I loved without any explanation, so there's that.

My cock is rock hard in my hand, throbbing with anticipation. I squeeze gently as I close my eyes, Ellie's face appearing in my mind. I imagine her kneeling before me, her blonde hair falling around her shoulders, her lips parted as she looks up at me with those bright green eyes.

"What do you want, Jamie?" she whispers, her voice sweet, her breath warm against my skin.

"You," I groan, my grip tightening around my shaft. "I want you."

A slow, seductive smile curves on her plush lips, and then I imagine her leaning forward, her tongue darting out to wet her lips. I pretend my hand is hers as I brush my thumb over the head of my cock. She looks up at me.

"Tell me what you want me to do," she murmurs.

"Suck me," I demand.

Imaginary Ellie doesn't hesitate. She lowers her mouth, her lips brushing the tip of my cock before she takes me in, her tongue swirling around the head. I groan, my head falling back against the pillow as pleasure surges through me. Fuck, it feels so real.

I imagine my hand tangling in her hair as I guide her deeper. I imagine her moaning around me, the sound sending a jolt of pleasure straight to my core. I can feel her hands on my thighs, her nails digging into my skin as she works her mouth up and down my cock.

My hips thrust slightly, needing more. Needing this to be real. As the tension builds, I let myself imagine her lips moving faster, her tongue flicking the underside of my cock as her head bobs. I can feel myself losing control, my breath coming in short gasps as the pleasure intensifies. I'm so fucking close, but I don't want to stop imagining her this way. Once I cum, I know I'll feel guilty as hell for thinking of her like this, but right now, I can't bring myself to feel anything other than pleasure.

My hand moves faster, and I imagine Ellie sucking me faster and harder. I finally feel the tension coiling in my stomach, the pressure building to an unbearable point. I can't hold it back anymore.

My body tightens, my muscles clenching as I cum harder than I have in months. The thick, hot stream lands on my stomach, but I can't bring myself to care.

My dick throbs and my mind races as the image of Ellie on her knees for me disappears.

I am so fucking screwed. There is no way in hell that I'm going to be able to sit with her week after week and talk hockey and theatre and events. There's no way I'll be able to control myself knowing she's right down the damn hall from me every night. I need to distract myself somehow. Get my mind off of Ellie and back on me and healing. I just don't know how when she's at the forefront of my mind most days.

I decide that instead of beginning to spiral, I should probably get some sleep. Tomorrow is going to be a long day, and I'm going to need a clear head. I begin to doze off, tossing and turning slightly until I'm in a comfortable position. Finally, my thoughts fade, and sleep overtakes me.

My alarm wakes me with a start at eight thirty in the morning. I take a quick shower and throw on some jeans and an Ellington Wolves hoodie. I have a bit of a pep in my step this morning, and I suspect it's due to the fact that I'll be meeting with Ellie in an hour. I'm probably a little too amped up about this, but I'm grateful for the excuse to be around her.

The house is quiet, and when I walk into the kitchen, it's empty. Ellie must have already left. A pang of disappointment rushes through me.

Just then, my phone goes off, breaking the silence. Mom's contact lights up the screen.

"Hello?"

"Hi, honey. How are you doing?" mom asks. She's been asking me that since I got benched. Not that she didn't ask before, but it's been more often since I got hurt. I think she thinks I'm going to spiral out of control, which to be fair, I kind of did the other day in the locker room before Ellie found me. Mom doesn't need to know about that, though. She'll just worry more, and I don't want that for her. She's been through enough, and she has her own shit to deal with.

"I'm good. Just about to head out for a meeting. You okay?"

"Of course. I just wanted to check in and see how you were doing. I know you've been under a lot of pressure lately with your new team," she says, her voice soft and motherly.

I run a hand through my hair. "Yeah, it's been a lot but I'm fine. The team is shaping up, and my knee feels good," I lie. I can practically feel her smile through the phone.

"Oh, honey. That's great! You'll be back to playing in no time, I just know it. You know, Denise says that doctor you saw in Boston had no idea what he was talking about. She's super knowledgeable."

Shaking my head, I slide my shoes on and grab my keys off the hook by the front door. "Mom, she thinks she can see the future. I don't know how knowledgeable that is."

"Jamie, you know what she said about your father. She was right!" mom exclaims. Denise, her best friend and neighbour is convinced she's a psychic. She's been filling moms head with crap for years. I've tried to tell her that it's all bullshit, but she won't have it. I think she likes believing that someone can see what's going to happen.

"He had cancer, mom. We all knew he wasn't going to make it. We didn't need a psychic to tell us that," I say as I slide into my car and turn it on.

"Well, either way. I know you'll be okay. You're getting better every day. Now, have you met any nice girls up at that fancy college?" she changes the subject so abruptly I get whiplash. In almost every phone call, mom will ask if I've met someone, and in every phone call I tell her no. In all fairness, the answer usually is no. However, the answer is more complicated now. Because, no, technically I haven't met anyone. But I have been thinking about one girl in particular.

My mom loved Ellie, and she was devastated when I left her. She told me I was losing out on one of the best things that would ever happen to me. Back then, I thought the best thing that could happen for me was going pro. Now, I'm not so sure, because that's gone too.

Mom would probably be ecstatic that Ellie's here, but there's not much to tell her. Ellie seems like she would rather be anywhere else whenever we're in the same room, but I can tell there's a part of her that's affected by my presence. It may be a really small part of her, but it's there.

Shaking my head, I say, "no, mom. I have not met any girls."

Mom sighs on the other end. "You know, I would like grandkids someday."

I choke on air. I wasn't expecting her to say that. I haven't really put any thought to having kids or a family. I've been on my own for so long, and I kind of figured I would be forever. Except now with Ellie, I don't think I want to be alone anymore. Jesus, who the fuck am I?

Pulling into the parking lot in front of the hockey arena, auditorium, and tennis court, I end the conversation with mom by telling her I was late for a meeting, and I'd talk to her later. Thankfully, I'm not actually late because Ellie would probably kick my ass.

Before getting out of the car, I take a deep breath and try to focus on the purpose of today's meeting instead of the recurring images of my imagination last night. The last thing I need is to get a boner while I'm trying to discuss business.

Well, here goes nothing.

Chapter 20

ELLIE

I check my phone for the tenth time in a row. I swear to God, if Jamie is late, I'll kick his ass. He assured me he'd be here on time, and he has ten minutes to make sure that happens. I'd like to get this meeting over and done with so I can focus on the play. Not only that, but I don't want to be stuck alone in a room with Jamie longer than I have to.

Just then, the auditorium door opens and Jamie strolls in like he owns the place. He's all confidence and swagger in his dark jeans and Ellington University hoodie. Damnit, why does he have to look so good? This would be so much easier if he was ugly.

He stops in front of my desk, a smirk on his lips.

"I'm on time," he states as he peers down at the watch on his wrist. "With eight minutes to spare."

"Wow, I'm impressed," I say mockingly. His smile grows wider.

"You didn't think I would be, huh?" he asks, his arms crossing over his shoulders like a shield.

I shake my head. "No, honestly, I didn't."

"You wound me, Sweetheart," he acts as if he's being stabbed in the chest and tumbles a bit.

"That was good. You should join the play," I deadpan.

"Ha. No thanks, I'd rather take a skate to the leg than get on a stage and perform."

"It's not much different than what you do on the ice. You perform for an audience the same way I do," I tell him. His eyes widen a bit before his arms fall to his sides.

"You think playing hockey and acting on stage are the same? Last time I checked, you don't have to watch for pucks coming at you at one hundred miles per hour."

Standing from my seat, I slap my hands on the desk.

"I never said they were the same. I said they weren't that different. Listening comprehension is important, Jamie." I know I'm poking the bear, but I don't care. For some reason, getting a rise out of him is satisfying.

Jamie's palms land on the desk as we mirror each other. His narrowed green eyes stare into mine as if this is some sort of stand-off. As if we were wolves just waiting for the other to attack. The tension between us is palpable, and I can't tell if it's the kind that says we want to kill one another, or if it's the kind that says we want to kiss one another. I'd like to think it's not the latter, but there's a part of me feels like it is.

"Keep looking at my lips Sweetheart, and I'm gonna think you want to kiss me," Jamie grins cockily.

I can feel my cheeks heat with embarrassment as I look up from his lips and back to his eyes. I hadn't even realized I'd been staring at his lips, and I hate that he caught me. I don't need to inflate his ego even more.

"Let's just get to work," I tell him, sitting back down and gesturing for him to take the chair across from me. He sits slowly, never taking his eyes off of me. I feel his gaze as I sort through the paperwork and notes on my desk.

"Right, yeah. Let's do that."

Rolling my eyes, I read through some notes I'd taken with my ideas for the event. I decide I'll start with the easiest thing, a name for the fundraiser. I didn't exactly know what name would fit this sort of thing, but I think this one stood out the most to me, and I think Jamie will like it.

"Let's start with a name. I came up with a few, and this is the one I liked the best," I tell him, flipping the paper so he can read what I'm pointing to.

He stares at the page for far too long before his eyes narrow and he scoffs.

"You're kidding."

My head snaps up. "Excuse me?"

"Pucks and Props?" Jamie says, pointing at the paper like it personally offended him. "That's what you landed on? Really?"

My brow furrows and my fists clench. "It's catchy," I say defensively. "And brings together both groups."

Jamie shakes his head. "Sure, we'll go with that."

Leaning back in my chair, I cross my arms. "Oh, I'm sorry. Did you have a suggestion?"

"Yeah," he says easily. "Literally anything that doesn't make me sound like an ass when announcing it."

I chuckle. "Well that eliminates, hmm, everything.

Jamie's eyes narrow, and he smirks sarcastically.

"That was a good one. I'm offended. Ouch," he mocks.

I knew this was going to be challenging, us working together. However, I didn't expect it to be like this. There's just so many unresolved feelings between us, and we've both got our own shit going on. That's why we need to put our feelings for each other aside and focus on work. Easier said than done, I guess.

"Fine," Jamie says finally. "Pucks and Props it is."

A slow grin crosses my face and my brow arches. "That sounded painful."

"It was," he says. "I'm going to complain every time I say it."

My smile is victorious. "I'll take that as an agreement."

Jamie leans back in his chair, shaking his head.

"You always did have a way of getting what you want."

I freeze, the smile fading into a flat line as I take in what he said. He's talking about the past. About us. Why would he bring that up? He doesn't have a right to bring up our relationship as if he has fond memories. He's the one that ruined it.

"Don't do that."

"Don't do what?" he asks innocently, like he doesn't know he just shoved a dagger into my heart.

"Try to act like you care about our past. You don't, and that's fine. But don't bring it up like you give a shit."

His brows furrow and he looks at me inquisitively.

"Ellie, I didn't m—"

"Do you have any ideas for the event? Like, what we actually want to do?"

Jamie clears his throat and nods. "Yeah, a hockey game."

"A hockey game. That's your big idea? A regular hockey game?"

"Not just a *regular* game. One that offers more." He stands from his seat and begins to pace back and forth. My stomach twists as I watch him do something I've seen him do a million times. This is what he's always done when he's thinking. He used to tell me it helps him think better.

Shaking my head, I say, "I don't understand."

"What if," he says slowly, "mid-game, right when people think they know what's going on...we stop."

My eyes narrow. "Stop what?"

"The game," he says as if it's obvious. "The lights go down. The music hits. Everyone's silent because they have no clue what's about to happen."

"Jamie..." I have no idea where he's going with this, but the smile on his face screams mischievous.

"Hear me out." He sits back down and looks me dead in the eyes. A small shiver runs down my spine from how intense it feels. I haven't seen him smile like this since he got here. He's been broody and sad for the most part. "We're in full gear. We're on the ice, and instead of a play..."

He pauses, watching me.

"...the team performs a choreographed dance," he finishes with a goofy smile. He's screwing with me, right? There's no way this man just offered up his whole team to dance in front of an audience.

I stare at him, unblinking.

"You want the hockey team to dance," I say flatly.

"On skates," he adds.

"In front of a crowd."

"Yes."

I open my mouth to speak, close it, and then say, "Absolutely not."

Jamie grins. "I knew you'd say that."

"This isn't a joke, Jamie," I tell him sternly.

"No, it's not," he replies. "It's unexpected. People would lose their minds."

He's not wrong. Seeing a bunch of jocks perform a dance routine would be pretty entertaining. The girls would go crazy for it, and the guys would probably find it hilarious.

"Fine," I say reluctantly, crossing my arms over my chest.

His eyes light up. "Yeah?"

"Only if you join them," I say, my eyes daring.

Jamie guffaws. "Yeah, okay."

"I'm serious. You have to participate as their coach. You have to lead them."

"Ellie, I—"

"That's the only way I'll agree to it. Do we have a deal, or not?" I ask, waiting for him to either tell me to get lost or agree to my terms. He lets out a deep sigh, and I know I've won.

"Fine, okay. I'll do it too," he pouts in defeat. I smile a victorious smile. He rolls his eyes.

"And my drama students will choreograph it."

"Sounds good to me," he agrees.

I write everything down in my notes before moving on to the next order of business.

Placing my pen down on the paper, I interlace my fingers on the desk and look across at Jamie who's watching me intently, like he wants to jump across the table and do something we'll both regret.

Clearing my throat, I say, "My turn."

Jamie straightens. "The floor is yours."

"During intermissions, the drama club performs a scene from our upcoming play."

He frowns. "A whole scene?"

"Well, a curated one," I say. "Five minutes each. We don't want to give too much away."

"What's the play about?" he asks, actually seeming curious.

"It's a sweet story about a woman who travels far from home for a new life and meets a man who changes her perspective. She learns that she doesn't have to be independent all the time. It's okay to ask for help and have someone to lean on."

He watches me, his eyes narrowing as if he's trying to read me like a book.

"Sounds... thrilling," he says. "How does it fit exactly?"

"That's the point," I tell him. "We'll perform it mid-ice with a minimal set. My actors and stage crew will get everything ready. The ice becomes part of the environment."

"And you think people will go for it? It'll keep them entertained?"

I nod. "Oh, they'll be entertained. We'll only do scenes that have humor, or cliffhangers where people can't wait to see what comes next," I explain with excitement. This idea might just actually work.

He smiles brightly, and I know I've got him.

"And it promotes the play," he says slowly.

"Yes."

"And brings in donors who like the arts."

"Yes."

"We can even sell tickets at the rink," he shrugs and I nod.

"Or we could raffle them off!"

"Alright, Sweetheart," Jamie said. "Seems like we've got a plan."

My eyes narrow at the nickname that keeps making a comeback. "Don't call me that."

"Whatever you say, Sweetheart. You know you like it," he winks.

Looking down at my lap so he can't see the way my face is absolutely blushing, I reluctantly admit to myself that yes, I think I might enjoy it.

Probably more than I should.

Chapter 21

JAMIE

"Jesus... oh fuck," I groan, a bead of sweat running down my forehead. The bed creaks from my weight as I'm pushed farther into the cushion. "Oh my god, yes. Right there."

"Alright, please stop with the sex noises," Jared pleads, causing me to laugh hysterically.

"I'm laughing through the pain, Jared. If I don't, I'm gonna start cussing and throwing fists. Neither of us want that."

"You already are cussing."

"Yeah, but not at you," I point out.

"Yeah, well not yet anyway. You might be in a second though. Get up. Time for—"

I sit up quickly, giving him a desperate look. "Not the bands..."

Jared nods, a sinister smile forming on his face, probably because he knows these are my least favorite thing to do. They hurt like a bitch, and that's crazy for me because it's something that used to be so easy. Oh, how the mighty have fallen.

"Yes, the bands. Now get your ass up and on the mat," he points to black yoga mat on the floor.

Groaning exaggeratedly, I reluctantly move from the bed to the mat. Jared hands me the bands and directs me on what to do with them.

I count the reps in my head the way I used to count shifts.

One.

Two.

Three.

Four.

The resistance band bites into my quad as I extend my leg, sweat slicking the back of my neck despite the rooms aggressive air-conditioning. I push through the searing pain in my knee, trying to picture anything else in my mind to keep me from thinking about how much it hurts.

"Don't rush it," Jared tells me for the third time.

I exhale through my nose and slow the movement, my jaw tight. My knee burns, but my need to get back on the ice is hotter.

As I huff and puff, I stare up at the ceiling.

And of course, like she's a freaking beacon of light, Ellie's face is there. All gorgeous with her pink lips and green eyes and perfect smile. Fuck, the way she was talking to me the other day, all demanding and straight to business. The way she smiled when the details finally came into place. Shit, I had to jack off in the shower as soon as I got home. She's a goddamn vision, and I don't understand what my eighteen-year-old self was thinking. Cleary he wasn't considering I left quite possibly the most beautiful girl I've ever laid my eyes on. I had her. I had her and I fucked it all up. Now, I have to work like hell to try and get her back.

Jesus Christ, this hurts.

I finish the set and let my leg flop down on the mat.

"What were you thinking about?" Jared asks, curiously.

"How much I wanted to punch you for making me do that again," I say with a straight face. He chuckles.

"You're improving," he states. "Your strength's coming back."

"Yeah," I mutter. "Slowly."

Everything's been so goddamn slow lately. My healing, earning Ellie's trust, my team.

The one thing that hasn't been slow, though, is how much I want Ellie. It's like having an itch I can't scratch.

See, wanting her isn't the problem. The problem is wanting her and knowing I don't get to touch her.

That pain is worse than any pain I've felt in this room, and the worst part is, it's all my fault.

Later that day, I'm in the locker room with the Wolves.

It's loud and chaotic, and the energy is palpable. They're pumped for tonight's game, and honestly, I am too. They've been practicing their asses off and I'm actually a little proud of them. Ridgewood Academy is good. They have some skilled players, and their coach is a hardass. I can also be a hardass, but not as bad as Sean Morone. I'm not completely sure what the outcome will be, but I'll be proud either way.

I do hope they win though, because I have to break the news to them that they're going to be dancing in front of quite a big audience in a few weeks. Can't wait to see how that goes. But for now, we need to focus on the game.

After my pep talk, the boys are fired up and ready to go. The arena is loud when the guys take the ice. There's cheers and screaming, the sound of hands banging on the glass. Ridgewood's guys enter the ice, and the stands erupt with boos. I miss this. This feeling of adrenaline pumping through my veins. The rush of heat before a game.

Scanning the stands, I try to find the one person I want to see, but she's nowhere to found. Not that she has a reason to be, we're not together.

Skates carve into ice, sticks clack together, and I take my spot behind the bench. It's definitely odd being behind the bench instead of on it. I don't know if I'll ever get used to this, but with any luck, I won't have to. I cross my arms over my chest and watch as the guy's skate back and forth, hitting pucks at the goal and stretching. Warmups are always chaotic. We chirp at each other, make snide comments about sleeping with someone's mom or girlfriend to get them riled up. It's the best part of the game, aside from winning of course.

The time starts on the clock and they start off strong. For the first ten minutes, they hold their own. They've got smart passes, our defense is tight, and Levi Petrolla, our mammoth of a goalie is guarding that net with his life. It's a promising start, and although I should be completely focused on the game in front of me, I can't help but check the stands every few minutes in case Ellie miraculously decides to show up.

Get your head in the game, Jamie.

Shaking my head, I refocus on what's happening on the ice, barking orders and definitely some words that should probably not be said at a college game.

I watch as one of Ridgewood's forwards comes barreling down the ice with the puck. Jacob Rostolvic gets in front of him, effectively stealing the puck and heading in the other direction. Ridgewood's players are tough. They're aggressive and they don't hold back. It's like they can sense fear, and right now, my guys are acting scared. Their pulling back on shots, not getting close enough to the goal, and making stupid mistakes.

The first goal comes from Ridgewood after Logan Bergström loses the puck in the neutral zone. One second he had possession, and the next, the puck was in the back of our fucking net.

I take a deep breath through my nose as I try not to react. I watch Levi as he slams his stick against the ice in frustration.

If I had a stick, I'd be doing the same thing. These guys are not giving it their all. I don't care if it's practice, I don't care if it's a beer league game. You show up and you give it one hundred and ten percent of everything you've got. You prove to yourself and to others that you are meant to play hockey. You're meant to be there. Ridgewood seems to have gotten that memo.

"Move," I snap as Paul, one of my wingers, hesitates to steal the puck. "Jesus, Novak, move your god damn feet."

That makes him move faster. He races toward Ridgewood's net while their goalie is distracted and dumps the puck deep inside. Fucking finally!

The score is finally one to one, and by the looks of it, Ridgewood is not playing around. They came to win, and that's what they're going to try to do.

When the end of the second period comes around, I feel like I'm about to have a coronary. My heart is racing and I'm sweating. I wasn't even on the damn ice but with the way I've been shouting and pacing back and forth, it's no surprise that I'm dying of a heat stroke.

"Gap! Close the gap!" I bark for what seems like the thirtieth time today.

But it's too late.

The shot rings off the crossbar, the sound sharp enough to rattle teeth. I lean over and take calming breaths, as if that's going to help me right now.

"You okay, coach?" one of the Wolves asks, looking a bit concerned. Is he shitting me right now? With the way this team has been playing, how could I possibly be okay?

"Shut up and turn around." He does. I know, that was an asshole move, but I'm so riled up right now. I can't tell if it's because they're playing so poorly, or if it's because I wish it were me out there on the ice.

By the third period, the game is already lost. I turn my back on the ice and drag a hand over my face.

"Unreal," I mutter.

I make the decision to take Petrolla out of goal with over two minutes left. It's risky, but I'm putting in one of my best guys.

"Congratulations," I tell him. "You get one more chance to prove you deserve this damn jersey, do you hear me?"

"Coach, there's no way we're winning this. It's four to two. It's over."

I grab him by the collar and bring him close.

"It's not over until the damn buzzer goes off, kid. Get out there," I spit, shoving him toward the ice. He recovers quickly, hopping the barrier and skating into the chaos.

Of course, he was right. Ridgewood beat us four to two. The buzzer signifies the end of the game, and I try my best not to break my clipboard over my damn knee.

Silence swallows the rink as the boys make their way off the ice and into the locker rooms. I follow after them, my adrenaline boiling at an all time high.

"Did that feel good? Huh? Did it? Because that feeling is only gonna get worse if you keep this shit up. We've worked and worked for weeks. That shit out there? That looked like deer on skates."

The locker room is so quiet you could hear a damn pin drop.

"Drills at six a.m. tomorrow. If you're not here you're off the team. If you bitch, you're off the team. I don't care how much money mommy and daddy throw at this school. I won't have this bullshit again. Got it?"

No response. They all stare at me as if I've got three heads.

"I said, *got it*?"

"Yes, coach," they say in unison.

"Get the hell out of here. NOW," I growl.

And then I'm alone, pacing and trying to catch my breath.

I'm pissed off, annoyed, and not all because of the game. Ellie wasn't there, and I don't know why it bothers me so much. I don't know why I expected her to.

Chapter 22

ELLIE

When the final buzzer sounds, I watch as Jamie says something to the team, and by the angry look on his face, I doubt it was anything good. I've never seen him like this. So pent up and full of rage. Why do I find it attractive?

He was pacing behind the bench like a live wire the entire game, his jaw set. I couldn't hear everything he said over the noise of the rink, but I didn't need to. I could see that he was pissed off just by his body language.

His team seemed like they were afraid of him. Although, I would be too so I can't really blame them. Except, his anger wasn't pointed at me, and from afar, he looked good. Crap, Ellie. No, you do not think he's hot. He's a jerk. Right?

I hid behind a pole pretty much the whole time so he couldn't see me. I watched him look up into the stands several times, but I doubt he was looking for me. He has no reason to. I didn't want him to know I was here, watching him.

But God, control radiated off him, like he was born to be in charge. Like he was thriving. I know he wants to get back on the ice, but he'd really be a great coach. His team just needs a little pep.

When he finally turned and walked toward the tunnel, relief should have followed, but of course it didn't. Relief was the last thing I felt. Instead, something pulled tight in my chest. This grown-up version of Jamie is harder, rougher.

He's got a temper and all this rage inside of him that I don't quite understand where it comes from. Even when his father died, when I expected him to blow up and crash and burn, he stayed strong. Humble. It was like he had no emotion. It kind of used to scare me, the way he'd be able to just walk away from things. I guess that's why it was so easy for him to walk away from me.

I don't know what forces me to be standing here like an idiot outside of the locker room. Maybe I'm a masochist. Maybe I like the pain. Or maybe I'm just an idiot. All I know is that I shouldn't be here, yet something in me is telling me to check on him. To make sure he's alright. Taking a deep breath, I push the door open and automatically feel the change in the air. It's heavier, sadder. It's weighed down by years of guilt and heartbreak.

As I make my way further into the room, I see him. Jamie Patterson, sitting hunched over on a bench. I watch for a moment as his body rises and falls with his rapid breaths.

His white undershirt clings to him, and as I grow closer, I see the beads of sweat trickling down his cheeks and his arms.

For a second, I think he might be so out of it that he doesn't even notice me. But then his breath hitches.

I make my way in front of him, kneeling down to be level with him. This feels all too familiar, like we've been here before. I should let him deal with this on his own. He probably wants space and here I am, not giving him any.

"Jamie," I practically whisper.

He flinches, as if he'd been somewhere else and I've just brought him back to reality. He straightens too quickly, immediately favoring his knee, and that's when I see it.

The way his hands tremble and the tight, unfocused look in his eyes.

Oh. Oh no. He's having another panic attack. Shit. I reach out to touch him but decide it's probably not a great idea. I pull my hand back quickly.

"You shouldn't be here," he says breathily.

"I know," I reply. "But here I am."

He drags a hand through his hair and turns away from me. "I'm fine, Ellie. Just go."

It's a lie, just like the last time.

"Jamie, you're not. You're shaking and dripping in sweat. That's not fine."

His chest rises sharply, then stalls. He presses his palms flat against the bench like he needs the solidness of it to keep himself upright.

"I fucked it up, Ellie," he tells me. "I fucked everything up."

A part of my heart cracks at the utter sadness in his voice. Shit, I'm not supposed to feel this way. Not about him.

"Fucked what up, Jamie?" I ask, curious as to what he could be referring to. It couldn't be all about the game, could it?

"I should've got help sooner. I should've told someone about my knee when it first happened. But I didn't. I thought I had it handled," he cries, his breath catching. "Now I'm here, my career is over, and I can't even coach this fucking team. I can't help them the way I should. And I..."

He sucks in air like he can't get enough.

My chest tightens.

"Hey," I say softly. "Look at me. You what?"

He looks up through wet lashes, his eyes searching mine. God, he's beautiful. I really have missed those eyes looking at me like this. Like he needs me.

"I fucked up with you."

My heart stops and everything goes silent. That's the last thing I was expecting him to say.

"Jamie..." I begin.

"Please forgive me, Ellie. I know I don't deserve it. I know I'm fucking shitty. But I need you to forgive me." His head falls to my shoulder, and he cries. He cries harder than I think I've ever seen a man cry. For once, he's showing emotion. He's showing me the real him. Not the hot, cocky hockey star image he's built up for the world. But him.

"Shhh...Jamie," I coo. "Jamie, breathe with me."

I feel his jaw clench.

"Come on," I demand, firmer now. "You're spiraling. You need to breathe."

His eyes lift to mine, and they're dark and frantic.

"I'm not supposed to fall apart," he says with a sniffle. "Not now. Not in front of them. Not in front of you."

"You're allowed to be human, Jamie," I say quietly.

He shakes his head, breath still uneven.

"I can't stop thinking about everything at once. The game. My knee. My team. Fuck!" His laugh is broken. "You. I can't stop thinking about you, Ellie. It's driving me fucking insane. You're just... you're always there and you're perfect and knowing I'll never get the chance to... it's killing me."

My heart stutters at his unexpected confession. I understand him being stressed and upset about the team and his injury and what not. But me? Sure, he's been flirty, but I figured that was just him trying to get under my skin. Was it real?

Jamie watches me, waiting for my response.

"Say something, Ellie," he begs.

I'm frozen in place. My brain has left the building, and I am incapable of speaking. What the hell am I supposed to say to that?

After a moment, I finally make it back to reality.

"Do you know how unfair that is to me? Do you know how long I waited for you to come back? Do you have any idea how many nights I spent crying myself to sleep? No, you don't, because you weren't there, Jamie. You weren't there!"

"Fuck, I know!" he shouts. Tears begin to run down my cheeks before I even realize that I'm crying. "Okay? I know I wasn't there. I was eighteen and I didn't know how to handle it. I... I made a split-second decision. Packed my bags, got in the car, and drove. I didn't tell anyone where I was going, not even mom," he explains, his voice hoarse from crying and shouting all night.

"Is that supposed to make this better?" I practically sob. Jamie shakes his head, grabbing both of my hands in his. I want to pull them back, but I miss his touch. I didn't realize how much I craved it until now.

"No, it's not. Nothing can make it better. All I can do is tell you how sorry I am. How badly I regret what I did. I can't take it back. I can't change it, but I can spend the rest of my life proving to you how sorry I am. I have no problem doing that."

That makes me sob. How many times did I wish he'd show up and say this? How many times did I stare at my phone late at night waiting for him to text or call?

"This isn't happening. I've walked into the freaking Twilight Zone," I laugh manically, running my hand through my hair.

How did this go from me helping him through a panic attack, to him confessing he can't stop thinking about me?

"I can't fix my knee. I can't control how my guys play. But I can do this. Let me, Sweetheart."

Sniffling, I say, "don't call me that."

Jamie chuckles, running his index finger down my cheek and catching a stray tear.

"I... I have to go. I have an early rehearsal," is all I can say. I slip out of his grasp and quickly walk to the door. It opens an inch before it's slammed shut. I jump, turning around to see Jamie leaning over me, his hand on the door.

My heart is beating a million miles a minute, and I feel like I can't breathe. He smells like sweat and cologne, his hair is disheveled, his eyes are full of fire. My chest rises and falls as I watch him lean closer to my face. He's inches away now.

"I let you walk away last time. This time, I'm not letting you go," he states before grabbing my face and smashing his lips to mine.

Chapter 23

JAMIE

What the fuck, what the fuck, what the fuck?

I'm kissing Ellie Monroe. I'm kissing her and she's kissing me back. She's not pulling away; she doesn't seem repulsed. So far, so good.

The kiss is fierce and desperate. It's fueled by frustration, built up tension, and something else I can't describe. I pull her closer, my hands tangling in her hair as her arms wrap around my neck. Her lips are soft, fitting with mine just like they used to. I take the risk of sliding my tongue against hers, and it pays off. She kisses me back with fervor. It feels so familiar, yet so new at the same time.

I pick her up easily, her legs circling me like they've done a million times before as I deepen the kiss. Her body molds to mine, her curves fitting perfectly against me. I can feel her heartbeat racing against my chest, mirroring the frantic rhythm of my own.

"Jamie," she gasps, breaking the kiss momentarily. Her eyes are dark with desire, her breath coming in short, ragged gasps. "We can't—" she begins, but I cut her off before she can continue.

"We can," I murmur, my lips brushing against hers. "Give in, Sweetheart."

She surprises me when she doesn't argue, and I watch as her resistance crumbles around her as I kiss her again. My hands move down her body, tracing the curves I've missed for so long. I lay her down on the bench, hovering over her. I know this is risky. I know this could cost us both our jobs. Yet, I can't stop myself. I'm afraid that if we stop, she'll run, and we'll never have this chance again. It's selfish, I know. But God knows, I'm selfish.

I assist her with taking her blazer off, tossing it to the floor. She pulls off her shirt next, letting it land with the blazer. My lips trail down her neck and down over the swell of her perky tits. *Fuck*, I've missed this.

She moans, her head falling back as I suck at the sensitive skin, leaving a mark that's both a claim and an apology. Jesus, I hadn't realized how much I've missed hearing that moan.

"Fuck, Jamie," she whispers, her fingers digging into my shoulders. "What are we doing?"

"Making up for lost time," I growl, my mouth finding hers again. My hands move to her jeans, unbuttoning them seamlessly with one hand. My hand moves into her warmth, and I trace the edge of her panties. After a few seconds of torture, I pull her jeans and panties off, flinging them away.

She's already wet, her arousal evident as I slip a finger inside her, her walls clenching around me.

"God, you're so fucking wet," I groan, my voice thick with desire. "Tell me you've been thinking about this too."

Ellie moans and shakes her head, her eyes closing as I begin to move faster inside her.

"Oh, you haven't?" I ask with a teasing lilt to my voice. "How many times have you dreamt of me since we reconnected? How many times have you played with yourself to the thought of me? Tell me, Sweetheart."

It's a dare more than a demand. I want to make her squirm, for reasons other than my fingers diving into her pussy.

"Jamie..." she says breathlessly. "Please."

Her hips buck against my hand as I add a second finger, thrusting into her with slow, deliberate strokes. Her head falls back, her tits heaving as she bites her lip to stifle her moans.

"What, El? What do you want from me?" I ask, tilting my head.

"I..." I stop, beginning to pull my fingers out slowly. "I want you." she practically whispers.

Oh, that won't do. "What was that, Sweetheart? I couldn't hear you."

"I want you. Please... please make me cum," she whines, and my erection grows tenfold. Fuck she's gorgeous.

I nod and resume pushing my fingers into her pussy. She pants and moans and writhes under me like she can't get enough. I can't believe I walked away from this. What the fuck was I thinking?

With a swift motion, I unbuckle my belt with my other hand, my pants sliding down my legs as I free my aching cock. It's been too long, too many years of pretending leaving her was easy. I need to be inside her.

Positioning myself at her entrance, her eyes meet mine as I push inside her. She's tight, so fucking tight, her body welcoming me like it's been waiting for this moment just as long as I have.

"Fuckkkkk," I groan, my hands gripping her hips as I begin to move. She moans loudly, and I cover her mouth with my hand. She breathes through her nose, inhaling and exhaling rapidly. I move slow at first, each thrust deliberate, savoring the way she feels around me. Her nails dig into my back, her eyes widening as I fill her completely.

"Do you want more?" I ask, making sure she really want this.

Ellie nods.

Removing my hand from her mouth, I kiss her hard. She kisses me back, her fingernails running down my arms and leaving goosebumps in their wake.

With a low growl, I pick up the pace, my hips snapping against hers as I pound into her with relentless force. The sound of our bodies slapping together fills the locker room, the scent of sex and sweat mingling in the air.

"Oh my god," she cries, her head tossing back as she clenches around me. "Jesus, Jamie... fuck, don't stop."

I won't stop. Not now, not ever. I'm lost in her, in the way her body moves with mine, in the way she moans my name like it's a prayer. My balls tighten, the pressure building as I feel my orgasm approaching.

"Cum with me, Ellie," I grit out, my voice raw. "Let me feel you fall apart on my cock."

Her eyes meet mine, her expression a mix of desire and vulnerability as she nods. With a final, desperate thrust, I push her over the edge, her body shaking as she cries out, her walls milking my cock as she cums.

I follow after her, pulling my dick out quickly and painting her with my release. Holy shit, what just happened?

For a long moment, we just stay like this, our breaths intertwining, our hearts pounding in unison. I leave a gentle kiss on her forehead, and she smiles. Grabbing a towel from the closet, I help her clean up. When that's done, we frantically get dressed. I temporarily forgot we were in the damn locker room. As I pull my pants on and fasten my belt, I watch Ellie's face go from rosy cheeked and bright, to ashen and worried. Or regretful. I can't really tell.

"I have to go," she says softly, backing away toward the door. What the hell?

"Ellie, wait," I reach out to grab her wrist. Her eyes move down to where I'm holding her, then back up to my face. I see the tears forming in her eyes, and it's like a gut punch. "What's wrong?"

She shakes her head, a lone tear running down her cheek. "We shouldn't have done that..."

"Why, Ellie? I say it's been a long time coming."

"Because Jamie. There're a million reasons we shouldn't do this. One, I may have forgiven you, but I haven't forgotten. Two, we work together. Three, we're housemates. Four, how do I know you won't bolt again when you heal and go back to your pro hockey life? And five, if we continue, I don't think I'll be able to stop myself."

My eyes narrow in question. "Stop yourself from what?"

She sniffles, peering up at me with big green eyes and wet lashes.

"I don't think I'll be able to stop myself from falling in love with you. Again. And the last time I loved you, you broke my heart."

Chapter 24

ELLIE

"You *what*?!" Lainey screeches as I watch her jaw drop so far, I'm surprised it didn't hit the floor. I probably should have kept this to myself for a while, but I couldn't keep this from my best friends. It was driving me crazy hiding it, and I knew they'd be a little pissed about it, but they're my family. They know everything about my life, just as I know theirs. I called them as soon as I got home.

The whole drive home, which is only five minutes, I sobbed. I sobbed like a freaking baby because I just dug myself a hole I don't know if I can crawl out of. I don't even know if I want to get out of it. The whole thing is overwhelming and completely unexpected.

"Oh, honey..." Gwen sighs. I can feel their disappointment through the phone.

I fall back onto my bed, throwing my arm over my face and holding my phone above me.

"I know, I know. I fucked up. I made a mistake."

"In the locker room?" Lainey asks, a grin growing on her face. I nod, cringing in embarrassment.

"Lainey, seriously? Ellie, you could have gotten caught!"

"Okay, miss chemistry room," Lainey rolls her eyes and Gwen glares into the phone.

"Oh, whatever. I'm just saying, you both work there. If you'd have gotten caught, you would have been fired."

Gwen, ever the voice of reason.

"Guys, that's not the point! I'm freaking out here!"

Lainey stifles a laugh and Gwen rolls her eyes.

"Hey, El. I have a question." Lainey says, and I know it's not going to be serious by the way she's trying to keep her smile contained.

"What?"

"Is it as big as you remember?"

Lainey laughs hysterically as if that's the funniest thing she's ever said.

"Lainey!" Gwen and I say in unison.

"Oh, calm down, I'm kidding," she waves her hand dismissively. "On a serious note, Ellie. Like I said before, you're too good for him, and he doesn't deserve your forgiveness. But if this is what you want, you know I'll support you no matter what. I can't say the same for Holland though."

Gwen scoffs. "Oh, no. Holland's definitely going to kick his ass."

"I don't even know if it *is* what I want! I mean, yes, he's attractive. He's been nothing but kind to me since we moved here. He's apologized every chance he's had. But it's a bad idea, right?" Absentmindedly, I play with a strand of my hair as I wait for their reply. Gwen takes a deep breath.

"Look, El. We can't make this decision for you. You need to let your heart decide what it wants. Clearly, a part of you still has some sort of feelings for him or you wouldn't have slept with him. Plus, Lainey and I can't really judge because we both went for questionable men. Hell, both of you tried to talk me out of being with Ryker. Now look at us. We're happy, we're thriving—"

"You're pregnant!" Lainey interrupts with a shout. My eyes widen as I watch Gwen's reaction. Her cheeks turn red, and my eyes begin to fill with tears.

"You are?" I ask, practically whispering. Gwen nods slowly, a tear dripping down her cheek as her hand instinctively move to her belly.

"Yeah, I am," she sniffs, a smile growing on her face.

"Oh my effing god! You're having a baby!" Lainey squeals, throwing her hands in the air and having her own little freak out moment.

"Wait, does Ryker know?" I ask, and Gwen shakes her head.

"Not yet. It's pretty new, but I'm going to tell him this weekend. I just don't know how he'll react," she grimaces.

"Well, have you guys talked about kids?"

"Of course. I just didn't think it would happen this fast."

"I call Godmother!" Lainey exclaims. That girl can't read a room for shit.

"Are you happy, Gwenny?" I urge, hoping to get her honest answer. She looks down at her belly and rubs circles, a small smile on her lips. She's glowing, and I'm incredibly happy for her and Ryker, if Gwen is happy.

Gwen nods. "Yeah...I think I really am."

Grinning, I say, "I'm really happy for you, Gwen. You'll be a great mom."

"You will, and I'm happy for you too," Lainey smiles.

Sniffling, Gwen wipes away a few stray tears, then straightens. Her face turns serious.

"Now, back to you, Ellie. You deserve to be happy, and if Jamie makes you happy, then I say go for it. Just make sure it's really what you want first. Spend some more time together, feel it out. Everyone deserves a second chance. It's been what, nine years? He's not the same guy he was when he was eighteen, and you're not the same girl. You're adults now," Gwen urges. I know she has a point. I can tell Jamie's not the same guy he was all those years ago. I just don't want him to break my heart again.

"Just be careful, El. Take it slow. Get to really know each other again. And remember we're always a call away if you need us, okay?" Lainey tells me. I know they are. They always are.

"Just, don't tell my brother. Not yet," I beg Lainey. Lainey is terrible at keeping secrets, but I really hope she keeps this one. I don't need Holland finding out I might potentially be falling for Jamie. We'll cross that bridge when we come to it, but for now, he doesn't need to know.

Lainey nods. "Of course, mum's the word." She motions zipping her lips and tossing the key.

A while later, I'm off the phone and finally lying down. I have an early rehearsal, and I already have so much on my mind. I don't need to be exhausted too. Tomorrow is also the day I have to tell the kids about the fundraiser and working with the hockey team. That will go one of two ways. Either they'll take it really well and all will be fine. Or they'll be pissed and argue. Guess I'll find out.

Chapter 25

ELLIE

My alarm goes off causing me to roll over and groan loudly before turning it off. I tossed and turned all night, thinking about Jamie and the way his lips felt on mine. How his fingers felt inside me. How his dick filled me so completely.

"How many times have you dreamt of me since we reconnected? How many times have you played with yourself to the thought of me? Tell me, Sweetheart."

How could he make me so wet by just the tone of his voice? He was so... demanding. When we were younger, we didn't really know what we were doing.

But now that we're adults... a lot has changed. I cringe at the thought of him with other women. I'm not stupid. He's a hot hockey player for a professional hockey team. Of course he's slept with plenty of women, just as I've slept with other men. I just... I don't like thinking about it.

I think back to my talk last night with Lainey and Gwen. One thing I left out was how I found Jamie there in that locker room, having a panic attack and being so vulnerable. That's the second time I've found him in that condition. I don't remember him having panic attacks before, but I can't imagine the pressure he's under.

His knee, the kids, getting back to his career. That's a lot for anyone, but especially for Jamie who's only dream since we were kids was the NHL.

Although sometimes I question if it was his dream, or his fathers. Yes, Jamie always liked hockey. He loved watching games with his dad, and he grew up playing on the pond in his backyard in the winter. But he got more serious about it after his dad passed. I wonder if he promised him he'd go pro, and now that he's not, Jamie feels guilty.

Or I'm way off base and it has nothing to do with his father and everything to do with the fact that he loves the sport. Either way, he's under a lot of stress. Was fucking me just a way to release that stress? Did he use me?

Oh, shut up, Ellie. No, he didn't use you. He told you how much he wanted you.

Shaking my head, I try my best to start thinking about how I'm going to bring up the fundraiser to the kids. I'll do it at the end of class, that way, they'll wait until after rehearsal to hate me.

I've already submitted the plan to Dean Ashby, and he was all for it. He loved the idea of the two departments getting together to create something memorable. He mostly loved all the way the school would make money.

So, it's a go. Now I just have to get through several weekends working with Jamie to make this night perfect. What can go wrong, right?

When I walk into the kitchen, Jamie is standing at the island eating a plateful of scrambled eggs. My eyes skim his toned body in his black athletic pants and a black zip up that hugs his muscles so tightly, I could probably count every one of them. His brown hair flops to one side and his eyes are focused on his phone that lies on the counter.

I make my way over to the coffee maker and pull out a mug from the cupboard above. I feel his gaze on my back and my cheeks heat. Then, I feel his presence behind me, his body heat enveloping me like a hug. He reaches above my head, grabs a mug from the cupboard, and places it down on the counter, his arm brushing mine. Goosebumps break out all over my body. It was barely a touch, but it hit me like a live wire. And then I feel him move my hair from my right shoulder and slide it over to the left before his mouth is next to my ear. I feel his hot breath on my cheek.

"Would you mind pouring me a glass, too?" he says in a husky tone that makes me want to turn my head slightly and let him kiss me. I nod. "Thank you, Sweetheart."

And then he walks away, back to his eggs that are probably cold by now.

"Was it necessary to get that close to me to ask that?" I ask, trying my best to keep my breathing under control.

He chuckles. "Don't pretend you didn't like it."

I roll my eyes, watching the coffee pour into my cup.

"Maybe I didn't," I shrug as I remove my cup and put his under the machine, clicking the button again and waiting for the coffee to pour. The scent of sandalwood and vanilla assault my senses, and when I turn around, Jamie is right there. He boxes me in, his hands on either side of me planted on the counter. My heartbeat skyrockets, and my breath hitches. What the hell is he doing?

"You sure enjoyed me being close to you yesterday in the locker room," he taunts. "In fact, you were *begging* me to touch you."

I can feel how hot my cheeks are. My pussy clenches and I already know I'm wet. He doesn't even have to touch me. I'm pathetic.

"I was not begging," I lie. Jamie rolls his eyes.

"Come on, Sweetheart. There's no need to deny it."

"I... I'm not," I stutter. "I don't have time for this. I have to go to rehearsal."

He moves an inch closer, his body practically against mine, and holy god, why do I want it to be?

"I bet that if I bent you over this counter right now and fucked you until you screamed my name, you'd let me."

His eyebrow raises as if he's challenging me. Do I like the sound of that? Yes, yes I do. Will I let that happen? No. Because I need time to think about whether or not I want to even pursue anything with this man and having sex with him again will not help.

"You're wrong," I tell him, even though we both know it's not true. "Now let me go. I have to get to work, and so do you."

Jamie tilts his head. "Alright, Sweetheart. If you say so."

He pushes off the counter, and I immediately miss the warmth the closeness of his body was providing. I inhale shakily, my morning completely thrown off due to the unexpected closeness to Jamie.

Get it together, Ellie. You don't let men distract you. You are smarter than that, stronger than that. You didn't come here looking for a man. You came here to work.

I walk hastily out of the kitchen, leaving my coffee behind. I can feel Jamie's eyes watching me as I go which makes me move faster.

Once I'm safely in my car, my head falls to the steering wheel. I shouldn't be letting Jamie in my head like this. It's not healthy. I need to tell him that the sex was a one-time thing, and we can't let it happen again. That's what's best for both of us.

Starting the engine, I make my way down the driveway and head toward campus. My phone begins to ring over the loudspeaker. When Freddie's name pops up on the screen, I grin like an idiot. We text here and there, but we've both been so busy that we haven't been able to have an actual conversation. Not that we can have one now since I'm on my way to work, but a few minutes is better than none.

"Hello? Is this Professor Monroe?" Freddie teases. I roll my eyes with a smile.

"Hey, Freddie. I've missed you and your sense of humor."

"Hey babes. It's been too long. How's your new life at the University? How's directing? Everything you thought it would be?" he asks as I pull into the parking lot.

"Directing is good. My students are really talented, and they listen to me so that's good..." I say, my voice fading off.

"Umm, what aren't you telling me?" Freddie asks, and I can imagine his face with his eyes narrowed and a curious smile.

"Okay, you remember how I told you I was being forced to live with my asshole ex?"

"Yes...oh my god. You guys fucked. You dirty little—"

"Hey! Yes, we uh... we had sex. But now it's weird and awkward and I don't know how to act!" I say, a bit of panic in voice.

"Wait, okay. Where did you guys do it? Like in his room or yours? Or maybe right on the couch?" he inquires and my face heats as I think of that night. Me lying on that bench, naked and completely bared to him. Him standing over me, all muscle and power. Completely opposite of how vulnerable he'd been when I found him.

"The locker room..." I cringe.

"Ellie Monroe! Who are you?" Freddie asks facetiously. I cover my face with my hands, my head shaking.

Groaning, I say, "I know, I know. I don't know what came over me. He was there, he was saying all the right things, and he looked... God, he looked so good. It was like I couldn't stop myself."

"Well, why is it awkward?" he asks.

I sigh. "I think it's only awkward for me. Jamie seems to be flirtier, and I think he thinks it's going to happen again," I explain. Actually, I don't think. I know. If what happened in the kitchen this morning is any indication, he most definitely wants it to happen again.

"And it's not?" Freddie prods.

"No. It can't. We work together."

"Is that the only reason?"

"No." Shit. Is that the only reason I don't want it to happen? No, because I'm still worried about what will happen if he heals and goes back to his team. Will he just leave again? Does he assume this is just sex and he's not going to take it further? My mind spins with different scenarios. This is exactly what I was trying to avoid. This spiral.

"El, you know I love you. I want what's best for you. I know what he did to you was shitty, and I totally get it if you're questioning things. In fact, you should be. Men suck. But if there's any part of you that wants to give it chance, I'll be here for you. Whether the ending is happy or everything crashes and burns. Got it?"

A stupid tear escapes my eye and runs down my cheek. "Thank you," I say, sniffling. My eyes catch on the time on my dash. "Shit, Freddie. I'm late, I have to go. I'll call you soon, okay?"

"You better. I need weekly updates, Bitch. Love you."

"Love you too," I tell him before hanging up. Staring out of my windshield, I watch as students walk into the building in front of me. I remember when I was one of them not too long ago. Everything was so much simpler then. I partied with my friends, I had fun, did some stupid shit. Yes, my father got arrested, but that was a long time coming. But most importantly, I'd forgotten Jamie and my past. I'd moved on. Now look where I am. I'm a freaking mess, and I have to go and direct for several hours while trying not to think of the one man I shouldn't want.

Closing my eyes, I take a long, deep calming breath. And then I jump so hard I almost hit my head on the car ceiling when a tapping sound comes from my window.

Chapter 26

JAMIE

When I pull into the parking lot, I spot Ellie's car immediately. I park a bit further back so she doesn't see me. I flustered her this morning, and although that was my intention, I kind of felt bad for making her squirm before work. Not bad enough to not do it again, but still. I know she's trying to avoid me; I can tell by the way she didn't say a word to me and avoided eye contact with me this morning.

She let herself go with me last night, and now she's rethinking all of her life choices. I saw it in her eyes this morning when I had her pinned against the counter. She doesn't know what to think. I knew it wouldn't be easy to get back into her good graces, and I knew she was going to make this difficult. All I want is for her to see that I'm making an effort. I'm really trying to be the man she needs. I just hope she can see that.

Grabbing my hockey bag from the back seat and locking my car, I walk toward Ellie's car. I was just going to go in and leave her be, but then I see the screen in her car. The name Freddie is there. Who the fuck is Freddie? Why is she on the phone with him at nine in the morning?

Before I can stop myself, I tap on her window, causing her to jump an inch in the air. Fuck, she's cute. When she sees it me, her face goes from scared to annoyed real quick. I seem to have that effect on her. She slowly rolls the window down, glaring at me.

"What the hell are you doing? You scared the crap out of me," she seethes. I want to chuckle at her attempt at being intimidating, but I'm too annoyed by the name I saw on her fucking screen.

"Who's Freddie?" I ask, straight faced. Her mouth opens, then closes. She blinks a few times before answering me.

"Are you stalking me now?" she asks. My impatience grows.

"Who is Freddie, Ellie?"

"That's none of your business, now move."

My jaw tenses, and my hands turn into fists at my side. I want to keep her here so I can keep interrogating her until she gives me an answer, but we're both late and I don't want to get her in trouble. So, I back away so she can swing the door open.

"Thank you," she says, her voice steady, as if she's completely unbothered.

I watch her walk to the building, her hips swaying and her ass looking just as fine as it did this morning in those tight yoga pants. Part of me hates that she wears those in public so other men can ogle at her, but then I remember I can't tell her what to wear, especially because she's not mine.

When the guys are suited up, they join me on the ice. I've been going back and forth with myself on if I should mention the fundraiser before or after practice. I choose before. That way, they can work off some of that aggression and annoyance. They're going to be pissed, I already know they will be. I don't care. I promised Ellie we'd do this, so we're doing this.

The guys gather in a clump in front of me. They're smiling and laughing with each other, and I know that's all about to come to end. I should feel some sort of guilt for that, right?

"Alright, listen up!" I blow my whistle and the rink goes silent. Everyone's eyes are on me. Here goes nothing.

"We've got a fundraising event coming up in a few weeks. It's to bring in donations, and to raise money for a new hockey arena on campus. It will no longer be shared with the other facilities. We'll have our own space to play."

The guys nod, some even smile.

"Now, this event is mandatory. That means, unless you're on your fucking deathbed, you better be here."

Groans hit immediately.

"Well, what do we have to do? Play a game?" Logan asks. I nod.

"Yep. But that's not all."

Their curious looks watch and wait for me to continue.

"This fundraiser is for athletics *and* the arts. Meaning, we'll be working alongside Professor Monroe's theatre class. They will be choreographing a dance for us to perform during the first period of the game. Everyone will participate. If you do not show up, you're off the team.

"You're joking, right?" Jacob asks.

"There's no way I'm getting up in front of the whole school and dancing like a circus monkey. Hell no," Issacc Anders states, his expression one of disgust and anger.

"You will if you want to be part of this team. This program exists because of donors and sponsors. We need to do this."

"Coach, come on," Levi groans.

"Show up," I spit. "Or you explain to Dean Ashby why you didn't."

Their jaws drop, but no one dares to say another word.

"Our rehearsals start tomorrow at six p.m. sharp. Do not be late. Now, warmups. Go!" Blowing my whistle, the team scatters across the ice. I take a deep breath, glad that's over with. I knew there would be pushback, I just hope I still have a team after tomorrow.

For the rest of practice, the guys play angry. Their passes are sloppy, their stickhandling sucks ass, and their teamwork is pathetic. I thought breaking the news to them would help, but it seems like it only made it worse.

Finally, I decide I've had enough of this for one day. I've put them through the ringer, and it's not just because they were playing like shit. It's because I haven't been able to stop thinking about Ellie and who Freddie is. She would have told me if she was seeing someone, wouldn't she?

I head to my office and shut the door. Attempting to push the Ellie thing out of my mind, I focus on my players and what I can do to really shape them up before Friday's game against Atlantic Academy. We have to win this one. Ashby won't keep me around if we keep losing, and this is all I have right now.

My phone lights up with a text from the group chat.

Rhode Island Stormies

Theo Cramer: *This team isn't the same without you, Patty.*
Billy Callahan: *Yeah, it's better.*
Billy Callahan: *Jkjkjkjkjk. Love you.*
Connor Grieves: *We need you back, brother.*

It's then that I get a really great idea. It's a little crazy, a little unconventional, but it might help.

Me: *How would you guys feel about going back to college?*

Chapter 27

ELLIE

By the time I lock the theatre doors behind me, my voice is shot and my patience is hanging by a thread.

Fundraiser announcement: done.

Hockey team collaboration explanation: done.

Fielding questions that ranged from 'Do we have to?' to 'Is this thing mandatory?': also done. One of my students even called the hockey guys sweaty neanderthals with sticks.

This is going to be the longest three weeks of my life; I can already tell.

I drag my bag higher on my shoulder and head across campus. I am in desperate need for coffee right now. The late afternoon sun casts long shadows over the quad. Around me, students laugh with their friends, professors walk to their respective buildings, and no one seems as stressed out as I feel right now.

I hate that I'm thinking about how it went for Jamie. I hate that I care. But no matter how hard I try, I can't seem to stop. Whether I like it or not, our worlds are officially coming together, and it doesn't appear that I can stop the inevitable crash.

As I sit in the café, I sip on my hot latte and stare aimlessly out the window. My thoughts are scattered. The play, the fundraiser, Jamie. One thing in particular stands out from the rest of my jumbled thoughts. Why did Jamie ask who Freddie was? Was he standing by my car the whole time? Why did he seem so pissed off? Could he be... jealous? No, that's ridiculous. He couldn't be jealous, because we're not even together.

Yet he seemed like I had slapped him in the face. I can't lie, the thought of Jamie Patterson being jealous over me is an attractive one. Little does he know, the man he's jealous of doesn't swing for my team.

When I get home, the house is quiet. I'm assuming Jamie's in his room, thank God. I don't think I can have a clear conversation with the man right now if he's still acting the way he was earlier.

I kick off my shoes and drop my bag by the stairs, heading straight for the kitchen. I halt in my tracks when I see Jamie standing there, his muscular arms crossed over his broad chest. His face is serious, his jaw clenched. Okay, so I guess he's still pissed. So much for grabbing a snack and heading to bed. He's so quiet, I'm not sure he'll ever speak. But then he does.

"How was work?" he asks, and I'm taken aback by the question because that's not what I was expecting him to say. My weight shifts from one leg to the other as I stand awkwardly at the island, too nervous to move.

"It was fine..." I say slowly, watching him carefully.

"Aren't you going to ask how my day was?" he inches forward slightly. I instinctively take a step back. I'm not afraid of him, but I am feeling a bit intimidated at the moment.

Clearing my throat, I ask, "how was your day?"

He smiles slightly, but it's not a real smile. It's more of a dangerous one.

"It wasn't great, honestly. I couldn't really concentrate. I was too distracted by the guy you were on the phone with this morning. Freddie, was it?" he lifts an unhinged brow. I want to laugh, however, that doesn't seem like the smart thing to do right now, so I keep it in.

"Jamie, I—" he cuts me off.

He closes the distance between us in three long strides. "Who is Freddie?" he demands, his eyes narrowing as he studies me for my reaction.

I'm frozen in place. He's right there, and he looks so serious. My heart skips a beat. Jamie's never been the jealous type. He was never one to throw a punch off the ice. Yet, right now, he looks like he could punch a wall, and the cold edge in his tone sends a shiver down my spine.

When I finally having my breathing under control, I tell him, "He's a friend back in New York.

Why?" I shrug casually as if his closeness and attitude aren't affecting me in the slightest.

"And you two just casually have phone calls early in the morning?" he questions in an accusatory tone.

"Sometimes, yes." I don't know why I haven't told him the truth yet. Maybe because it's kind of hot to see him all worked up and envious. Maybe I like the way his body hovers against mine, or the way he's now gripping my arms. Not tight, not aggressive, just holding.

I watch his nostrils flare. He clearly didn't like that answer.

"Does your little friend know about us?"

My brows furrow. "Know what about us, exactly?"

He looks offended, as if I've just told him that he smells like dog shit. He doesn't of course.

"That we're—"

"We're not anything, Jamie. We're not together," I say sternly, but I immediately regret it when I see his face fall before turning angry again.

Without another word, he lifts me up and places me on the counter. My breath hitches as his hands grip my thighs, holding me in place. Well, this took an unexpected turn.

"Jamie," I gasp, my voice shaky. "What the hell are you doing?"

"Showing you what we are," he replies with a growl.

Suddenly, he grabs the hem of my shirt, pulling it up and over my head in one swift motion. My bra follows, my breasts exposed to the cool air. I try to cover myself, but he grabs my wrists, pushing my arms down to my sides. I'm in shock. I've never done it on a kitchen counter. Then again, I've never done it in a public locker room either until I was with Jamie.

I didn't expect this conversation to head this way, and I know I should stop it. I should tell him to fuck off and leave me alone. I should, but I won't. Because I think I'm going to like what comes next, and I can't hide how my body reacts to his touch.

His hands slide over my stomach and up to my breasts. He squeezes them in his warm, rough hands, before his mouth lands on one of my nipples and he sucks hard. He plays with my other nipple between his fingers, pinching and squeezing, and the sensation is almost too much. My head falls back.

"Jamie, I...oh god," I cry. I told myself this wouldn't happen again. I told myself it was a one and done situation, just exes catching up. However, here we are. I'm half naked on the kitchen counter with Jamie sucking on my tits. Way to hold out, Ellie. Great job.

He pulls away, his eyes peering up at me with hunger. When he stands, his lips crash against mine, rough and demanding. I don't even pull away. I just let him kiss me, his tongue invading my mouth and staking his claim.

Despite the fact that this is wrong, and I'll probably regret it later, my body responds to him. My nipples tighten and my core aches with a familiar heat. Jamie's hand slides down my back, gripping my hip and pulling me tighter against him. I feel the hardness of his cock pressing against me, and my breath catches in my throat.

He breaks the kiss, his breath ragged as he watches me. "You're mine, Ellie," he tells me, his voice hoarse with desire. "Do you understand? Mine. Not Freddie's, or any other man."

My eyes meet his, and instead of anger, I find hope and lust in them. I don't respond, because I'm not completely sure how to. I don't want to admit to him that I'm enjoying this. That deep down, I do want to be his. But I'm scared as hell to let him in again.

Jamie's hand slides down, cupping me through my jeans. I gasp as he squeezes me, his touch both rough and tender.

"Tell me, Sweetheart," he demands, his lips brushing against my ear. "Tell me you're mine."

My breath is unsteady and my body trembles with need. I can't tell him that. I can't be his.

He grabs my chin between his fingers and forces me to look him in the eyes.

"Say it, Ellie," he says again, unbuttoning my jeans and pushing his hand inside.

My vagina is screaming at me to give in so he'll give me what I need, and my brain is saying to stop this madness and run. But in the end, my vagina wins.

"Y-yes," I practically whisper. "I'm yours."

"You're not just saying that so I'll make you cum, are you Sweetheart?" he asks.

I shake my head as his hand moves lower and hovers over my panties.

"No."

A dark smile curves his lips as he pulls his hand out of my jeans and steps back.

"Prove it," he commands, his voice a challenge.

He hooks his fingers into the waistband of my jeans, pulling them down along with my panties in one swift motion.

I blink at him, unsure of exactly how he wants me to prove it to him. "H-how?"

He licks his lips seductively and I swear I almost fall apart. He looks so... strong. So completely in control that I totally forget how vulnerable he looked in the locker room. Right now, he doesn't resemble that man at all. This man looks like he's ready to destroy me.

His eyes darken as they focus between my legs.

"Open those legs and show me that pretty pussy. Let me devour you, Sweetheart," he murmurs.

Holy mother of—

Jamie uses his index fingers to lightly push my legs apart, exposing my pussy to the relentlessly cold air in the kitchen. Is this happening? On the counter? All because he's jealous of a man he's never even seen?

My cheeks flame when Jamie crouches down so his face is eye level with my bare vagina. His gaze is hungry and full of need. His hands grip my hips as he pulls me toward him.

"You look delicious, baby, and I'm famished," he growls before his head dips between my legs. His lips brush against the sensitive skin of my inner thigh. He nips, and I squeal at the unexpected feeling. My breath catches as I feel his warm breath on my center.

"You're already soaking wet for me, Sweetheart, and we're just getting started."

My hands grip the edge of the counter as his tongue flicks out, tracing a path along my folds, and I can't help the gasp that falls off my lips. My head falls back, and instead of pretending that I'm not enjoying this, I let myself feel it. I give myself permission to let go.

"Oh God," I moan, my body arching toward him.

I feel his smirk against my skin before he continues his assault with his tongue, delving deeper. One hand tangles in his hair, my nails scraping his scalp as I hold him close.

"Holy shit," I groan, my hips bucking against his mouth. "Jamie, please."

He hums his approval, his fingers digging into my hips as he holds me still. His tongue is relentless, his mouth devouring me just as he said he would. God, I've missed feeling wanted. I've missed the feeling of a man falling at his feet for me.

My breath comes in sharp gasps, my body tightening as pleasure coils low in my belly.

"Tell me again," he demands, his voice muffled against me. "Tell me you're fucking mine."

My eyes squeeze shut, my body on the brink of release.

"Jamie," I growl. Screw him for making me say that when I'm in such a vulnerable position. Yet, I say it anyway.

"Ellie..." he whispers against me before he enters one finger inside me. Oh my God. I'm going to cum. "Tell me, baby."

"I'm yours," I pant, my voice desperate. "I'm yours, Jamie. Please..."

"Please what, Sweetheart?" he coaxes.

"I'm going to cum," I tell him, my eyes watering at the intense pressure building inside me.

"Good. Cum for me, baby girl."

His finger and tongue begin to move faster and I'm a goner.

I let out a sharp cry as I have the most powerful orgasm I've ever had, my body shaking as waves of pleasure wash over me.

Holy shit. My vibrator never made me feel like *that.*

Chapter 28

JAMIE

She's incredible.

Ellie Monroe is fucking incredible.

And she's *mine*.

I don't think she's completely over what I did, and maybe she never will be. However, I'm not going to ever stop trying to turn that around.

I know she probably only said it because I was tongue deep in her pussy, but I don't even care. One day she'll mean it. I know she will.

I watch as she comes down from her high, her breasts moving up and down as her breaths begin to calm, her blonde hair falling around her.

My cock stiffens in my pants and strains against my jeans, begging to get out.

Don't worry, buddy. You're about to get your turn. I'm not done yet.

When she opens her eyes, they fall on me before moving down to the very obvious bulge in my pants. Her eyes widen.

I begin to undo my button and zipper as she watches, her cheeks red and face flushed. I let my jeans and briefs fall the floor, stepping out of them and pushing them aside. My cock twitches eagerly as I look at her wet pussy dripping for me.

Stepping forward, I place my hands on her waist, my fingers tracing the curve of her hips. "You're so fucking beautiful," I murmur. "And you're mine. Only mine."

Ellie shivers at my words, goosebumps appearing on her pale skin. I can tell she's internally panicking at the thought of that, but I'm not worried. She knows what she wants, she just doesn't want to admit it yet, and that's okay. I'll wait until she does.

I lean down to kiss her, her lips soft and melting into mine. My fingers brush against her pussy, teasing her before I position myself at her entrance. I feel her hold her breath as her body tenses with anticipation.

"Ready?" I ask, my voice a low growl.

She nods but doesn't speak. I pinch her chin between my fingers, forcing her to look at me. I don't want to do this without her full permission.

"Answer me," I demand, my grip tightening on her hips.

"Yes," she whispers, her voice barely audible.

With a swift thrust, I enter her, filling her completely. Ellie gasps, her head falling back as I stretch her. I still for a moment, giving her time to adjust, and me time to revel in the feeling of being inside her again. Then I begin to move, my hips snapping forward in a steady rhythm.

"Fuck," I groan, my voice hoarse with need. "You feel so good, baby."

Ellie moans, her body moving with mine, her hands gripping the counter as I pound into her relentlessly. The kitchen fills with the sound of our flesh slapping together, our breaths coming in ragged gasps.

I grip her hips tightly, my fingers leaving bruises as I claim her. My thrusts quicken, my control snapping as I near the edge. Fuck, I'm not going to last.

"Jamie," Ellie moans.

"Are you gonna cum again for me, Sweetheart?" I prod, my voice a harsh whisper.

"Yes," she pants.

"Good girl. Cum on my cock."

Ellie's body obeys, and I watch as her release takes over her body. She cries out, her walls clenching around me, milking me as I follow her over the edge. My hips still, my cock pulsing as I fill her with my cum. A groan of intense pleasure escapes me.

Jesus Christ, I want to do that for the rest of my life.

For a long moment, we stay like this, our bodies connected, our breaths slowly evening out. My hands slide up her back, my fingers tangling in her hair as I pull her to me, kissing her slow and deliberate.

"Mine," I say against her lips, making sure she knows who she belongs to one more time. To my surprise, Ellie nods, her cheek resting against my chest.

"Yours," she whispers, her voice steady.

Kissing the top of her head, my arms wrap around her as I hold her close, realizing this is the first time I've held her like this in years, and she's allowing me to.

Pulling back, I look her in those big green eyes. She looks at peace, yet somehow, also conflicted. Like she doesn't know how she's supposed to feel right now. I understand her hesitancy, I do. I just hope one day she doesn't look at me with confusion and distain. I want her to look at me like she did before I fucked everything up.

"You never asked about protection," she says, and my heart stops. Fuck, she's right. I was so caught up with everything that I didn't even think about fucking protection. What a fucking idiot.

Seriously, Jamie? Is this your first day? How the fuck didn't I think about that? The last thing I fucking need right now is a baby. I've got too much going on, and I'm trying to get back to my team. I can't have a baby.

"You can stop spiraling. I'm on birth control," she smirks as if she enjoyed watching me internally panic. "You should have seen your face."

"Not funny," I tell her, pointing my finger in her face.

"A little funny. Now hand me my clothes," she demands. I love when she gets bossy. Might be the hottest thing I've seen her do.

Once we're dressed, Ellie stands in front of me, her hands locked in front of her. I don't know why she's acting shy now. I just fucked her on the kitchen counter.

"One more thing," she says, a smirk forming on her lips.

My brows narrow. "What?"

"The guy you're jealous about, he's gay."

With that, she walks out of the kitchen, and I listen to her footsteps as she goes up the stairs. I stand there, completely taken aback and kind of in shock.

Gay? Freddie's gay?

What the actual fuck?

Chapter 29

JAMIE

It's been a week. A week since I fucked Ellie on the kitchen counter. A week since I claimed her as mine, and all I can think about is the sound of her moans and the feeling of being inside her.

"I'm yours, Jamie."

I still don't know if she was being genuine or if it was just a heat of the moment thing, but I'm letting myself believe she meant it, because if I don't, I might fall apart.

Who the fuck am I? Fall apart? Over a girl? I don't do that shit. I don't let chicks dictate my feelings or distract me from what really matters. Except, Ellie's not just some chick, and she's what really matters.

Because if I never get hockey back, at least I'll have her. Even if I'm not able to play again, Ellie will be there, and she'll have forgiven me for the shit I put her through. The goal since I got benched has been to rehab, recover, and get back to my team, but I have a new goal now. Get Ellie to be mine. Like, actually mine. Although, it would be nice to get both.

I stare at my watch, the cold chill in the air hitting my cheeks, wondering when this day is going to be over, because the sooner I can get home, the sooner I see *her*.

Honestly, watching these guys practice is giving me a migraine, but hopefully that's all about to change. They're dragging, as always. Except, it's not physically. They're skating hard enough, hitting the drills, and running the plays I've drilled into their heads for weeks now. But the edge is still missing. Maybe it's because they're not confident. They've been losing for so long now, maybe they've just flat out given up.

What we need is something that will separate us from the rest of the teams. Something that will make them fear us. The Wolves don't need to be good. We just need to pull off a miracle. No pressure.

I blow my whistle, the sound echoing off the walls of the rink.

"Again!"

Collective groans roll across the ice.

"If you have enough energy to complain," I call out, "you've got enough energy to run drills."

Frustration coils tight in my chest, mixing with the steady throb in my knee. I push it down like I always do because the pain doesn't matter. What matters is getting these guys in shape to win the next game, and I have a little something that might motivate them.

Blowing the whistle one more time, the guys make their way over to me, dripping in sweat and looking exhausted.

"Alright, listen up!" I call. "I'm gonna tell you what I've noticed the last several weeks, and you're gonna listen."

They straighten, every eye focused on me.

"Number one, you've got no team morale, and that's reflected on the ice. It's like you're not communicating with each other at all out there. That has to change, today. Number two, you're relying on Bergström and Rostolvic to get shit done, when in reality, you should be working as a team. If you're not connected out there, you've already lost. I don't care if you hate each other. On the ice, you're a unit. Is that understood?"

"Yes, Coach," they all say in unison.

"Good. Now, I have some people I'd like you to meet."

I hear the footsteps coming up behind me as the entire rink goes silent. Some of the guy's jaws hit the floor, while some look starstruck.

Theo Cramer, Connor Grieves, Billy Callahan, and Wilder Ranslavic walk onto the ice, each of them looking smug and confident. They stop, forming a line at my side. It's kind of entertaining watching Callahan try to look intimidating when I know he's a huge softie. Last year for Halloween, he dressed as a princess with his niece. Yet when he gets into hockey mode, he doesn't fuck around.

"No fucking way..." Logan breathes.

"Holy shit, that's Wilder Ranslavic," Levi states in awe.

Straightening, I begin to walk back and forth, making sure I have everyone's attention. Once I'm confident they're all looking my way, I step back in line with my men.

"As you all may know, this is Callahan, Ranslavic, Grieves, and Cramer. They're some of my buddies from the Storm, and they're gonna show you dipshits how to play some damn hockey. Got it?" I announce, and the Wolves all nod. They're in for a treat. I just hope my friends can keep it together and get this shit done. I'm counting on them to help me get the Wolves set for the rest of the season.

"Yes, Coach!"

I look at my buddies and give them a nod, letting them take over. I don't know if this is the smartest idea I've ever had or if it's about to be one of the dumbest, but I guess I'm about to find out.

Theo steps forward, eyes scanning the room like he's sizing up a rival team on game night.

"We watched your last game film on the way here," he tells the Wolves. They share some looks and whispers before their attention snaps back to Cramer. You could hear a fucking pin drop in here it's so damn quiet.

"And?" Logan asks. Kid's snarky, and I know Callahan's going to have a field day with him.

Wilder shrugs. "You want the polite answer or the honest one?"

There's no response. My team looks terrified.

"Honest," Logan mutters.

Wilder nods once.

"You've got talent, size, speed, and a shit ton of money backing every inch of this place," Theo says.

"But you don't play like a team that *needs* to win," Callahan states.

I watch the Wolves faces shift from awe to defensiveness and maybe a bit of embarrassment. Good. They need to know what the pro's think of their skills as players. If they're not going to listen to me alone, now they've got five of us telling them the same damn thing. They need to be told like it is, or they're never going to get better. They'll never succeed.

"Okay," Theo claps. "We're here for the weekend. Your coach here asked us to run some sessions and scrimmages with you guys and talk strategy. Help you figure out what Patterson's been trying to beat into your skulls for weeks."

"You want the NHL?" Connor asks, his tone serious. "Then stop acting like this is guaranteed. Nothing is. It doesn't matter how much money mommy and daddy make. They can't buy your way in. You've got to be fucking great."

Damn, Grieves. I didn't know he had it in him to give a pep talk like that.

Honestly, I'm glad they agreed to this, because I was at my whit's end with these fools. I needed backup. The awesome thing about my friends is they've always got my back, just like I've got theirs. Even if I'm not out there playing with them right now.

Two hours later, we're in full scrimmage mode. Connor, Theo, Wilder, and Billy rotate in every once in a while, demonstrating how things should be done.

The Wolves skate faster and hit harder, trying to prove my guys wrong. This is what they needed. They needed to want to prove themselves.

Before long, the Wolves are gasping for air as Theo steals the puck clean from Jacob, passing it to Connor who buries it into the net flawlessly.

Wolves players stand around looking like they've just witnessed a miracle. I think they're starting to see that this is the level they need to be at. This is what it takes to be the best. To get to the top.

After a few more games, the Wolves finally look like they're playing like a team. It seems like they're communicating, they're staying on each other, and they're confident. Just then, I feel something loosen in my chest for the first time in weeks. Maybe I made the right decision by bringing the Storm here. Maybe this is what the guys needed. Some fresh faces and some new strategies.

By the time we finally step off the ice, everyone's exhausted but the mood feels lighter. It feels like, for the first time since my injury, there's hope.

Theo bumps my shoulder as we walk toward the locker room. "You weren't kidding. They've got potential."

"Yeah, well potential doesn't *win*," I mutter.

"No," Billy says behind us. "But the right energy does. They've got it in them. They just needed a little nudge."

I nod in agreement.

"Yeah, well, thanks for helping out. I appreciate you guys. I was going crazy over here."

"We've got your back, you know that," Theo says, a hand landing on my shoulder. "Now, let's go eat some grub. I'm fucking starving."

Chapter 30

ELLIE

Exhaustion has caught up to me. Between play rehearsals, fundraiser rehearsals, and all the extra stuff that comes with being director slash professor, my body is spent. Not to mention thoughts of Jamie swimming around in my brain, taking up more space than I care to admit. I've slept with him twice now. I've let myself fall victim to his charm and his magical dick.

I'm supposed to be smarter than this. I'm supposed to be the one with the answers, the sounding board for my friends and family. I'm practical. At least, I was. That is, until Jamie fucked it all up.

Except this time, it wasn't by breaking my heart. This time it's him trying to win it back.

God, the second Holland finds out, he's going to freak. He's bound to find out sooner than later since him and Lainey are coming to the fundraiser. Mom's not feeling well, so she's decided to stay home. It's better that way anyway, since she and Holland had a big argument last year about a situation that I wasn't privy to.

This week is the last week of rehearsals for the fundraiser, and there's only three more weeks until the play and the end of the semester. Everything feels chaotic and my stress levels are at an all-time high. I know I can do this; I've proven to myself that I can, I just need to get through it.

Except, instead of being completely, one hundred percent focused on all of that, all I keep thinking about is the way Jamie demanded I was his. The way he demanded I say it back. The way that I think I may have actually meant that. Am I his? Do I want to be?

He's been... tolerable the last several weeks since we started planning and rehearsing the fundraiser. It's actually been quite endearing watching him work so hard to get me to forgive him. Like I said when we first got here all those weeks ago, I'd forgiven him a long time ago. I just needed to see that he was actually sorry. That he really did feel bad about what he did.

I see that now. I see how guilty he's felt. I see how much he wants to make up for it. I've seen his demons, the way they affect him. I've witnessed his vulnerability. I know he's not a monster. And that's why I think I've fallen for him.

I've fallen for Jamie Patterson. Again.

With that realization, I take a quick shower and lie in bed, once again staring up at the ceiling. Right as sleep begins to take over my tired body, I hear... laughter?

But it's not just one laugh I hear, it's multiple laughs, and male voices.

What the hell?

Slipping out of bed, I throw my robe on and head down the stairs. I should have grabbed a weapon for defense, but in my haste, I forgot to arm myself. If anything, I'll run and hide. The house is big enough.

Slowly, I make my way into the kitchen, and that's when I see it. The glare from the tv, the popcorn bowl on the coffee table, and the five men sitting in the living room.

My heart rate slows as I recognize at least one of the faces. When we make eye contact, Jamie smiles brightly. That smile makes my want to melt into a puddle. But right now, I'm actually kind of pissed. My eyes wander over the other four very large men sprawled across my couch.

"Hey, Sweetheart," Jamie drawls, and the four other men turn to look at me as I stand in my freaking robe in shock.

I could murder him.

"Why," I say slowly, "are there strange men in my living room?"

One of them sits up straighter. "Oh shit. Is this the roommate?"

"Yes," Jamie says, completely unbothered. "And before you ask, no, they're not staying long."

My eyes flick between the four of them. "You didn't think to... I don't know... *ask*?"

He shrugs. "They're helping me out with some hockey stuff. It's not a big deal; they'll be out of here soon. Plus, I thought you were asleep."

"I was about to be, until the obnoxious laughter scared me awake."

Jamie rolls his eyes before standing and gesturing to his friends.

"Ellie, meet Theo, Connor, Billy, and Wilder. They're my buddies from the Storm," Jamie explains. How is he not understanding why I am not happy right now? I should have been notified that there would be other men in the house, right?

Taking a deep breath, I try to center myself.

"Jamie, I don't care if you have friends over. But it's after midnight, I have class in the morning, and I'm in my freaking robe!"

"It's a fashion statement, for sure," the tall blonde one says. I think he's Billy.

Jamie shoots daggers in his direction before looking back to me. His eyes soften, and it seems to finally click in his head.

"Guys, give us a minute."

They sit back down on the couch as Jamie leads me through the kitchen and up the stairs into his bedroom. He shuts the door behind us.

Jamie turns back to me, his hands in his pockets, eyes searching my face.

"Look, I'm sorry I didn't tell you the guys were coming. I realize now how that could make you uncomfortable," he says, his blue eyes looking like crystals as they search my face.

"I thought someone had broken in, Jamie," and when I say it out loud it sounds impractical. Of course no one broke in. I do live with a roommate, and he is allowed to bring people over. I just would have appreciated the courtesy of knowing they'd be here.

Jamie's lips turn up into a smirk as if he's trying his best not to laugh at me. Placing my hands on my hips, I do my best to look stern.

"Jamie, it's not a joke!"

He composes himself, straightening and stepping closer to me.

"I'm sorry. It's not a joke. I will tell you if I have anybody over next time, okay?" he says, and it's hard not to fall for his charm. "How can I make it up to you?"

A grin forms on his face, and I have a feeling I know exactly what he's thinking.

I point at him. "Jamie, your friends are waiting for you downstairs."

He takes a few slow steps toward me as I begin to back away until I can't anymore. The back of my legs hit his bed causing me to fall to a sitting position as Jamie stands in front of me looking like some sort of freaking god.

"And?" he asks, as if his friends being downstairs doesn't bother him in the slightest.

"They'll hear us," I state, hoping that will deter him. I don't want them listening to us having sex. That's just weird.

"Let them," he says, shrugging. What the fuck?

He leans down so that his hands are on the bed on either side of me and his face is inches away from mine. The scent of him makes me rethink my choice.

"Jamie, I—"

"You're mine, Ellie. I don't care what they hear, because you are mine, not theirs. Let's make them jealous," he grins.

"You're insane," I tell him.

"I've been called worse," he winks. "Now lay down, Sweetheart. Let me make up for my mistakes."

Chapter 31

ELLIE

I've never really believed in seeing fireworks or feeling sparks when you kiss someone. Probably because it's never really happened to me. But right now? It's happening with Jamie. I'm feeling all the sparks, seeing all the fireworks, experiencing the butterflies. The way Jamie's kissing me right now makes me a believer.

How did we get here? Just a few weeks ago I was trying to talk myself out of falling for this man, and now I'm letting him fuck me? What does that say about me? That I'm weak as hell and incredibly naive? Maybe. I don't even think I care anymore. Right now, kissing Jamie feels like the place I need to be.

His lips are insistent, his tongue teasing the seam of my mouth until I open for him. As the kiss deepens, I feel my resistance melting away. One hand moves to my waist and he squeezes gently. I can feel the heat of his body against mine, and I've officially forgotten why I was even mad in the first place. Jamie breaks the kiss, his breath hot against my ear.

"Will you let me show you how sorry I am, Sweetheart?" he murmurs, his voice rough.

I nod, even though I should say no. My body says the opposite, and I choose to listen to it. His hands move to the tie on my robe, slowly pulling it so the robe falls open. Since I was already in my pajama's, I'm not wearing a bra, so my nipples are perfectly visible through my thin tank top. I sit up so Jamie can pull the tank over my head. I shiver as the cool air hits my skin, but Jamie's hands are quick to warm me, sliding down my bare shoulders and landing on my breasts. He plays with each nipple, pinching gently.

"You're beautiful, Ellie," he whispers, his eyes dark with desire. "I don't fucking deserve you."

My friends would agree with that statement, and I probably should too. But I've seen how much he's changed, they haven't.

I bite my lip, not knowing exactly how to respond to that.

"I know I've said this a million times already, and I sound like a broken record, but I'm sorry, Ellie," he says, his hands stilling.

I don't know what possesses me to say it, but I look him directly in the eyes and say, "Prove it."

Jamie's eyes widen a bit, shocked by my demand. He doesn't stay that way for long. His hands move down to the edge of my sleep shorts, and I lift my hips to help him slide them down, leaving me in nothing but my lace panties. Jamie's gaze lingers on my body, his appreciation evident in the way his breath hitches.

"Fuck, Ellie," he groans, his hands moving to my hips, pulling me closer. "You're killing me."

A smile pulls at my lips. Knowing that I have him all riled up turns me on more than it should. Sex with Jamie was always good. I mean, back then we were practically kids and we didn't exactly know what we were doing. Yet every time with him made me feel wanted. It still does. Even after everything, I still feel wanted by him.

His lips meet mine, kissing me softly before he trails a path of kisses down my neck, his teeth grazing my skin as he moves lower. His hands go back to my breasts, his thumbs brushing over my peaked nipples, and I arch into his touch, a soft moan escaping my lips.

"Jamie," I whisper, my voice trembling.

He looks down at me, and I almost cum just from the look in his eyes.

"What do you want, Ellie?"

I hesitate for a moment, not wanting to voice it out loud.

"I'm not going to touch you until you tell me what you want me to do, Sweetheart," he drawls, his deep voice sending shivers down my spine.

With a sudden boldness, I tell him exactly what I want.

"I want you to fuck me."

His eyes widen, and a slow smile spreads across his face. "Even if my friends are right downstairs?"

"Yes," I practically whisper. Jamie leans down closer, whispering in my ear.

"Even if they can hear you moaning my name?"

My cheeks flush with heat. "Yes."

His smirk grows daring, and my pussy clenches. I want him. I want him inside me, I want him on me, and I want *him*, which is extremely hard for me to admit to myself, but I can't think about that right now.

He reaches for the waistband of his jeans, unfastening them with quick, eager movements. I watch as he pushes them down, his boxers following, revealing his thick, hard cock. My mouth waters at the sight, and something inside me compels me to reach for him, my fingers wrapping around his shaft. I haven't tasted him yet, and I want to. His hand lands on mine, pulling me off of him.

"Not yet," he says, his voice hoarse. "I want to taste you first."

"You already have," I pout. He chuckles to himself.

"Yeah, and I can't fucking get enough."

He pushes me back onto the bed, his hands moving to my panties. He slides them down my legs. When I'm completely bare to him, his gaze wanders up and down my body, his tongue darting out to wet his lips.

"You are..." he pauses. "God, Ellie. You're fucking stunning." His hands move to my thighs, spreading them apart. I feel exposed and vulnerable, but the way he's looking at me makes me feel powerful and desired.

He begins to kneel, but pauses, taking a sharp inhale. Sitting up on my elbow, I watch as his expression turns from desire to pain.

"Jamie? Are you okay?" I ask carefully. He nods, gritting his teeth.

"Yeah, it's just my knee."

I sit up quickly, concerned.

"Well, get on the bed! You shouldn't be crouching like that anyway," I scold. He shakes his head, standing from his position and hovering over me once again.

With a smile, he says, "Aw, Sweetheart. Do you actually care about me?"

I glare at him, not saying anything. Of course I care about him, and that's the internal problem I'm having here. Because caring about him means getting attached, and I'm already pretty much there. It might be too late for me to go back now.

He climbs onto the bed, patting the pillow next to him.

"Come here, baby."

I crawl up the bed, lying next to him, and he moves to hover over me. Leaning down, his lips touch mine. It's a brief, soft touch before he kisses his way down my body, landing right on my clit. My back arches as his tongue begins to work. Oh, God.

"Jamie," I moan, my voice desperate. I gasp as he licks a slow, deliberate path up my pussy, his mouth hot and wet. His hands grip my thighs tighter, holding me open as he delves deeper, his tongue flicking over my clit, then dipping inside me.

"Fuck," I groan, my head falling back into the pillow. "Yes, right there."

I don't think I've ever been so vocal during sex. I'm usually reserved and quiet, only moaning every once in a while. Maybe I've just been with guys that don't make me feel the way Jamie does. Jamie's tongue is magic, and don't get me started on his dick. I'd forgotten how perfect it was.

He hums against me, the vibrations sending shivers through me. His tongue is relentless, his mouth devouring me, and I feel my orgasm building.

"Jamie, I'm close," I warn, my voice shaky.

I feel him smile before he says, "cum for me, Ellie," he urges, his fingers pressing into my thigh as he sucks my clit into his mouth.

I cry out, my back arching off the bed as my orgasm crashes over me. God, it feels like ecstasy. I've never felt a better feeling, and it's because of the man in front of me. The one man I never thought would make me feel like this again.

Jamie groans, squeezing me harder. When I finally come down from my high, he lifts his head to look at me. His mouth is glistening, his eyes are full of fire and lust, and he wears a devilish smile.

Right then, I make a decision. I decide that it's time to give him something in return. Something I've imagined doing since the first time I saw him naked again.

With a newfound confidence, I sit up, giving him an innocent expression.

"Your turn," I whisper. His brows furrow, as if he believes he heard me wrong.

"My turn?" he asks, and I nod.

"Yes. Lay down. I want to taste you," I tell him. I don't even know who I am right now, but I know what I want and that's him.

He does as I say, climbing up the bed and lying on his back. His perfectly erect cock stands, ready for me to take control. When my palm wraps around his length, Jamie inhales sharply. I begin to pump slowly at first, keeping a steady rhythm that seems to be satisfying him by the way his eyes roll into the back of his head. When his eyes shut, I lean down and wrap my lips around him. He's warm and large, and the salty taste of him makes me want more.

Jamie groans. "Fuck, Ellie. God, you're amazing."

I hold back my smile as I let myself sink deeper onto him. I gag a bit as he hits the back of my throat, but after a few seconds, I'm used to it. I move faster, peering up at him through my lashes. He's beautiful. He always has been but seeing him reveling in this feeling that I'm giving him is beyond hot. His abs flex and his muscles coil as he lifts himself just enough to hit the back of my throat again.

"Jesus, Sweetheart. You're going to make me cum before I get to fuck you," he tells me through gritted teeth. I pump him into my mouth a few more times before pulling off of him reluctantly. As soon as I'm off, Jamie grabs me, flipping me onto my stomach. I yelp at the fast action.

"What are you doing?" I ask in a screaming whisper.

I feel him climb off the bed, and suddenly he's grabbing my hips and hoisting me backwards, hips in the air. I feel his hard cock near my entrance.

"I'm going to fuck you now, and you're going to let everyone in this house know who you belong to, right Sweetheart?"

I nod frantically, hoping he'll give me what I need right now. But instead of him entering me, his hand slaps my ass, leaving behind a hot sting. I yelp at the sudden pain.

"What the hell, Jamie?" I've never been spanked during sex, not because I'm against it or anything, but because no other guy that I slept with ever tried. Is it bad that I actually kind of liked it?

"Use your words, baby girl," he orders in a low, gruff tone.

"Yes," I say quickly. "Everyone will know. Please fuck me, Jamie."

Without hesitation, he positions himself between my legs and slides in with one hard thrust. I grip the covers, trying to hold onto something while Jamie pounds in and out of my pussy.

"Fucking hell, Ellie," he groans, his voice thick with need. "You're addicting."

I moan louder than I mean to. The bed creaks beneath us, making it obvious that we're not up here just to talk. But I don't care. All I can focus on is the way he's filling me, the way his cock is stretching me, the way his hands are gripping my hips as he drives into me.

"Jamie," I pant, my voice breathless. "Harder."

He obliges, his thrusts becoming more urgent and desperate. I begin to move back onto him, meeting him stroke for stroke. God, he feels incredible. The sound of our flesh slapping together fills the room, and I can hear his friends laughing downstairs.

"Tell them, Ellie," Jamie growls. "Tell them who you belong to."

"You," I gasp, my body beginning to tighten around him. "I belong to you, Jamie!"

"That's right. And I'm not giving you up, not ever again," he grits out as he thrusts deeper, his hips snapping against my ass. I feel his cock twitch inside me, and that's what tips me over the edge. I clench around him as I cry out his name.

A few moments later after we're both cleaned up, we lie in bed, staring up at the white speckled ceiling. Jamie rolls onto his side, pulling me into his arms, his lips pressing a soft kiss to my forehead. I want to melt into a freaking puddle. Who is this man and what did he do to the jerk that screwed me over?

"I meant what I said, El. I won't give you up. I can't," he practically whispers. His fingers absentmindedly move up and down my arm, giving me goosebumps. "You're the good. I need good."

My heart melts a bit at his confession. "Who knew Jamie Patterson, the hockey god, could be so sweet?" I ask, hoping to break the tension between us. There's a wall there, and I'm not sure if it's his or mine.

"Not quite the hockey god anymore," he states flatly.

I place my hand on his cheek, and it feels surreal to be lying here in bed with him. I know we've screwed a few times, but this is different. Lying here like this is intimate. It's real.

"You still are, even if you're not on the ice right now. You will be again."

His eyes meet mine, searching for something. For what, I'm not sure.

"How do you know?"

A small smile falls on my lips as my thumb moves slowly against his face. He looks so calm, yet so troubled. He's fighting a war in his head, and it doesn't seem like he's winning.

"Because you're you. You don't let anything hold you back."

Not even me.

Chapter 32

JAMIE

The room feels brighter today as I lay on the bed waiting for Jared to come in and ruin my day. Maybe it's because I slept better than I have in months last night and I actually feel rested. Or maybe it's from the fact that I finally feel like Ellie and I are in a good spot. She's not holding herself back anymore and I love that.

It's crazy to think about how far I've come.

Not wanting anything to do with relationships and shit for years.

I wanted to focus solely on hockey and forget about everything else, and I left Ellie all those years ago to get rid of distractions.

But now that she's back in my life, albeit unexpectedly, I can't imagine being without her.

Of course I still care about hockey, and I really do hope my knee heals so I can get back to my team, but maybe I'm realizing now that hockey isn't the only thing I have in my life.

Christ, if my teammates could hear me now. Some of them might understand how I'm feeling considering they've settled down. I wonder if they felt like their world was shifting around them. Maybe I should ask them. Or would they just think I'm a pussy? No, they wouldn't think that. I didn't think that when Callahan got so drunk one night that he cried on my couch for two hours about Kelly because they'd gotten into an argument earlier that day.

I found it slightly amusing, yes. But I didn't think he was a pussy for caring about the woman he loved.

By the time Jared walks in, I've talked myself into calling Calli after my session.

The last session I had, Jared told me my injury was healing well, and I should be back on the ice in no time. I've learning to take everything the doctors say with a grain of salt. I've also learned not to get my hopes up for things I really want, because that's when the exact opposite happens. Today he'll tell me that I'm regressing and his words from last week will mean nothing.

"How we doing today?" Jared asks, trying to strike up a conversation before he begins his torture.

"Ready to get this over with," I tell him honestly. After this, I have to head to the school for a fundraiser rehearsal.

We're closing in on the big day, and we only have a few more rehearsals to go. It's been a challenge for all of us. My guys have had a bit of trouble getting the dancing down, and I've struggled to get all of the steps without needing to rest my knee. I probably should have told Ellie I couldn't do the dance, but I knew it would make her happy and I want to do that. I want to make her happy to make up for the times I made her the opposite.

The drama kids have been doing well with their part, and I love watching Ellie in her element. She was meant for this life, and knowing her, she doubted it. Ellie is confident, don't get me wrong. However, she still questions herself. A sharp pang in my chest reminds me that she wasn't always that way. She used to be so sure of herself and her abilities. I suppose I might have had something to do with that part of her diminishing. Or maybe I'm giving myself too much credit and it has nothing to do with me. I did read a few years back that her father was arrested. Maybe it has to do with that.

Either way, I think I'm starting to see that spark coming back to her now, watching her lead these kids and helping them realize their full potential. I love that for her.

Fuck.

I think I love her. I don't think I ever actually stopped.

"Well, then let's get going. Show me what you got," Jared says.

I push myself off the table and plant my feet on the mat, and for the first time in months, I don't feel that sharp pain that usually radiates up my leg.

Jared's eyebrows lift. "Well, would you look at that."

"Don't jinx it," I mutter, but there's no bite in it, because I finally don't feel so broken.

We start with balance drills. Six weeks ago, I couldn't stand on this leg without feeling like the floor was trying to swallow me. Four weeks ago, I could walk and stand for short periods of time before the pain became unbearable. Two weeks ago, I could shift my weight without wanting to throw up.

The panic attacks slowed, and even though I wasn't feeling like everything was going to be okay, I was able to think of what Ellie told me. Hockey isn't who I am. It doesn't define me. There is more to life than hockey. I wouldn't say that I began to accept the fact that my professional career could be over, but I was more focused on the Wolves and Ellie than I was about my knee.

Today, I'm able to put pressure on my leg instead of limping and trying to keep from taking a full step. It trembles a bit, my muscles trying their best to remember how to work without the pain they'd become so accustomed to. Yeah, there's a little residual pain there, and it's not completely healed, but it's finally at a place where I allow myself to have some hope.

Air leaves my lungs in a shaky rush.

"Holy shit," I breathe.

"I know," Jared says softly. "Big difference, isn't it?"

Big difference doesn't even begin to cover it. I know this is just standing, but this means that I'm one step closer to getting back to the Storm.

"Try a controlled squat," he says. With a deep breath, fully ready for the pain to make its way back, I slowly make my way down into a squatting position, hold it for a few seconds, and carefully make my way back up. There was a pinching sensation, but not one that made me want to fall over and writhe in pain.

I haven't been able to do a squat in weeks, and I revel in the strain I feel in my legs. Fuck, I've missed being able to do that. Jared smiles, watching as I do one more squat for good measure.

"Okay, big man. Let's not overdo it. Take the brace off."

My breath gets caught in my throat.

"Are you sure?" I ask, not confident that what I just did will be possible without my safety net.

Jared nods. "Yep. Take it off and see what you can do."

My fingers hover at the Velcro. I've been living in this thing for weeks. Wearing it at practices, wearing it at rehearsals, often times wearing it to bed in fear that I'd bend the wrong way in my sleep.

Shaking my head, I clear my throat and undo the brace, setting it on the table behind me. I look at the large, pink vertical scar in the middle of my knee and get chills. I'd been avoiding looking at it, because every time I do, I remember how it got there.

I feel naked and exposed. Yes, of course Jared's seen it plenty of times as my physical therapist, but he's never made me take it off for drills.

"Shift your weight," he orders.

With a deep breath in, I do, and nothing happens. There's no buckle, no lightning bolt of pain, no shock that makes me want to scream.

It just... works. My laugh bursts out, rough and disbelieving.

"Are you fucking kidding me?"

Jared chuckles. "See, and you thought I was torturing you just for fun."

Rolling my eyes, I say, "Oh come on, some of it was definitely for your enjoyment."

"Yeah, you're right," he shrugs. "Listen, Jamie. This is progress, but you're not one hundred percent healed. You still need to be careful. Don't be getting cocky, now."

"Right, yeah. I know." I hesitate before asking the question I really want an answer to. "Do you think I'll play professionally again?"

Something flickers in Jared's eyes before he nods once. "Yeah, Jamie. I think you'll play professionally again."

He pats my shoulder with a smile, squeezing once, and then he leaves the room.

For the first time, I leave physical therapy with smile on my face and hope in my heart.

Cold air hits my face when I step outside the clinic. I flex my knee on the sidewalk, stretching and making sure it's still solid.

A grin pulls at my mouth before I can stop it. I feel like I'm seeing parts of my old life again, and I'm so ready to get back to it. Except, this time, Ellie will be by my side.

She's the first person I think about telling the good news to. Not my mom, not my team, not even Callahan. It's her. Of course it is.

Dragging a hand down my face, I let out a breath of frustration and relief.

I don't know how she'll react to the news. The last time I got the chance to play, I left her. I think she'll be happy for me, because that's just who Ellie is. But I don't think she'll continue what's happening between us. Me getting better might mean the end for us.

"Get it together," I mutter to myself. It's going to be fine. This is a good thing. This is the best news I could have gotten. I can't let what Ellie might think or do take away from that.

Getting into my car, I grip the steering wheel and stare out the windshield.

Things just got a little more complicated.

Chapter 33

ELLIE

Cold air curls into my lungs as I stand on the ice in the middle of the empty rink mapping things out in my head. We've been rehearsing in the rink the last few rehearsals, and it's time to make sure everything is finalized and ready for Pucks and Props night.

It's in four days. The hockey team has a game tomorrow night, and then we have one more rehearsal before the final dress rehearsal. This night has to be perfect and I'm going to make sure it is.

Fifteen minutes later, the rink is full. Skates scrape softly across the ice as the hockey students warm up. They glide through the opening formation of the dance number. Just weeks ago, they could barely keep a rhythm without tripping over each other, and now it seems like they could do this in their sleep. To be fair, we kept the dance pretty simple, so they didn't have to learn too many steps. Plus, they are on skates, so it couldn't be super complicated anyway.

I look over to the bleachers where my students are bundled in their coats and gloves running lines as the tech crew tests portable lighting rigs aimed toward center ice. Set pieces on wheels wait near the Zamboni entrance, ready to roll into place during transitions.

It's coming together better than I imagined it would. It was definitely rough at first, getting these two groups to work together peacefully, but we did it. Jamie and I, we did it.

It's been strange working so closely with Jamie while simultaneously screwing occasionally. Don't get me wrong, I'm enjoying the screwing. It was unexpected, but maybe it was inevitable. Living together, working together... there was no hope for us. This was going to happen no matter how hard I tried to pretend that he didn't affect me the way he used to. But that's the thing about old feelings. They die hard.

Clutching my notebook close to my chest, I take a deep breath before calling out, "Full run in five!" Everyone pauses where they are before heading off the ice and going to their separate corners of the large arena.

Jamie stands near the players' bench, talking quietly with two of his forwards. He came in slightly late, but I think he was at a physical therapy appointment. We haven't really seen each other since last night. He was gone when I awoke, and then I came here. Something about his posture looks loose, like nothing seems to be holding him down. The weight he'd been carrying for weeks, gone. And then I see why.

Where is his brace? He's always wearing it, especially on the ice.

Everything inside me stills, the air suddenly feeling heavier. For a short moment, the entire rink fades to background noise. I watch him put pressure on the leg that he's been working so hard to heal, and a selfish thought becomes very clear in my mind.

If he's better, he can leave. Leave Ellington, leave the Wolves, leave me.

I don't notice I've started walking toward him until he looks up and catches me staring. The players beside him go quiet before walking off, talking about how they're going to kick ass at tomorrow's game.

I smile, trying to act as if this isn't going to hurt like hell.

"How was PT?" I ask. He shrugs, like it was no big deal.

"Good. Really good," he tells me, a small smile on his lips. There's a gleam in his eyes, something I haven't seen in a long time. Hope.

"You're not wearing it," I say.

His gaze flicks down to his knee, understanding what I'm referencing. "Yeah," he chuckles.

"How?" The word slips out before I can stop it. How? Seriously, Ellie?

"Jared says we're almost done," he explains. "A couple more weeks and I'll be cleared to skate. Not sure at what level, but I'll be back on the ice."

Suddenly, I feel like I could sink into the ground, and I kind of wish I would.

Cleared to skate, meaning cleared to go back, cleared to leave me behind again. It's selfish, I know. I should be incredibly happy for him. That's what he's wanted since he got here. I knew he wasn't going to stick around forever, which is why I didn't want to get feelings involved, but my stupid heart just had to go and fall in love with him, again.

Shit. I'm in love with him.

Forcing a smile, I say, "That's amazing, Jamie. You've worked really hard."

His eyes seem to search my face as if he's trying to read between the lines.

"Yeah," he says quietly. "I did."

Silence stretches between us, filled with everything we're not saying.

"Ellie, I'm not—" he begins, but I don't let him finish.

"Well, I'm happy for you, Jamie," I say quickly. "I really am. Now let's get back to rehearsal."

His jaw tightens. He knows what I'm doing. What I always do. I'm avoiding. Pretending that whatever just happened between us doesn't matter, that my feelings for him don't matter.

"Ellie, wait—"

I walk away before he can say whatever it is he was going to say, because no matter what he says, I know that if he has the chance to go back to the NHL, he's going to jump at it. And I'll be left alone.

"From the top of the dance!" I call, and everyone takes their places, including Jamie. The music echoes through the open space as the guys begin to dance. Jamie does his best, not putting too much pressure on his leg, but doing more than he could do a few weeks ago. I really am happy for him. I'm so glad he's on the mend. However, I'm not dumb. I know that if he goes back, he's not going to want me there to distract him.

After the dance, my students take the ice, the tech crew shuffling in all of the props and sets. They deliver their lines perfectly, April and Leo stealing the show with their beautiful performance. It's short and sweet, and I think it will make people want to know what happens next.

The doors at the top of the bleachers creak open and when I look up, I spot Dean Ashby stepping inside, hands clasped behind his back as he watches quietly from the aisle. Why is he here?

I clap at the end of the performance, congratulating my actors and tech crew for an outstanding rehearsal.

"Alright, great rehearsal everyone. Two more before the big night. Get some rest tonight, and good luck to the hockey team on their game tomorrow," I say before dismissing everyone. Jamie makes his way over, stopping beside me. We both peer up to see Dean Ashby walking down toward the boards, smiling wider than I've ever seen.

"This," he says warmly, voice carrying across the rink, "looks phenomenal. You two did a fantastic job at putting this together in such a short time."

Relief crashes through me.

"I cannot wait to see the full thing on fundraiser night."

Emotion tightens my throat, and I look to Jamie, seeing that he's smiling too. Except, he's not looking at Ashby, he's looking down at me. I quickly look away, clearing my throat.

"Thank you, Dean Ashby. It really was a team effort," I say.

Once he leaves, Jamie and I collect our things in an awkward silence. Just as I'm about to head out, Jamie calls me.

"Ellie, please talk to me," he begs. I turn back to look at him. He looks desperate, like he needs me to tell him what I'm thinking. I don't want to, though. I don't want him to know that I've gone and fallen for him after I've told him so many times that I wouldn't. That I couldn't. I don't want to admit that thinking of him getting better and leaving to go back to the Storm might actually break me to pieces.

"About what Jamie? I'm proud of you. Really, I am so happy that you're healing and that you'll be back on the ice soon. You deserve it."

"I'm not going anywhere yet. I'm not one hundred percent, and I have to finish out the semester," he explains. Oh, so those are the only reasons he wants to stay. Nothing to do with me or our, whatever this is. Relationship, situationship, whatever you want to call it.

"Right, well best of luck at your game tomorrow."

With that, I walk out of the rink, leaving Jamie behind, where I should have left him in the first place.

Chapter 34

ELLIE

My room is silent. The only sound I hear is the beat of my heart and my breathing. I'm allowing myself one night of self-pity before I go back to being a boss ass bitch and throw all my focus into the end of the semester and the play.

I know nothing's official yet, and Jamie isn't fully ready to get back to playing professionally, but it's better to rip off the Band-Aid now than wait until he inevitably makes the decision to leave.

He looked so conflicted, like he didn't want to tell me, but he was excited to tell someone.

Of course he was, this is huge for him. He deserves to feel excited and relieved that he's healing from his injury. He thought his career was over and he's just learned that it might not be. I would never take that away from him, and I'd never make him choose between his career and me.

Picking my phone up, I press Lainey's name. It rings a few times before she picks up, her smiling face filling my screen.

"Oh my god, hi bitch! I see you in three days!" she squeals.

Chuckling, I say, "Hi to you too."

"Holland has decided to come too," she tells me, and I roll my eyes.

"You mean, you're forcing him to come against his will," I say. Lainey shrugs.

"Tomato, tomahto. He misses you."

"I miss him too. Is he home?" I ask, and she nods.

"Yeah, he's in the shower. Now, enough about him. How are things over in Jamie land?" she asks with a mischevious smile.

A broken laugh slips out of me, thin and tired. Lainey goes quiet instantly.

"Oh no. What happened?"

I swallow, but the lump in my throat doesn't move. "Nothing happened. He's just... he's almost healed, Laine."

She doesn't say anything, but I can tell she already understands where this is going.

"Physical therapy's almost done," I practically whisper. "He'll be cleared to skate soon. To go back to the NHL, back to his real life."

Her expression softens. "El..."

My chest tightens, pressure building fast as I try to hold it together. But I'm so tired of pretending I'm fine.

"I was careful this time," I say, my voice shaking. "I kept my distance. I told myself it was in the past, and the closeness wouldn't bring back any old feelings." My eyes begin to burn as they fill with tears. "I told myself I wouldn't let this happen again."

A tear spills out and runs down my warm cheeks, and I finally say the words that I've been trying my best to avoid.

"I fell in love with him, Lainey."

The confession hangs in the air between us for a few seconds before I continue.

"And I'm so mad at myself for it," I choke. "Because I knew how this would end. I knew he'd leave. He always does."

My shoulders begin to shake as I let the tears spill. Lainey stays quiet, letting me get my emotions out into the open. This all seems ridiculous because he hasn't even said he's going to leave. But I know where it's going. I just know.

"I just got him back," I whisper. "And now I'm losing him again."

After a few deep breaths, I wipe my tears.

"You falling in love isn't a mistake, Ellie."

"It is if he doesn't stay."

"No," she says gently. "You can't help who you love, El."

I squeeze my eyes shut.

"You warned me, Laine. You told me not to let my guard down, and I did it anyway. I let him worm his way into my heart again."

Lainey sits up straighter, pulling her long, curly hair over her shoulder.

"Have you told him?"

My laugh is hollow.

"God, no. Why would I do that?"

"Because he probably feels the same. He pursued you, El."

"He might," I shrug. "But even if he did, it wouldn't matter. Hockey will always come first for him."

"Is that Ellie?" Holland's voice asks in the background. My heart stops. Oh fuck.

Lainey's head whips around.

"Yeah, it's—"

"Who's she in love with?" he asks, and Lainey blanches. Holland appears on the screen next to Lainey. His expression is stone, his jaw tight.

"Who are you in love with, Ellie?" he asks, his voice low.

"Holland, come on. This is girl talk," Lainey tries. Holland doesn't even look her way.

"It's him, isn't it? Jamie fucking Patterson. It's him?" I can't answer. I don't want to disappoint my brother. I know he wanted to kill Jamie back then for what he did to me. He saw how broken I was, and now he's seeing it again.

"Holland, I—"

"He broke you," Holland snaps. "Do you remember that part? Or did we all just hallucinate the months you couldn't even get out of bed?"

My throat tightens painfully. "Holland, of course I remember."

"Then why are we doing this again, Ellie? Why are you letting the same guy hurt you twice?"

"Because I love him, Holland!" The words burst out before I can stop them. "Okay? I love him and I tried not to and I fucking failed. I failed."

Holland's anger flickers, his nostrils flaring.

"He's going to leave again," he says quietly. Not cruel, just certain. "And you're going to be shattered all over again."

"Holland..." Lainey starts.

Tears begin to run again, but I do my best to hold strong.

"No, Lainey. He's right. I should just... cut my losses. Walk away first, you know?" I sniffle. I know that's what I have to do. I can't let him break me again. I just... I can't.

"Ellie, wait—" Lainey begins, but I don't want her to talk me out of the decision I've just made.

"I'll talk to you tomorrow," I tell her with a tearful smile before hanging up and throwing my phone onto the carpet.

I've done it once, I can do it again, right? I can live without him. He's not the center of my world. I have friends and family, and I don't need him. I don't.

I end up crying myself to sleep, once again, over the boy who broke me nine years ago. The next time I see him, I'll tell him it's the end, and everything will go back to the way it was. He'll go back to his team, and I'll... I don't know. Maybe I'll stay here for another semester. Maybe I'll go home. But whatever I do, it's going to break my fucking heart.

Chapter 35

JAMIE

I tossed and turned all night. My mind is on one million things, and I'm stressed as fuck when I should be fucking thrilled. I saw the way Ellie looked at me, like I was about to shatter her world all over again. I hate that look. It's well deserved, I guess. However, I made the decision that I'm going to ask her to come with me. When all is said and done, I want her by my side. No, I *need* her. I don't plan on leaving her behind. I could never. Not after everything that's happened between us this past semester.

Taking a deep breath, I shake my body out, getting rid of all the tension and all the thoughts that don't have to with the game tonight.

It's one of the last games of the semester before winter break, and this might be one of the last times I get to be their coach. These guys need a win. We've worked our asses off, and after Cramer, Callahan, Grieves, and Roslavic came and showed the Wolves how to get shit done, they've been playing harder than ever. They have drive, they have energy, and they have the want to win. This is it for them. We're playing Atlantic Academy again, and this is the Wolves time to fucking shine, so they better play their asses off.

The energy in the rink feels electric. I think this might be our biggest crowd yet. I wanted my friends to be here tonight, but they had to get back home. I was also kind of hopeful that Ellie would show up, but as far as I can see, she's not here. I can't let that distract me from what's happening right now though.

The hype music blasts loudly as I lean against the boards during warmups, arms folded, trying to ignore the familiar ache building in my chest. The one that usually symbolizes the beginning of a panic attack.

I take a few deep breaths, shaking my hands out and focusing on the ice. I've never seen a therapist, and I never plan to. The only person that knows I even have panic attacks is Ellie. I won't let my enemies know I have a weakness, and I won't have my team thinking I'm undeserving of my captaincy, which I *will* get back once I return.

Feeling my adrenaline slowing down, I give the bleachers one last look to see if Ellie might have shown up, but she's not there. She's not. She's come to almost every game this season, but she's not at one of the most important ones?

"Coach," Logan says, gliding up beside me and distracting me from what was about to be a rabbit hole of bad thoughts. "You think we can actually win this one?"

I meet his eyes, and for once, I see determination and hope there.

"Yeah," I tell him confidently. "Yeah, I do."

Ten minutes later, Braydon, our star center is at the faceoff. He looks more ready than I've ever seen him. The music in the rink stops, and the quiet makes the air feel thicker. It seems like everyone's at the edge of their seats, waiting to see who gets possession.

Braydon taps the blade of his stick once against the ice.

The Atlantic player across from him leans in. The ref lowers the puck, and time stops as it falls to the ice.

Clack.

Braydon wins it clean. The puck snaps back to Andersson who passes it to Logan. The Wolves keep possession of the puck for a minute or two before Paul Novak sends it flying in the other direction, giving it right to one of Atlantic's players. Fuck.

We get it back, but it's not long before there's another turnover. My palms are sweating and my heart is pounding inside of my chest as I watch the game play out, knowing I have no control over the outcome.

By the end of the first period, the score is still zero to zero, which isn't terrible. We've still got a chance to change that in the second.

The second period begins with a rush. A new sense of urgency and hope spreading through the team like wildfire.

Atlantic's guys are intense. They're like sharks, and they smell blood in the water. I watch helplessly as one of the Wolves loses the puck, and by the time anyone is by him to help, the Atlantic player shoots it right past Levi. Fucking shit.

The light flashes, the buzzer goes off, and for a split second, I see it. The shoulders dropping, the hope leaving their bodies, and I know I need to step up and be their coach for this one. I know what they're feeling. Well, maybe not exactly because I've never experienced a losing streak like this, but either way, I get it. Falling behind sucks ass. Losing sucks worse. But there's still more game to play, and they're not allowed to give up yet.

I step forward, my voice cutting through the noise. "Look at me!"

The whole bench turns.

"It's one goal," I say. "It's not the end yet. There's ten minutes to go in the second, and then we've got the third. Keep your heads in the game and your sticks out of your asses, you hear me?"

Something seems to shift in their eyes, like they're actually hearing what I'm telling them, thank fuck.

"Next shift," I yell as the next line jumps over the boards and onto the ice.

The rest of the game is a blur.

We score twice in five minutes, Logan gets a penalty for a high stick, which I try to argue but to no avail, and the other team scores on the powerplay.

At the end of the second, we're tied two to two. The guys are more hyped up in the locker room, and I'm feeling more confident and less like I'm about to be sucked into the ground. This is good, I just wish Ellie could be here to see it. Shit. I don't remember the last time I wanted a girl to be there to witness these moments with me. When did Ellie become the one person I want to tell everything to? When did she become my person?

With five minutes left and still tied, the tension is unbelievable. God, I miss that rush at the end of a game where it's all or nothing and everyone's revved up. And then it comes, the moment that seems to have been building the entire game.

One of the Atlantic players, skates by Braydon, his stick getting caught under Braydon's skate, and he goes down hard. The wolves gather around and before he's even off the ice, Logan's gloves fly off. The ref blows the whistle, the crowd is on their feet, cheering like this is the best thing they've seen in their lives.

My guys on the bench erupt, their sticks banging against the boards as they shout at their teammates on the ice. As much as I should be yelling at them to stop fighting like idiots and play the goddamn game, I'm actually enjoying this. My heart pounds, and for a brief moment, I remember what that feels like. The adrenaline and anger surging through my veins.

The refs dive in, grabbing jerseys, and trying to pull bodies apart. By the time they finally get them apart, the Atlantic player has a bloody nose, and Logan sports a nice gash on his cheek.

I probably should be angry, but I'm actually kind of proud. They stood up for their teammate. Their brother. That's what this whole thing was about. Getting them to play as a team, a unit. And they did.

Logan and the Atlantic player get five minutes in the box. They're out for the remainder of the game. My anxiety spike, knowing Logan is probably one of the best players on the team, but I'm confident the remaining players can do this.

It's five on five, and the crowd is going crazy. Everyone is on their feet, girls are jumping up and down, and I know it's giving the guys the extra push they need to get this win.

With seven seconds left, I'm sweating and my pulse is racing. Novak gets possession of the puck, and he gets a breakaway, skating down the ice faster than I've ever seen him go.

And then... the lights begin to flash and the horn goes off. The sound of cow bells, noise makers, and applause fills the arena. I let out a long breath, finally feeling like I can breathe again. The guys pile onto the goalie in a mess of limbs and disbelief.

My hands burn from clapping so hard, and I'm grinning from ear to ear like a fucking idiot. I'm proud of these guys. I'm proud of what they've overcome, and how hard they've worked to get here.

And once again, the only person I want to share this moment with, is Ellie Monroe.

Chapter 36

JAMIE

The drive home feels longer than usual. It's quiet and dark, and for once I finally let myself feel. A bit of peace. We won. I don't care if they sucked pretty much all season, because in that moment, in that game, they did what they needed to do. I need to send the guys a damn fruit basket because whatever they said to the Wolves, worked miracles.

My phone is blowing up with texts from the group chat, and I noticed a missed call from my agent. I'll call him back in the morning. Tonight, I'm going to revel in this success.

I want to get home and tell her the news, and I want to tell her I love her.

I want to tell her everything.

I want to tell her I wish she was there, that these past fourteen weeks made me realize that I was a fucking loser for leaving her. I want to tell her that healing scares me, because as much as I want to be back, I'm afraid I'll never play the same again.

I grip the steering wheel tighter.

Somewhere between the past and now, she stopped being this memory that I suppressed and started feeling like home. I always thought that the place I felt most at home was on the ice, where I could feel my dad with me, rooting for me. But now it's the girl I fell in love with when we were fifteen years old. The girl that I was lucky enough to have in my life for all those years. The only girl who looks at me like I'm more than what I do on the ice.

As I pull into the driveway, my heart picks up speed. I'm suddenly feeling nervous, but I can't pinpoint why.

The house is dark when I walk in, silent. Somehow it feels bigger, and yet I feel claustrophobic.

Tossing my keys on the kitchen counter, I throw my jacket over the back of one of the chairs at the island. For a second I just stand there, just listening, trying to hear footsteps or any signs that she's awake. It's late, so I'm sure she's asleep, but I'm hoping she's not.

I walk upstairs quieter than necessary, like the floor might betray me if I step too hard. Ellie's door is closed, a thin line of light underneath.

I should go to my room. Talk to her in the morning, but instead, I just stand here like a fucking idiot. My hand hovers near the wood as I debate on whether to knock or not.

Because if she opens that door, if she looks at me the way she did when she left the rink the other day after rehearsal, I don't know if I could keep myself from telling her everything that's going on inside my head, and I don't know if she's ready to hear it.

Back in my room, the silence feels louder. I sit on the edge of the bed, still wired from the win, from the future, from her. We won tonight. It's the biggest moment of the season so far. I should be ecstatic, but instead I just feel disappointed.

A slow breath leaves my lungs as I stare at my phone, reading through the messages from the guys.

Rhode Island Stormies

Billy Callahan: *Aye, that's that shit!*

Connor Grieves: *awoooooooooo.*

Theo Cramer: *What the hell is that?*

Connor Grieves: *I'm howling, like a wolf.*

Wilder Ranslavic: *Go to fucking bed. I'm trying to sleep.*

Billy Callahan: *Uh oh. Someone's a grumpy pants.*

Wilder Ranslavic: *I'll kill you. And no one will be able to find the body.*

Billy Callahan: *I'm feeling threatened.*

Wilder Ranslavic: *Good.*

Connor Grieves: *Congrats on the win, Patty!*

Theo Cramer: *I knew those kids could do it. Just needed a kick in the ass.*

Billy Callahan: *Hell yeah. Congrats, buddy.*

Jamie Patterson: *Thanks guys.*

Connor Grieves: *I bet the boys were hyped.*

Jamie Patterson: *Yeah, they were. Logan and Jacob more than anyone. They busted their asses out there.*

An incoming call distracts me from the chat. Billy's name flashes across my screen. It's almost midnight, why the fuck is he calling me?

"Why are you calling me?" I ask as soon as I answer the phone. I'm honestly not in the mood to talk right now. I want to wallow in whatever the feeling is in my chest.

"Well hello to you too, Patterson," Callahan replies, chuckling to himself. "I just wanted to congratulate you on the W tonight."

Rolling my eyes, I turn onto my side, my phone on speaker. "You already did. Why are you actually calling?"

I can see him rolling his eyes through the phone. "Fine. I'm nosy as fuck and I want to know what's happening between you and the chick."

I pause, my heart stuttering at the slightest mention of Ellie.

"What chick?" I ask, playing dumb. I mean, he obviously knows we fuck, considering I fucked her in my room the night the guys were here. There's no way they didn't hear Ellie screaming for me while she came on my cock.

"Come on, Patterson. The roommate, the girl you were fucking while we tried to ignore all the sounds coming from upstairs. Rude, by the way."

I clear my throat. "Right. Uh, well first of all, she's not some chick. Her name is Ellie," I start, trying to determine whether or not I want to dive into this with him right now.

"She's hot, man. I don't blame you for—"

"Shut the fuck up before I rip your head from your body, Callahan," I growl, and I hear him laugh immediately on the other end. He loves his wife and would never disrespect her. Kelly's a great girl. She's pretty, she's sweet, and she puts up with Callahan's shit. They've been together for years now.

"There it is," he says through laughter. "You like her. You wouldn't get that possessive over someone you're only fucking. So, are you guys like, dating? Is she your girlfriend? And if so, why the fuck didn't you tell me?"

Fucker. He was testing me, and I did exactly what he wanted. Guess we're doing this.

Rubbing a frustrated hand down my face, I sigh. "She's... well... I don't know what she is, man. We dated in high school, and after my dad died, I threw myself into hockey. I don't know why I did it, but I left. I left her, Billy," I explain, feeling completely deflated.

"Okay, so you broke up with her, and now she's there?" he asks.

"I didn't just break up with her, Calli. I abandoned her. I fucking left without saying a word. No explanation, just poof. Gone. I went to a hockey camp for a bit and then came to the Storm. Hockey was my focus, and I didn't think about how it would affect her."

There's a long pause before Callahan speaks.

"Shit," he exhales sharply. "Damn, Patty. That's like, fucked up."

Rolling my eyes, I pull myself into a sitting position, the covers falling off and leaving me exposed in just my boxers.

"Yeah, thanks. I know I fucked up. But seeing her again, being with her... I think I love her, Calli."

"You think?"

I stare at the window, coming to terms with the wicked truth.

"I know. I'm in love with Ellie."

"So what's the problem?" Callahan asks, and I realize now that I haven't told anyone but Ellie about the good news.

"I'm almost cleared," I tell him.

"What do you mean?"

"I'm almost done with PT. I'll be coming back to the Storm to start practice soon. They'll start me slow, but Jared says I'll be back on the ice in no time," I explain, but I don't sound as excited as I should. Because I know what it could really mean.

Callahan howls on the other end and I have to pull the phone away from my face so he doesn't pierce my fucking eardrum.

"Fuck yeah, brother! That's awesome! The guys are gonna be stoked," he exclaims. "I don't see how this is a problem though."

Huffing out a breath of frustration, I climb off the bed and begin to pace back and forth. If Ellie would just let me talk to her about this.

I'd tell her I don't plan on going anywhere without her. I know I don't have a great track record, but this time it'll be different. This time I know what I have in front of me and I'm not ever going to push her away again. She's been my rock, a constant reminder these past few months that hockey isn't all I have.

"Ellie thinks I'm gonna disappear again. I don't even know if she has actual feelings for me. We really haven't talked about it. But the way she looked at me the other night, I could tell exactly what she was thinking. She expects me to walk away again." I don't know why I'm telling him all of this like he's my goddamn therapist. I sound like a fucking loser.

"And you don't want to?" he asked, attempting to figure out what I'm rambling about.

"No. I want her to come with me," I state, feeling so sure of my choice.

"Well then tell her. Make her listen. There's no way she doesn't feel anything for you. You've been cooped up in a house together for three and a half months, dude. And from the sound of it, she really likes when you do the horizontal tango," he proclaims, and I can literally see him wink at me through the phone. Idiot.

He's not wrong though. One thing I can say for certain is I still know how to please Ellie when it comes to sex. I can read her body like a fucking book. She's reactive as hell and she can't hide when she's turned on. Her cheeks flush and her body tenses. And she always gets this look in her eye, like she doesn't want to give in, but her body betrays her.

My mouth begins to water and my dick hardens as I visualize Ellie all wet and ready for me. Fuck, she's a goddamn dream, and I never want to wake up. Shit, stop thinking about sex right now.

After talking about the team and discussing what I've missed in my time away, Callahan and I hang up, and I'm left alone once again, contemplating all of my life's decisions.

If nothing else, these past few months with Ellie have made me realize that maybe healing wasn't just about my knee. Maybe it's been about figuring out what kind of life I actually want if hockey wasn't the only thing left standing.

I don't know what choosing her looks like. I don't know what it'll cost. I don't know if she even wants me to ask her to come with me. But for the first time since the injury...I know what I'm afraid of losing, and it isn't hockey.

Chapter 37

ELLIE

Tonight's the night.

It's Pucks and Props night, and I feel sick to my stomach. Not because I'm nervous, but because I've been thinking about Jamie for two straight days and I haven't been able to focus on anything else. I should be completely immersed in this production, in the play, but instead I'm thinking about how to tell Jamie that we can't continue whatever is happening between us because in a week and a half, he'll go back to his life, and I'll stay here.

In a week and half, we'll go back to being strangers, ex-lovers, and I'll go back to pretending he never existed. That he never broke my heart.

It's about to be a long night, and I'm already over it. I just want to get this thing over with and be done with it all. The only thing I am excited about is seeing Lainey. She and Holland will be here tonight to cheer on the hockey team and my theatre students. And for moral support. God knows I'm going to need it.

As I stand in the middle of the rink, my clipboard in hand, I look around the arena. It's huge for a college campus, but I wouldn't really expect anything less from a university that costs an arm and a leg in tuition.

I'd never really been in here before all this. Before Jamie. The only thing I ever did in this building was use the auditorium for shows I was in. Now that I'm alone, I'm taking it all in. The ceiling is high, with banners hanging down from past championships. The ice gleams under my feet reflecting the school crest right in the center.

Tiered seating rises steeply on both sides, and though I've never seen a professional hockey arena, I'm pretty sure Ellington's arena is close to the same size.

Each individual seat had the crest stitched into it. They look clean and crisp, just as everything on this campus does. Despite everything being clean, you can still smell the scent of hockey. It's not as repugnant as the men's locker room, but it's definitely there.

Along the walls, framed photographs and plaques hang showing off teams from years past, famous alumni mid-celebration, and newspaper clippings immortalizing last-second victories.

It feels different when you're in here all alone. When the lights are off and you're standing smack dab in the middle. It's almost like a stage, except there's no lights and no one's here. I guess hockey and theatre aren't all that different. Well, minus the hitting, slamming, and all-around competitive nature that hockey entails. But we're both performing for an audience. So maybe that's the only similarity.

And now I'm rambling in my head. God, I don't think I've ever been this nervous and I'm not even the one performing. I just want this night to go smoothly. I need it to go smoothly. Because I'm already trying to hold myself together and if anything goes wrong, I'm afraid that will be the last straw.

My mom called this morning to wish me good luck. She couldn't be here since she's got the flu or something. I don't know how true it is. She hasn't come back to Ellington since dad got arrested. I think it makes her upset, so I didn't push her.

The light click of a door opening causes me to jump, almost slipping on the ice. I don't see who's walking toward me in the dark, and for a moment my skin prickles and my heart begins to race. Oh god, am I about to be murdered in the hockey arena? This is not the place I want to die in. I want to be surrounded by my family and friends when I'm old and senile.

As the footsteps grow closer, my vision begins to adjust, and I see that it's not a murderer. It's Jamie. Which somehow feels even worse right now.

One hand in his pocket, the other carrying a cup of what I assume is coffee. His hair is disheveled, and he looks like he hasn't slept in days. I don't know why he'd be unable to sleep. He's getting everything he wanted.

His knee is almost better, he'll be able to get back to the NHL, the Wolves won their game the other night. So why does he look like he's struggling to keep it together right now? Why do I care? My heartbeat reminds me exactly why I care. I love him. Stupid heart.

"Hey," he says, his voice low, and I hate how his voice makes my entire body shiver.

"Hi," I reply softly.

He shifts nervously. "Are you nervous?"

"A little," I say honestly. There's no point in lying, it's probably written all over my face.

"Don't be, it's going to be great. Everyone's worked really hard. Especially you."

I watch his face, his eyes looking down at the coffee cup in his hand before reaching it toward me. I stare at the cup for a moment, wondering why he's giving it to me. Looking up at him, he gives me a small, unsure smile.

"I got you coffee," he tells me, and I almost melt into a puddle. Seriously? He brought me coffee? He's really not making this any easier. Is he trying to hurt me more?

"You didn't have to do that."

"Just take the damn coffee, Ellie. Don't be stubborn," he demands. I reach out and the cup from his hand, our fingers brushing slightly, and it instantly warms me.

"Thank you," I mutter.

"Ellie, look. Can we talk about the other day at rehearsal?"

My brows furrow, acting as if I have no idea what he could possibly be talking about. Except, I know exactly what he's referring to. Me finding out he'll be going back to his team and leaving me behind.

Okay, he didn't actually say that, but I know how this plays out. He's going to want to put all of his focus on a full recovery and getting back in the game. He won't have time for me.

"What about the other day?" I ask and he shakes head with a scoff.

"You know what I'm talking about, El."

"Jamie, there's nothing to talk about. You're healing, and that's great. I'm so happy for you. You won't have to slum it here anymore. You get to go back to your life, back to hockey, back to pretending I never existed."

He looks as if I've slapped him across the face, as if I've just offended him with the truth. He takes a menacing step closer.

"Ellie, I was never pretending like you didn't exist. It's not like I just left and never thought of you again. I thought about you every goddamn day for months," he seethes.

"Oh, is that supposed to make me feel better?" I ask, completely shocked as to why he thought admitting that he'd thought of me would bring me any comfort.

His head falls back as he lets out a frustrated groan. "I was eighteen, Ellie!" he shouts. "Dad was dead, and I got the offer of a lifetime, so I took it. I should have talked to you. I know I should've talked to you. But you had plans to go to college and my plans were bringing me away from home, away from you."

Taking an angry step closer, my finger pokes at his chest.

"We could have worked something out! It didn't have to end. There were a million other options, and you chose the wrong one, Jamie. How could you stand here and tell me that you thought about me when you never even tried to reach out. And then you come here, and you make me fall in love with you all over again, for what? Just so you can break my heart again? Jesus, Jamie. Was it not enough the first time?"

I hadn't realized I'd started to cry until I taste the tears on my lips. I don't have time for this. I cannot be thinking about this right now when the event starts in a few hours and there's so much that needs to be done.

Jamie's face goes from frustrated to bewildered, stepping closer until there's no room between us and I can feel the heat of his body pressing into mine. I should push him away, tell him to leave me the hell alone, but I don't. Instead, I stand there against him, my breathing unsteady and my heart racing.

His eyes move rapidly over my face, as if he's trying to memorize every pore, every freckle, every detail.

"You love me?" he asks.

"Seriously? That's what you—"

"I love you, too," he rushes out. I swear my heart stops. My breath catches, and time freezes. He walks us backward until I hit the boards. "I'm in love with you, Ellie. I may have lost my way, and I know I don't deserve you. But I fucking love you, and I told you I'd never let you go again."

The tears flow faster, Jamie's confession pulling them out of me. We stand there for what feels like hours as my mind reels and all rational thoughts leave my body.

His hands fly to my face, his thumb gently brushing a tear away. He lets out a breath, as if he's contemplating something.

"Fuck it," he mutters, and then kisses me so hard I think I might bruise.

Lifting me up in one swift motion, I wrap my legs around his waist, my arms wrapping around his neck, the coffee cup falling onto the ice. I guess we'll worry about that later.

Jamie begins to move, but I'm too busy kissing him to pay attention to where he's bringing me. When my back hits the cold ground, I open my eyes and realize we're hiding in the teams' bench area. I should be grossed out by lying on the filthy ground, but right now I'm too distracted to care.

Jamie hovers over me, his lips finding mine again, his hands tangling in my hair. The feel of him is exactly what I need. The slight pressure his body applies to mine is electrifying. There's so much need, so much desperation in his kiss, as if he's trying to prove to me that he's serious.

What am I doing? We're in the arena. Anyone could walk in. How in the hell does he keep getting me into these situations? And why do I kind of love it?

Chapter 38

JAMIE

Ellie Monroe loves me.

She fucking loves me. She loves me despite everything I've done to make her hate me. She loves me even though I don't deserve it. I was shocked when she said it. At first, I didn't think I heard her right. Surely, she couldn't love me. Not me. Not the guy who broke her heart. But I did hear her correctly, and she did tell me she loved me. I wasn't lying when I'd told her I'd never be without her again.

She's coming with me back to Rhode Island, back home. She just doesn't know it yet. But I don't want to think about all that right now. Not when she's lying underneath me, kissing me like she's starving.

We probably shouldn't be doing this here, but what's life without living on the edge every once in a while? I let out a groan as her tongue slides against mine. I can feel the same desperation I feel in every movement. My dick throbs in my jeans, begging for release. Ellie's hand moves from underneath me, finding my hard cock and rubbing me up and down.

Don't cum in your pants, Jamie. Please don't cum in your pants.

A jolt of pleasure rushes through my body, and I bite her lip, causing her to moan.

"Fuck, Ellie."

"Is this okay? Do you like it?" she asks, her voice shaky.

"I like everything you do, Sweetheart," I tell her truthfully. Of course I fucking like it.

Ellie moans again when I settle between her thighs, the hard evidence of my arousal pressing against her core. She arches up instinctively.

I kiss and nip down her neck, wishing more than anything that she wasn't wearing several layers right now.

"I need you," I mutter against her throat, kissing the rapid pulse point I find there. "Can I have you?"

She nods quickly, like she's just as desperate to have me inside her as I am to be there. "Yes."

I pull back to look at her face. Her cheeks are flushed, lips swollen from kissing, and her eyes shine bright with want in the dark arena. She's the most beautiful thing I've ever seen.

"Are you sure? Cause I mean, we could—"

"Jamie." She grabs my face in her hands, her thumb moving slowly back and forth, and even though her hands are freezing cold, I've never felt warmer. "I'm sure."

I lean down to kiss her as I work at her jeans. The button gives way, then the zipper. I slide my hand inside, groaning when I feel how wet she already is through her panties.

"You're soaked," I growl. "All this for me?"

"No, it's for Freddie," she teases before breaking out into a small fit of laughter.

My eyes narrow. "You think that's funny, huh?" I ask before sliding her panties to the side and slipping my fingers into her. Her back arches off the ground and her laughter stops immediately.

"N-no," she stutters and cries out as I add another finger. I pump in and out slowly, watching her eyes roll to the back of her head.

"That's what I thought."

"Oh God, Jamie. More, please," Ellie begs, and I oblige, adding a third finger and curling them to find that spot inside her. Her walls clench around me, hot and tight.

"Jamie," she whimpers. "I need you inside me."

I've never heard a sweeter sound in my life.

"Okay, Sweetheart."

I pull my fingers free and make quick work of my belt and zipper. My cock springs free, hard and aching, the tip already slick with precum. Ellie's eyes drop to it as she licks her lips.

I pull her jeans and panties down her thighs, not bothering to get them fully off. She spreads her legs as wide as the bunched fabric will allow, and I position myself at her entrance.

"Look at me," I demand. Her green eyes meet mine. "I love you."

I push inside her and we both groan at the sensation. She's so fucking tight and wet. I bury myself to the hilt, then still, letting us both adjust. The feeling is overwhelming, her walls fluttering around me, her fingernails digging into my shoulders. Fuck, I could cum right now. But I won't because I want Ellie to feel how much I care about her. I want her to know how much she means to me.

She squirms a bit before she says, "Move. Please, move."

Pulling back until just my tip remains inside her, I watch her as I slam forward. She cries out, her back arching off the concrete, and I rush to cover her mouth with my hand.

"Shhh, Sweetheart. You can't be too loud. We're not at home, remember?"

She nods. Keeping my hand over her mouth, I do it again. And again. Ellie's head falls back and her eyes screw shut. I feel her moaning underneath my hand, and it drives me to go faster, harder.

"That's it, baby," I grunt, driving into her. "Take it, Sweetheart. Take my cock like a good fucking girl."

I remove my hand and lean down to kiss her, her lips soft and warm and wet. Her nails rake down my back, surely leaving marks through my shirt.

Hooking one of her legs over my shoulder, I change the angle, and she screams. Well fuck. My hand flies back to her mouth.

"Quiet," I hiss, though I don't slow my thrusts. "Unless you want someone to find us with my cock buried inside you."

Her eyes widen, and I feel her clench around me. The idea turns her on and I can't help my smile. My dirty girl.

"Well, well, well. Ellie Monroe, do you like the thought of that?" I whisper, leaning close to her ear. "The thought of someone walking in? Seeing you spread open for me? Seeing how good I fuck you?"

She whimpers against my hand, her hips bucking to meet each of my thrusts. Jesus Christ, she feels so good.

"There you go, baby," I coax, moving my hand from her mouth to grip her hip. "Cum for me, Ellie. Cum on my cock."

"I'm...I'm... oh fuck, yes. Jamie," she cries before her whole body seizes, her back bowing off the ground as her orgasm crashes through her. I fuck her through it, prolonging every wave, and watching her face contort in pleasure. She's stunning like this. Completely undone and completely mine.

When the waves finally come to a stop, I flip her onto her stomach before pulling her hips up and driving back inside. She moans into the concrete as I take her from behind. I'm not exactly gentle, but she lets me keep going.

I grip her hips hard enough to bruise as I pump into her, chasing my own release. The sounds of our ragged breathing and Ellie's tiny moans are the only thing that can be heard in the arena.

"Jamie," she whimpers. "I'm going to cum again."

"Then do it," I demand, reaching around and finding her clit. I rub tight circles over and over again, and then she shatters, her second orgasm seeming even more intense than the first. Her walls clamp down on my cock again, and that's all it takes to send me over the edge. Buring myself deep inside her, I cum with a groan, spilling inside her in hot pulses. My vision goes white at the edges and my whole body shakes with the force of my release. I collapse next to her, completely boneless. Holy fucking shit. That was intense.

For a long moment, we just lay there, tangled together on the cold concrete of the arena floor. My heart hammers against my ribs, and I can feel Ellie's pulse racing where our bodies remain connected.

"Wow," she finally breathes "That was..."

"Yeah..." I say, pressing a kiss to her shoulder. "Wow."

After we fix ourselves and pull our clothes back on, we lie back down, both on our sides so we're face to face. Ellie smiles, but it doesn't reach her eyes. The look makes my chest ache.

I reach for her, caressing her cheek. She leans into my touch, her soft skin feeling warm against my palm.

"I guess your knee really is almost healed," she says with a chuckle. I nod, just now realizing that I did all that and my knee didn't bother me at all.

"Yeah, I guess so." Ellie looks away quickly, and I think I understand what she meant by that comment.

"Hey," I say softly. Her eyes meet mine and I smile. "I love you."

Her small smile widens just a bit. "I love you."

"Come with me," I blurt out. Ellie gives me a questioning look.

"What do you mean? Come with you where?" she asks curiously.

"When I go back, I want you to come with me."

Her breath catches, and she seems to be at a loss for words. I don't think she was expecting me to say that. I don't think I can go back if she doesn't come with me. I'm in too deep.

"Jamie, I—" she starts, but I interrupt because I have a feeling she was about to tell me all the reasons she can't.

"Ellie, I told you I wasn't going to leave you. I need you to come with me. I have a place in the city. We can live there and I'll commute to the arena. You'll be able to go back to acting, and you'll be back with your friends. You'll be with me, and I'll be with you. It's a win-win."

"Jamie, that's insane. I can't just move in with you," she tells me, standing from our position on the ground. I follow, towering over her.

"Why not? We already live together. We've been living together for the past four months. What's the difference?" I ask.

Her arms cross over her chest. "It's not the same. Living with you, being with you, it's... we're..." she trails off, seeming to have no other argument.

"Please. Just come. After the semester's over, we'll pack up and go to New York. You can stay at my place, which would be our place, while I go to training," I explain, hoping she'll see how good of an arrangement this could be.

Her weight shifts from one foot to the other.

"What if I wanted to stay here? As the director?" she asks. I hadn't thought about that.

My brow furrows. "Is that what you want?"

Her hands fall to her sides, and she begins to pace back and forth in the small space.

"I don't know, Jamie. It could be," she proclaims. I move in front of her, stopping her pacing. Grabbing her arms and squeezing gently, I take a deep breath.

"Then I'd stay, too," I tell her, and I really mean it. Fuck it. Fuck hockey, fuck the pro's, fuck it all. It means nothing if Ellie's not by my side. I was too stupid to realize it when I was younger, too self-absorbed. I should have never just left her like that. I should have asked her to come with me. "I can't go back in time, Ellie. I can't change the past. But I can change the future. I should have asked you to come with me years ago and I didn't. So, I'm asking you now. And if you decide that you want to stay here and direct, then I'll stay too."

She blinks, her shoulders moving up and down quickly with her breathing. She honestly looks like she's seen a damn ghost.

"You'd just give up everything you've worked for? The life you've been talking about getting back to since you got here? To stay with me?" she asks in disbelief. I know, it's crazy, and it doesn't sound like me at all. I worked my ass off to get to the NHL, I trained for hours on end, I left my life behind. I don't regret any of it. The only thing I do regret, is not having Ellie by my side through it all.

"I think I'd do just about anything for you, Sweetheart," I tell her.

I lean down and kiss her gently and everything fades away. The arena, the thoughts in my head, the doubt and the fear. And for the first time in months, I finally feel completely free. I finally feel like my life is falling into place, and there isn't a piece missing.

Chapter 39

JAMIE

My pulse races and my hands shake as I stand in my office looking into the mirror that hangs on the wall. My face looks pale and my cheeks are bright red. I look like I've just skated twelve laps around the rink, except I haven't. In fact, I haven't done anything but sit here going over the routine for the fundraiser. The Wolves are in the auditorium with the theatre kids rehearsing one last time before they take the ice.

There's less than an hour before showtime, and I can't get my fucking breathing under control enough to feel like I can leave this room. I don't know what's going on. I've performed in front of way bigger crowds in bigger arenas.

This should be a piece of cake. So why does my brain think this is the end of the world?

Taking a deep breath in, I release it shakily as I stare back at myself in the mirror. I'm okay. Everything's okay. I'm okay. Everything's okay. I repeat this mantra a hundred times before ultimately giving up and fall back into my chair at the desk.

Fuck, I'm freaking out. I feel my heartbeat pick up, and my entire body is filled with adrenaline and the urge to vomit. I rub a clammy hand over my face and try to focus on my breathing. My leg moves up and down in quick succession under the desk.

Get it together, Patterson. It's just a dance. It's short, and it's for Ellie. Think about Ellie.

As if she heard my thoughts, she appears at my door, knocking once before opening the door slowly. When she sees me, her face drops and her smile turns to worry. She rushes over, kneeling in front of me, and her tiny hands cup my face as she tries to get my eyes to focus on her.

"Jesus, Jamie. What happened? Are you okay?" she asks, panic laced in her voice.

"I'm good. I just...I need a minute," I croak.

"You're shaking, Jamie," she says, and I turn away from her because she's already seen me like this far too many times for my liking. She pulls me back though, not letting me hide within myself.

"Hey, Jamie. Look at me. What is it? What's wrong? Is it the dance? You don't have to do it if you don't want to."

I shake my head, feeling completely fucking stupid. I rub my sweating palms on my jeans a few times before Ellie grabs them.

My adrenaline is at an all time high, my immune system shitting the bed on me. The loud ringing in my ears intensifies and my vision becomes blurry. Fuck, I'm going to pass out.

"Jamie, focus on my voice. Focus on me," she tries again. "Feel this?" she squeezes my hands. "That's real. Feel this?" she places her hands on my cheeks. "And this?" her warm lips meet mine, and she kisses me softly. I can feel the panic attack slowing, my pulse steadying. "I love you, Jamie."

My hands feel steadier, my brain quieter, the ringing is gone. Ellie's face comes into view as I open my eyes, and she looks like an angel. She loves me.

"Good, take some slow, deep breaths. That's it," she coos. I do as she says, taking a breath in and letting it go slowly. "Are you okay?"

I nod. "Yeah, I think so."

"Are you nervous about the show?" she asks, her worry still obvious.

Shrugging, I take a sip from my water bottle. "I don't know. I didn't think I was, but I guess I must be."

She clutches my thigh and peers up at me with those emerald eyes. "You don't have to do it if you don't feel comfortable. I won't be angry with you," she assures me.

"No, I'm going to do it. I just needed to freak out first. I'm good, I promise" I tell her with a smile. "Let's go kick some ass, yeah?

She nods, holding her hand out and helping me stand. Before we leave the room, I take a few more deep breaths. Let's do this.

The arena is full of life. Voices carry and echo off the walls, people walk up and down the stands as they find their seats. Burgundy fabric wraps around the boards. Gold spotlights sweep across center ice, highlighting the Ellington logo.

Students pack the lower sections, and faculty and donors fill the upper sections. It looks just like what Ellie had described in the meetings. The tech crew and hockey guys really outdid themselves.

Ellie comes up from behind, stopping next to me. She looks hot and professional in her black pantsuit and heels. I want to devour her here and now, but I contain myself. As much as I'd like to go for round two today, I have to keep it together for both our sakes.

"Oh my god," she breathes. "It's perfect."

I look down at her and my chest squeezes as I watch her smile grow wider, her cheeks pink from the cold and eyes wide as she takes it all in like it's magic.

"Told you hockey draws a crowd," I say with a chuckle.

The announcer's voice booms overhead. "Welcome to Ellington University's Pucks and Props night!"

The arena explodes. Ellie and I share one last look before heading to our respective areas with our students.

The theatre kids take the ice first, their first excerpt making the crowd laugh, and at the end, everyone's clapping. From what I could tell, it seems to be some kind of love story. The leads, April and Leo I think, did a great job at keeping everyone engaged. The props are awesome and everything went smoothly. From across the rink, I find Ellie standing proud and tall, her hands clasped together under her chin as she admires her students work and the response from the audience.

As soon as the music switches, the Wolves take the ice, jumping over the boards and getting set up for their scrimmage game. The crowd goes nuts, and it seems to fire up the boys even more. Half of the team wears our home jerseys, and the other half sports the away jerseys. They look like actual pros out there. I never thought I'd see the day, honestly. These guys were a total fucking mess. But it seems like whatever I did these past few months paid off.

When the scrimmage is over, the theatre kids come back out and perform again. We take turns going back and forth like this for an hour. By the looks of it, this crowd is loving every second of it, thank fuck. I didn't expect us to be able to pull something like this off. I don't think its ever been done.

I just hope that for as much as they seem to enjoy it, they dig into their pockets at the end of the night so all of this wasn't for nothing.

All night, I've caught Ellie watching everything like it's magic, and every time our eyes meet, my anxiety seems to dissipate. So, I'd say the real magic... is her.

This was all her vision. Sure, I helped execute it. I got the team ready. I helped where I could, but she did the rest. I'm so fucking proud of her. She's been busting her ass working on this and the play. I'm sure I made everything even more difficult for her, adding me into the mix. But she's handled everything with confidence and tenacity. She always has.

By the time we've finished with the scrimmage, and the theatre kids have finished their performances, we're all spent. But it's not over yet.

Shaking my hands out at my sides, I take few calming breaths before stepping out onto the empty ice where the crew has laid down a large tarp for us. I've never enjoyed public speaking. In fact, I've always kind of avoided it, but there's no avoiding it now, so here goes nothing. It's only a few words, Jamie. It'll be fine. You've done thousands of interviews; you can get through this.

I tap the mic clipped to my collar and fight the urge to say, 'is this thing on?'

Clearing my throat, I begin. "Thank you all for coming to Pucks and Props night. We appreciate you being here and donating to our Arts and Athletic departments. Now, you've seen the theatre department act. You've seen the hockey team show off." I pause, letting the crowd settle. "What happens when you combine them?"

As I walk off the ice and back to the bench, the lights drop and the arena gasps. Darkness swallows everything except for a single gold spotlight burning at center rink.

I watch Ellie from across the ice as she counts down to her cue. She doesn't look nervous or stressed. She looks calm and collected, the complete opposite of what I'm feeling right now.

This is it. This is the finale.

Chapter 40

ELLIE

The music starts and my heart pounds. We've rehearsed this for weeks, over and over again. These kids know this routine like the back of their hand. Half of them can probably do it in their sleep. I'm not worried about them as much as I am Jamie. That panic attack he had earlier scared me. It seemed worse than the other ones. Yet he didn't want to back out. He's determined to do this, and I wasn't going to argue with him. Let's just hope he doesn't pass out or throw up.

Bright colored lights burst across the rink in streaks of gold and purple. My theatre kids surge onto the ice first, confident and ready. They fan out in dramatic formation, arms slicing through the air in sharp, synchronized movements, exactly as we practiced. One they're in their places, the hockey team storms out onto the tarp and the crowd goes crazy. The song switches to 'Bye Bye Bye' by NSYNC and the choreography snaps into place.

It's no longer theatre versus hockey. They're working together, and it looks amazing. Jamie dances alongside them, doing exactly what he said he would. I laugh and clap along with the music as the crowd loses their minds. When I make eye contact with Jamie, he has a huge grin on his face that rivals my own. He looks completely carefree and I love that for him. He may not be the world's greatest dancer, but he's putting in the effort, and I appreciate that.

All of a sudden, Jamie cuts through center ice, never taking his eyes off of me, and I barely have time to register him before his hand is on mine.

"What are you doing?" I yell over the music. "This isn't part of the routine!"

"Screw the routine," he yells, breathless and grinning as he pulls me onto the ice. Well shit, I wasn't planning on that. I don't even argue, because his smile and joy are infectious and I can't help but want to join him.

My adrenaline spikes as I begin dancing to the choreography I've been watching for weeks.

The world around us blurs into lights and noise and laughter. The shouts and cheers from the stands are just background noise. When I look over to Jamie, he's already looking at me like I'm the center of his world. Like nothing else matters. My heart skips several beats. He asked me to come with him. To leave Ellington and be with him. Can I do that?

Can I live with Jamie? Can I trust him with my heart? I mean, we have been technically living together for months now, except we slept in separate bedrooms and tried to avoid each other at all costs. But even in doing that, we somehow always found a way to be near one another.

Jamie catches my wrist and spins me around like we're the only two on the ice.

And then everyone moves at once. A ripple of motion spreads across the rink and the song finally comes to an end. My lungs burn and I'm smiling so hard my cheeks hurt. Everyone hits their final pose and the music goes out, leaving only the sound of our heavy breathing.

The crowd is silent and unmoving. Oh god, did they hate it? Was it awful? Did I fail? I peer up at Jamie who still wears a huge grin as he tries to catch his breath.

After what feels like an eternity, the place explodes. People erupt out of their chairs and onto their feet. There's screaming, whistling, and stomping throughout the entire arena.

A relieved laugh rushes out of me and the weight of the world lifts off my shoulders. My laughter and excitement are uncontrollable. We did it. We pulled it off. This insane, elaborate stunt of ours worked.

The sound of Jamie's laughing beside me only makes my smile widen. He looks just as thrilled as I am. This big, burly hockey player with his cocky attitude and rough exterior stands next to me after admitting his love for me, asking me to live with him, and helping me pull off this fundraiser with a grin wider than I've ever seen him wear.

I turn to Jamie, breathless. "That was insane. We did it!"

He beams. "We fucking did it, Sweetheart."

Instead of the repulsion I used to feel when he called me that, my heart flutters and I want him to keep saying it.

The roar of applause keeps coming. I try to look for Lainey and Holland in the crowd, but there's too many people and it's impossible to tell where they are. I'll have to find them after we're finished here.

We all file off of the ice and into the changing rooms. The kids are ecstatic. They cheer and hug and it reminds me how it feels to perform your heart out and feel so proud and accomplished at the end. Listening to the audience scream your name, feeling the relief when you've performed your best. I miss that feeling.

When we're all done in the locker room, we head back to the arena to greet our friends and family. I search the crowd to see if I can find Jamie. When I spot him talking to a couple of his players, I can't help the grin that takes over my face. He turns around just as I begin heading toward him. His eyes light up, and butterflies erupt in my stomach. God, he's gorgeous. Even when he's all sweaty and tired.

"Hey," I say, suddenly feeling nervous, because I know what I'm about to say could change everything between us.

"Hey, Sweetheart," he licks his lips, and I wish I could kiss him right now, but I can't. Not here.

"Jamie, I—" I start but am interrupted by the sound of Dean Ashby's voice.

I take a step back from Jamie, hoping Dean Ashby didn't notice how close we just were. I know we only have a week left of the semester, but we still need to act professional.

Ashby looks as if he's just won the lottery his smile is so wide.

"Do you two have any idea how much you raised?" he asks.

Jamie and I shake our heads.

Ashby beams. "A little over two hundred and fifty thousand dollars."

The number doesn't compute at first.

"And that's after expenses," Ashby adds.

Jamie and I share a look that says, 'what the fuck?' before Jamies lets out a disbelieving laugh.

"You're kidding."

"I am not. You two did a phenomenal job. This was better than anything I could have imagined. Congratulations. You should be proud of yourselves. I knew you could do it."

Once Ashby's gone, I turn back to Jamie who is already looking at me.

I make a sound that's half scream, half sob before grabbing him by the arms.

"Two hundred and fifty thousand dollars! Holy shit!"

He chuckles at my excitement. "Hell yeah!"

"I'll come," I blurt out, as if my body couldn't hold it in any longer. I think my heart knew all along what I would say, but my brain tried to talk her out of it. I don't know which one I should be rooting for.

Jamie's brow lifts. "What?"

"I'll come with you," I tell him, almost breathless. "To New York. I'll live with you, and I'll go back to acting, and I'll be closer to Lainey and Gwen. I've made up my mind."

Grabbing my hands in his, his expression turns serious. "Are you sure? I don't want you to feel forced to do anything you don't want to—"

"I'm sure," I say with certainty. For once, I'm actually content with my decision. I'm going to do this. I let him go once, and I can't do that again. I hate to need him, but I do. I need him in my life. I need him in my soul. I need him physically and mentally. I'm done fighting it. I'm giving in.

"I fucking love you, Ellie Monroe. I promise, you won't regret this. I'll spend the rest of my life making up for what I did," he assures me, and I actually believe he will.

"I love you, Jamie Patterson."

"Ellie!" The squeal comes from behind me and I automatically know who it belongs to. I spin around so fast, I could've given myself whiplash.

"Lainey!" I squeal back as she runs into my outstretched arms. We jump up and down like teenagers as we hold onto one another. "I'm so glad you're here! I've missed you."

"I've missed you too! Gwenny was going to come but she's feeling a bit under the weather," Lainey explains. "I guess morning sickness isn't always in the morning."

I nod in understanding. "Of course, yeah. It's okay. I'll call her later. What did you think?"

"Oh my god, it was great! You did amazing. I can't believe you did all that in such a short period of time!" Lainey exclaims, her eyes focusing on something behind me. "Is that him?"

"Yes, I have some things to tell you later," I warn her. She gives me a curious look before I hear Jamie's name being called from somewhere down the crowded hall.

Oh shit. I know that voice. I turn just in time to see Holland storming toward us, his face red with anger. Oh no. Before I can stop him, Holland's fist connects with Jamie's jaw, his head flying back from the force. Everyone stops what they're doing and looks on to see what just happened.

"Holland!" I yell, my voice filled with rage. I can't believe he would cause a scene, here of all places.

"What the hell?" Jamie barks, crimson blood on flowing from his lip.

"That's for fucking breaking my sister's heart, asshole!" Holland seethes.

For the love of God, is he serious?

I cut in, my voice sharp. "Holland, stop. You're causing a scene."

Jamie straightens slowly, wiping the blood from his lip and looks utterly pissed, but he doesn't swing back.

Lainey grabs Holland by the arm and ushers him out of the building. I stop in front of Jamie, my hand reaching up to gently touch his face.

"I'm so sorry," I say, cringing with embarrassment. "I can't believe he did that."

Jamie shakes his head, the anger leaving his body as he looks at me. "I'm fine. It's fine. He's defending his sister, I get it."

"It's not fine. I'll talk to him."

"Ellie, it's okay. We don't need his approval. We don't need anyone's approval. Okay?" He caresses my cheek, his eyes searching my face.

I nod. "Okay."

"Good. Let's get out of here and go celebrate," he suggests with a wink, and I agree.

Chapter 41

JAMIE

When Ellie and I walk outside, the chill of the night air hits my face, my lip stinging from the punch I took. Well deserved, I guess. I bet he's been wanting to do that for a long time. I could have hit him back. I could've kicked his ass. However, I knew it wouldn't get me anywhere. Ellie would have been pissed, and it would have caused a much bigger scene than it already was. So I clenched my fists and held back, for Ellie's sake.

Ellie stops walking, feeling her pockets and huffing a frustrated sigh.

"Shit, I forgot my keys. You can head home, I'll meet you there," she tells me, letting go of hand, her hair flying in every direction from the wind.

Furrowing my brow, I say, “Are you sure? I can come with you.”

She shakes her head. “Yeah, I’ll just be a minute. We drove separately anyway.”

“Okay. Well, I’ll see you at home,” I tell her, planting a gentle kiss on her forehead. She smiles, then turns and heads back to the building.

I make my way toward my car, unlocking it and tossing my shit into the back.

“Patterson.” Fuck, not again.

Turning around slowly, I’m faced with Holland Monroe. This time, the girls aren’t here to put a stop to whatever stupid as fuck thing he’s about to do. If I have to, I’ll lay him out. Ellie can be mad all she wants, but I won’t let the guy beat the shit out of me.

“What do you want, Monroe?”

He huffs out a sarcastic laugh. “I want to kick your ass for what you did to my sister.”

I nod, pursing my lips. “Yeah, I wanna kick my ass for that too,” I say honestly. “Although, you seem to have forgotten the last time you and I saw each other.”

He blanches. Oh, good. He hasn’t forgotten.

“See, the way I remember it is that I tried to come back. Once I got picked up by the Storm, I came back. Do you remember that?” I ask, knowing by the look on his face that he does. “I showed up to your house, ready to apologize to Ellie, hoping she could somehow forgive me. But you answered the door instead.”

I take a menacing step toward him, and he doesn’t move an inch. He’s seething, his nostrils flaring.

"By the way your sister explains the situation, she doesn't seem to know the truth. And that truth is that you threatened me to stay away. You told me you'd ruin my career if I came near Ellie again. Knowing your family, you probably would have."

Holland's fists clench into fists at his sides. I watch his chest rise and fall as his breathing picks up.

"Why haven't you told her?" he asks.

I shrug. "There's no point. It wouldn't change anything now, and I didn't want her to hate her twin. We're in a good place now," I explain truthfully. Taking another step until we're inches away from each other, my expression turning threatening. "If you ever try to get in our way again, if you ever hit me again, she'll know everything."

His throat bobs as he swallows. He nods, backing away, exhaling hard.

"I still don't like you, and I sure as fuck don't want you with my sister," he spits.

I chuckle. "Would be weird if you did," I say before getting into my car and pealing out of the parking lot, leaving Holland standing there alone.

Wasn't the way I thought my night would end up, but there's still time to turn it around, and I know just the way to do it.

When I get home, I run upstairs and wash my face. Some dried blood sticks to my lip, but I don't think it'll bruise. I make my bed, and make sure the room is clean.

When I'm done, I run downstairs and pour two glasses of wine. We're celebrating tonight, and I intend to make Ellie feel amazing.

I won't tell her about the parking lot with Holland. There's no reason to. If Holland backs off, she won't ever have to know.

I wanted to tell her about Holland's threats for months, hell, years even after I left, but I knew it wouldn't change anything. I still left her. I still fucked up. So, I've kept that secret and will continue to do so. She'll be okay living in the dark about that one.

We just pulled off the impossible. The fundraiser was fucking awesome and the school made a shit ton of money. All thanks to Ellie. She also agreed to come with me back to New York. To live with me. There will be times where she'll have to sleep alone while I'm at away games, but I think she'll be okay.

My agent called before the event tonight. Told me I've still got a spot on the team if I want it. I told him I'd give him a call back when I had Ellie's answer. I wasn't going to tell him yes until I knew Ellie would come with me.

I called my mom on the way home too. She was ecstatic to hear the team won the other night and that the fundraiser went well. I wish she could have come, but she's been so busy and I didn't want her to feel like she had to drop everything just to come to a stupid fundraiser.

Taking a seat at the island, I scroll through my phone and wait for Ellie to get home. She should be here any minute now.

After sending a text to the group chat letting them know we absolutely crushed it tonight, the front door opens and I listen as Ellie takes off her shoes and drops her bag to the floor.

She heads directly to the kitchen like I knew she would. Her face lights up as soon she sees me. I'm thankful that she no longer grimaces every time she looks at me. Seeing her smile is so much better for my ego.

"Hey," she says, her voice sweet and quiet. She's back in leggings and hoodie, her hair thrown up in a bun on top of her head. She could be wearing a trash bag and still look stunning.

Grinning, I say, "hey, Sweetheart."

She walks toward me slowly, eyeing the wine glasses on the counter.

"Wine?" she asks. "My, we're getting fancy."

When she's close enough, my arms circle around her waist, bringing her to stand in between my legs.

"If you think this is fancy, wait until I take you to this steakhouse on the upper east side. It's the best fucking steak you'll ever have in your entire life," I whisper seductively. She hums.

"You're making me hungry," Ellie accuses, her cheeks turning pink. Taking a loose piece of hair that's fallen out of her bun, I twist it between my fingers. My dick hardens when she bites her lip.

"Would you like me to feed you, Sweetheart?" I ask, and I think we're both very aware that we're not talking about actual food right now.

Ellie nods. "Yes, please."

Standing from my seat, I pick Ellie up, her legs and arms wrapping around me.

"Let's eat," I say, heading up the stairs with her in my arms.

Chapter 42

ELLIE

Jamie's door barely closes before his hands are all over me, pressing me against the wall with a hunger that makes my pulse spike. I can smell the faint traces of his cologne mixed with the scent of wine on his breath, and the combination makes my head swim in the best possible way.

"I can't believe we really pulled that off. I though for sure someone would screw it up," I breathe, laughing as Jamie's mouth finds the curve of my neck. His teeth graze my skin, and goosebumps fill my arms. He pulls back just enough to meet my eyes. His brown hair is slightly disheveled from running his fingers through it all evening, and I freaking love that I can see the barely contained excitement practically vibrating through him.

"It's because of you."

"You helped," I remind him, reaching for the hem of his hoodie. He lets me pull it over his head. "We make a pretty good team, I guess."

"I agree. And to think you almost refused to work with me," he chuckles, and then his mouth crashes into mine.

It feels raw and desperate, all tongue and teeth, and I feel it everywhere. My nipples tighten into peaks, heat grows between my thighs, and my heart races. If there was some way we could be in each other's skin, we would be. We're pulling and tugging at one another and it's both chaotic and thrilling. Jamie groans against my mouth and the sound goes straight to my core.

His hands grip my hips, his fingers digging into the thin fabric of my leggings.

"Your smile tonight, after it was all over... I want to see that smile over and over again for the rest of my life, and I want to be the one that puts it there," Jamie drawls as he walks us carefully to the bed.

"I loved seeing your smile, too. I don't think I've seen you smile like that since we were seventeen."

He pushes me down onto the mattress, and I land with a soft bounce. He stands over me for a moment, and I stare at his sculpted chest and abs, the ones he's worked on since he was a teenager. I don't remember a day where he skipped the gym. Not even when his father died, and playing professional hockey all these years? I don't doubt the number of hours he's put into his physical appearance.

I watch his eyes travel down my body with an intensity that makes me feel like I'm already naked.

"Fuck, you're beautiful," he says, his voice rough. "You're my beautiful *girlfriend*."

My stomach flutters. Girlfriend. I'm Jamie Patterson's girlfriend. Again. This probably makes me seem like a freaking idiot, but I don't even care. People might not understand it, but I can't help the feelings I have for this man. As much as I wanted to ignore him, as much I wanted to hate him, it wasn't possible.

"I can't believe I agreed to move in with you," I chuckle softly.

"Having second thoughts, are you?" he asks, one eyebrow raised.

He climbs onto the bed, positioning himself over me, his weight supported on his arms.

Shaking my head, I say, "No. I don't think I am."

I reach up and pull him down to me, capturing his lips in another searing kiss. He pulls my hoodie over my head and tosses it to the floor, his hands finding the clasp of my bra immediately and tearing that off too.

His calloused palms caress my tits, his fingers pinching my nipples, and I gasp as his mouth replaces his fingers, his tongue swirling around one of the hardened peaks. He hums against my breast, the vibration making me squirm. His free hand slides down my body, pushing my leggings down. I lift my butt off the bed and use my hands to push them down all the way, exposing my lace panties. His fingers trace along the edge, and I can feel him smile against my chest when he discovers how wet I am.

"Someone's excited," he murmurs, his finger pressing the soaked fabric against my aching pussy. "I love how wet you get for me, Sweetheart."

"All for you," I say, my voice breaking as he rubs slow circles over my clit through the thin material. "Jamie, please..."

"Please what, baby?" He lifts his head from my breast, his blue eyes challenging me. "Do you need something from me?"

Dick.

"I need you inside me." The words tumble out, desperate and uncensored.

Jamie's answering grin is feral. "I can make that happen."

He hooks his fingers into the waistband of my panties and pulls, the fabric tearing easily under his grip. The cool air hits my exposed pussy for only a moment before his fingers are there, sliding through my wetness, teasing my entrance before pushing two fingers inside me without warning.

I cry out at the sudden intrusion, my back arching off the bed. "Fuck, Jamie..."

"You're perfect," he groans, his fingers curling inside me in a way that has stars exploding behind my eyelids. "You really want my cock, don't you?"

"Yes...god, yes," I reply, not even caring if it makes me sound desperate. I've never felt anything as good as when Jamie's inside me.

I'm panting, my hips rising to meet each thrust of his hand. "Please," I whine.

He withdraws his fingers suddenly, leaving me empty and aching. Then I hear the zip of his pants, and a moment later, he's kicking his jeans off along with his briefs. His cock springs free, hard and veiny, already leaking precum from the tip.

I reach for him, wanting to feel him in my hand, but he catches my wrist and pins it above my head. "Do you want to touch or be fucked?" he asks.

"The second option."

"That's what I thought," he says, positioning himself between my thighs, the head of his cock nudging at my entrance. I wrap my legs around his waist, pulling him closer. He slips inside easily, and I cry out, my hands grabbing the sheets.

Jamie fills me completely in one hard thrust, and we both groan at the sensation. My pussy grips him tightly, pulsing around his thick length as he stills inside me, giving me a moment to adjust. I don't need a minute; I just need him to move.

He pulls back until just the tip remains inside me, then slams forward hard enough to make the bed frame creak.

"Fuck, baby," Jamie groans.

He sets a brutal pace, each thrust driving me further into the mattress. His hands grip my thighs hard enough to bruise, pushing them wider and allowing him to sink even deeper.

"This pussy is mine," he growls, leaning down to bite my shoulder. "You are mine. Say it, Sweetheart."

"It's yours, Jamie. Fuck, I'm yours!"

Shifting his angle slightly, he hits that spot inside me that makes my vision blur. I feel my orgasm building rapidly, the tension coiling tighter and tighter in my core. My fingers dig into his back, leaving red scratches down his skin.

"Good fucking girl," he groans, his voice strained. He's close too. I can tell by the way his pace falters. "Cum for me, Ellie. I need to feel this pussy squeeze my cock."

His words push me over the edge. I cum with a scream, my entire body shaking as wave after wave of pleasure crashes through me. Not even a minute later, I feel Jamie follow me over, his hips stuttering as he spills inside me with a guttural moan.

We stay tangled together as our breathing slows, his weight pressing me into the mattress in a way that feels grounding rather than suffocating. When he finally rolls off me, he pulls me against his chest, his fingers tracing lazy patterns on my bare shoulder.

"So," he says, pressing a kiss to my temple. "Celebration part one complete."

I laugh, turning my head to look at him. "Part one? How many parts are there?"

"Well... this was to celebrate our win tonight," he says, kissing my shoulder. "Then we have to celebrate you moving in with me," he says, pushing my hair away from neck and leaving a kiss. "And the most important thing to celebrate, is you giving me another shot." He plants a kiss on my lips before pulling away and looking at me, his eyes full of admiration.

"It's your last one, you know. You don't get any more if you screw this up. I mean it," I tell him firmly. And I do mean it. I won't do this again with him...I can't.

"I don't plan on screwing it up. I don't plan on ever living without you again, Sweetheart."

Chapter 43

JAMIE

Something I've always loved to do is people watch. Not in like a creepy way or anything. It's more because I like to see that other people aren't perfect. It's also something my dad and I used to do together. We'd sit at the park near our house for hours, always sitting on the same old bench with the chipped piece on the corner.

Families would rotate in and out with their toddlers throwing fits or enjoying their time on the small playground. Joggers would pass us in steady loops, some focused and some clearly trying to outrun whatever their problems might've been. Sometimes we'd overhear someone talking on the phone. We'd make up stories about what their call was about. It was like having little pieces of other people's lives that weren't meant for us, that took us away from whatever we were dealing with at the time. I think that's what I like about it. You can learn a lot about people when they don't know anyone is paying attention.

And as I sit in the back row of the crowded auditorium, I watch as people enter and find their seats. Faculty, parents, students all coming to see the show Ellie helped build. She's been stressed about this all week, and I've been doing my best to keep her calm. Mostly that's been giving her earth-shattering orgasms which has seemed to do the trick.

It's been incredible getting to know her again. Not the version I remember. The real one. The woman she's become. Ellie Monroe has always been brilliant, that part never changed. But now I see everything I was too young and too stubborn to appreciate before. Every day she lets me back into her world and lets me witness the woman she's become, and every day I feel like the luckiest guy in the world to even be in her presence.

"Mr. Patterson? Are you here for the show?" a familiar voice asks. When I look up, Dean Ashby is heading down the aisle, taking the empty seat next to mine. I want to tell him to go find another fucking seat, but that would probably be frowned upon. I'd also like to tell him that question is stupid. What other reason would I be here for? The popcorn?

"I am. I assume you are too?"

He nods. "Of course. I've been looking forward to this all semester. Ms. Monroe is very talented."

"She is," I agree, turning back to face the stage. The red curtain sways under the slight breeze from people walking by. Ashby follows my line of vision, landing on the curtain.

"You did well with those boys this semester. They needed someone to take charge. They needed to learn to work together as a team. Whatever you did, I want you to do it again next semester."

What the fuck? That's the last thing I expected him to say.

Clearing my throat, I turn to face him, brows furrowed. "I'm sorry, Martin. I uh... I don't plan on returning next semester. My injury is just about healed, and I'll be going back to the Storm to start training. But I'm glad I could help."

His jaw ticks. "I understand. I figured that might happen. Can't blame an old man for trying though, can you?" he asks with a low chuckle.

"No, I guess not," I say with a shrug.

"Enjoy the show, Mr. Patterson. And good luck. The Storm is lucky to have you."

Ashby stands from his seat and walks off, his hands in his pockets.

Well, that was fucking awkward.

Fifteen minutes later, the auditorium is packed to the brim. I've been in arenas packed with twenty thousand people. I've heard playoff crowds roar so loud the ice vibrated beneath my skates. But this feels different. There's no yelling, no whistles, not loud buzzers or horns. It's just people having quiet conversations, waiting patiently for the show to begin.

A spotlight glows on the middle of the stage. The audience claps as the curtains rise, and when they do, the first thing I notice is Ellie standing just off to the side in the wings, a headset on and a clipboard tucked against her chest. She looks calm and determined. She looks like she's exactly where she belongs. I know she's said she prefers acting, and she's insanely talented, but directing might by another way for her to go.

I lean back in my seat, my knee bouncing despite myself. I don't get nervous watching hockey anymore; I don't usually get nervous before games. But watching something Ellie built from scratch? Watching the thing that she's carefully constructed for all these months?

Yeah, I'm a little nervous.

Halfway through, the main actor, April, begins her monologue to Leo, who sits on a prop bench, watching her pace back and forth. For some reason, I'm completely entranced. The guys would totally be giving me shit if they saw me right now.

"And you know what no one tells you about love? That it's terrifying. At first it feels easy. You'll have the butterflies and the late-night phone calls. You'll get that warm and fuzzy feelin' when you see their name light up your screen. You'll believe in all the promises and all the dreams." April pauses, walking to the other end of the stage, and whipping back to face Leo. "But the terrifying part is what comes after all that. The moment you realize that this person matters enough to hurt you, that they have the means to change you, that losing them would actually break something inside your chest."

Leo stands, but April, or Sherri, or whatever the hell her name is tells him to sit back down.

"I'm not finished, Charlie," she chastises. "Now where was I?"

"The terror of love," Leo's character says, and the audience chuckles.

"Right. That's when fear shows up. You keep one foot out the door, ready to walk away at any moment because it would be better to walk away than to get your heart broken. You realize that you have no control over what happens to you," she continues, tears flowing down her cheeks. Damn, this girl is good.

"Charlie, I see you. I see exactly who you are...flaws, fears, and all. And I choose you. That's the bravest thing you can do, you know. Choose someone, completely, no backup plans. I know you think your life is over because of the factory going under. But you are more than that place. There is more than one version of who you thought you'd be. And loving me? God, loving me doesn't change who you are. It just reminds you that your life is bigger when it's shared."

Suddenly, my knee isn't bobbing anymore, my palms aren't clammy, and my focus is on the woman in the wings. The woman that I love. The stubborn, determined, beautiful woman that I should have fought for all those years ago.

A few months ago, all I was worried about was when I was getting back in the game. I thought I'd never be whole again. Now? I've never been more certain of anything in my life. Ellie Monroe is it for me. She's my reason, and hockey is a bonus.

The curtain drops, and for a second the auditorium is quiet. No one moves; no one speaks. And when the curtains open again to reveal the cast, the auditorium explodes with applause and cheers. Everyone is on their feet. I'm already standing before I realize it, clapping so hard my palms sting.

While everyone looks at the stage, I look for her.

When the curtain finally closes for good, the audience begins to file out, and I head backstage. I don't know if I'm supposed to be back here, but who gives a fuck? I need to congratulate my girl.

Backstage is chaos. The cast is crying and hugging, parents are handing them flowers and telling them how well they did even if all they did was stand there the entire time.

I push my way through, hoping to find Ellie through all the craziness. And then I see her. Everything else fades. When she's in front of me, I see the tears in her eyes and the proud smile on her lips.

"You did it, baby" I say, my voice rougher than I expect.

Her breath shakes out in a laugh. "I did, didn't I?"

"You fucking crushed it. I'm so proud of you."

Her eyes search mine, like she's checking for doubt. For sarcasm.

Her throat bobs as she swallows. "You came."

I huff a quiet laugh. "Of course I came."

"I didn't think this would be your thing," she says softly.

I grab her face between my palms, forcing her to look directly at me.

"You are my thing, and I'll do anything for you, Ellie Monroe," I tell her, and her tears begin to flow freely down her pink cheeks. "I'm not going anywhere."

Not for a contract.

Not for money.

Not for fear.

I brush my thumb under her eye, wiping away her tears. "You know," I say lightly, "I've played in some pretty big arenas."

"I'm aware," she sniffles.

"But this?" I glance toward the stage doors. "This might be the best show I've ever seen."

She laughs, and it's the best sound I've ever heard.

"Let's go home," she says, taking my hand in hers.

As we walk out of the auditorium, I realize that for the first time, like ever, I feel completely whole. I can have both. It doesn't have to be one or the other. And having Ellie back in my arms again... It's the best fucking goal I've ever scored.

Epilogue

ELLIE

"Thirty-two seconds left in the third period! We're tied at four."

I don't think I've taken a breath in at least a minute. My heart is pounding so fast, and the adrenaline rush I have right now is not helping. I'm jumping up and down, screaming my head off. I'd say I probably look like an idiot, but almost everyone's doing the same thing. Including Lainey, Gwen, and Adaline, Gwen's baby.

She looks just like her mom, with her rosy cheeks and turned up nose. She's also stubborn like her dad. I love her. She doesn't seem to mind the loudness of the crowd or the chaos around her. She's been asleep in Gwen's arms for an hour now.

I was never into sports. My brother played rugby, so I'd go to his games just for something to do on a Friday night, but I never really understood what was going on. So, for me to be here in the front row right now is crazy. Thank God Jamie gave me a crash course about hockey. I still don't get all the lingo, but I've learned enough to know what certain positions are and what they do. I've also learned I love it when they fight. I especially enjoy watching Jamie fight. I've never seen something so hot and violent in my life.

The Rhode Island Storm have been on a winning streak for weeks now, and I've been to every single game since Jamie got back on the ice. It was definitely challenging at first, and there were days where I thought Jamie would just give up, but he never did. Now we're at the last playoff game of the season to see who's going to the Stanley Cup finals. I never realized how intense this was. People really go crazy for this stuff.

My attention goes to the ice as one of Jamie's close friends, Connor Grieves leans in for the faceoff.

"And Grieves wins it clean!"

The puck slides back to Wilder Ranslavic, who banks it hard off the boards.

"Ranslavic clears the zone!" the announcer says over the loudspeaker.

The other team, the Louisville Lazers surge forward again, but the guy I now know as Theo Cramer moves faster.

"Cramer closes the gap! Beautiful poke check. Here comes Callahan flying down the right side!"

The crowd rises all at once, and I watch as Callahan cuts toward the middle, one of the Louisville guys right on him.

"He drops it back—" the announcer begins. The pass glides perfectly into open ice. "And Jamie Patterson, who's had a tough season this past year with a knee injury really steps up!"

My breath catches as I watch Jamie with the puck.

Come on, baby. Come on...

"There he goes with a breakaway, and—"

He skillfully pulls the puck through his skates, not looking at all worried or rushed and when he gets close, he fakes a slapshot.

"The goalie drops!"

He shifts left, dragging the puck into a narrow lane, and my body feels like it's on fire. I'm like a freaking live wire.

"Patterson shoots—"

Oh my god, oh my god....

The puck lifts, and it snaps right into the top corner of the net.

"He scores! Jamie Patterson with seven seconds left! And that's a win for the Rhode Island Storm!"

The arena explodes and I watch as Jamie rips off his gloves, his teammates crashing into him along the boards. Billy tackles him from the side while Theo shouts something into his ear. Connor and their friend Wilder slam into the pile and it's nothing short of pure chaos.

Tears fill my eyes. Watching him come so far with his healing, seeing him doing the thing he loves, and witnessing him score the winning goal to get to the freaking Stanley Cup finals? I am so freaking proud of him.

As the crowd chants his name, Jamie's head lifts, but he doesn't look around to take it all in. He looks directly at me, and he points. My cheeks heat like they're on fire. Heads turn to looks at me, and I fight the urge to cover my face.

Jamie crooks his finger, indicating for me to come closer to the ice. I hesitate for a moment before finally getting my feet to move. He meets me at the door and pulls me onto the ice.

Is he really doing this right now?

He picks me up and spins me around like no one is watching, and I feel like I'm finally completely in his world. Everyone can see us, how stupid in love we are. All I ever wanted was for Jamie to allow me to be by his side while he succeeds, and now I'm here. And it feels pretty damn good.

When he sets me back down on the ice, I look up at him with a huge grin.

"You did it," I tell him, my voice shaky from crying. Jamie's grin grows wider.

"Hell yeah, I did. And I did it for you, Sweetheart."

Chuckling breathily, I say, "I'm so proud of you."

His eyes flicker with admiration and relief, as if he'd been waiting to hear me say those words to him his whole life.

"You came," he states.

"Of course I came," I tell him, reaching up to cup his cheek. My thumb moves back and forth slowly.

"I didn't think hockey was your thing," he shrugs sarcastically.

A single tear runs down my cheek as I stroke his. "You are my thing."

"I love you, Ellie Monroe," he says, leaning down until he's inches away from my lips. My eyes bounce between his blue eyes and his lips.

"I love you, Jamie Patterson."

His lips crash onto mine, and the whole world disappears. The sounds of the arena, the chaos around us, it all freezes. It's just Jamie and me.

Since I came back to Ellington, since I saw Jamie again, I fought with myself over how I felt. I told myself I couldn't love him. I couldn't possibly give him another chance after what he did. I thought loving him meant risking everything I'd rebuilt.

But loving someone doesn't erase who you are, it shows you that you can still be who you want to be, you'll just have someone there by your side to cheer you on.

Jamie pulls away, his hand tangled in my hair. "You ready for a lifetime with me, Sweetheart?"

I look around us at the fans cheering, the confetti falling, Jamie's teammates celebrating and nod.

"You sure that's what you want, Hockey Star?" I ask with a smirk.

"I've never been so sure of anything in my goddamn life."

Authors Note

First, I'd like to thank you for giving me a chance. I am so glad you're here. I truly hope you enjoyed reading Ellie and Jamie's story. As the final book in the Ellington U series, this story means so much to me, and I hope it can resonate with some of you.

When I started writing this series, I had no idea where it was going to go. I just knew I wanted to write. I'd like to take a moment to acknowledge some of the people that have helped me through this entire journey. I am so thankful for the people in my life that supported me every step of the way.

Thank you to my boyfriend for listening to all my crazy ideas and acting as my sounding board. I love you.

Thank you to my mom for always being one of the first people to read my stories, and for always cheering me on.

Thank you to my beta readers for your time and dedication to reading my story and helping me find things I couldn't see. I couldn't have done this without you.

Thank you to my ARC readers for providing such helpful feedback and amazing graphics. I genuinely appreciate your time.

Lastly, to my readers, I wouldn't be here if it wasn't for you. Thank you for your continuous support and encouragement.

I love you all!

Love always,
Rae Quinn

About the Author

Rae Quinn is a romance author, teacher, and screenwriter who lives in Georgia. When she's not writing sappy romance novels, she's consuming way too much coffee, reading a good book, or travelling.

Join Rae Quinn on social media to keep up to date on new releases, giveaways, and more!

Instagram: @authorraequinn_
Goodreads: Rae Quinn
Facebook: Rae Quinn – Author
Tiktok: @raequinn_author

www.ingramcontent.com/pod-product-compliance
Lightning Source LLC
LaVergne TN
LVHW100514110826
845146LV00002B/641

* 9 7 9 8 9 9 1 3 3 3 4 6 7 *